AMY
of the
NECROMANCERS

Jimena I. Novaro

Amy of the Necromancers by Jimena I. Novaro
Copyright © 2021 Jimena I. Novaro

Cover art by Lena Yang

ISBN: 978-0-9913850-6-5

For everyone who read along as I released this book one chapter at a time in 2020. Your encouragement and enthusiasm helped get me through a terrible year.

Thank you.

Contents

CHAPTER ONE

Mud

The night before my first day of junior year, I wake up with the Itch.

I slip down from my bunk bed, my bare feet soundless on the wooden rungs of the ladder. Sarah, my older sister by a year, snores softly in the bunk below mine. I watch her slack-jawed face for a moment before padding out of the dark room.

Moonlight illuminates the short corridor from our room to the living room. I pass the room that belongs to my oldest sister, Maddie, with its handmade sign on the front that proclaims, *Do not enter! Magic is happening.* I tiptoe through the living room and dining room and kitchen, a short trek, and pass my parents' bedroom and the bedroom shared by Aunt Betty and Grandma. I grab a key off the island counter as I pass.

Crossing the laundry room, I squeeze between plants Maddie has been repotting, bags of soil, piles of laundry for ironing, and a broken chair, and slip out the side door into the backyard of our double-wide. My bare feet enjoy the sensation of fresh, cool soil in the warm night air as I walk between tomato vines, rows of mint and rosemary, sunflowers with their heads bowed, and the bed of root vegetables sticking out their tufts of green. My nightgown flutters against my skin in the warm breeze, and my short auburn hair, tangled from sleep, brushes my shoulders. In the moonlight, my miles and miles of freckles stand out even more starkly against my pale skin than they do in the sunlight.

The garden sprawls on an uphill slope from our house with the garden shed looming over it, white against the dark, mossy tree trunks beyond our property. I slide my key into the padlock and click it open. The door, white-painted wood like the walls, swings open. I slip inside, close the door so no one can see the light from the house, and pull the chain to light the bare bulb above my head.

It's not as though I want to keep what I'm doing a secret—everyone in my family knows what happens when I get the Itch. But I don't want to be interrupted, and I don't want an audience. These moments are mine alone.

More potted plants, bags of soil and fertilizer, and empty pots clutter one side of the garden shed—the gardening things in our laundry room are the overflow from the shed. To the right is a chest full of tiny drawers, each with a hand-written label identifying the seeds nestled snug inside. The seeds come from a dozen varieties of roses, orchids, tulips, bougainvillea, daffodils, and carnations, none of which I would have been able to identify by sight; others, from every type of squash and pepper you could imagine along with tomatoes, eggplants, and berries. Garden tools hang from the wall, most of them cast-iron heirlooms with wooden handles passed down to Maddie from Grandma and maybe even from *her* Grandma.

In front of the door and below the light bulb stands a hand-made table so covered in work stains, weather stains, burn marks, and dents that the original color is almost indistinguishable. I approach the table and lay my hands palm-down on the surface, feeling the urge that drove me from my bed fill me like hunger, or a fever—no longer just an itch.

I take a bucket from below the worktable and set it on top. Then I empty a bag of soil into the bucket. I take a watering can and fill it from the faucet outside the garden shed, careful not to let too much light escape through the door as I go out and back in. Standing before the worktable again, I water the soil. I feel confident in my every move, driven and sure the way I almost never feel when I don't have the Itch.

I don't have to think. In fact, if I tried to think, it would disrupt my confidence and make me forget what I'm doing and how to do it—how much soil, how much water, how much time. The Itch doesn't operate on logic and has nothing to do with my brain; the Itch is a knowledge nestled somewhere inside the coils of my gut or the folds of my muscles. Mama says that's probably why it strikes most often at night, when my conscious mind has less of a hold on me.

I water the soil in the bucket until it becomes muddy sludge. Then I set down the watering can and slowly lower my hands into the bucket. I knead the dirt, combining water and soil until it's an even, black mud that makes you want to curl your toes in it, or rub it on your skin to feel the silky residue it leaves behind. I let my hands rest in the mud for a moment, my eyes closed, breathing in the scent, like freshly tilled earth after a spring shower, and feeling the heavy, smooth texture, like cake batter. Gradually, other scents waft from the bucket into my nose: lemonade on a summer's day, old carpet, motor oil, baby shampoo, wet dog. It must be a household pet, then; a well-loved one. The mud grows warmer, and shapes begin to form under my hands, like clay molding itself into the form it was meant to have.

I've brought back pets before. They usually want to go back to their houses, but of course, that's a bad idea. The children might be happy if their beloved cat or dog or bunny came scratching at their door, but the parents would be terrified, would dig up the patch of dirt where they had buried Spot or Lady or Chase and find the corpse still there, rotting. And their pet would *also* be nuzzling the delighted children, wagging its tail, eating the kibble if the parents hadn't gotten rid of it yet, disputing its territory with any new pet the family had found to replace it. Who knew what would come after that? Even if they are accepted back into the family, any pet I bring back can't stay forever; they often fade away in the night when it's time to go, leaving nothing but a pile of garden soil. If they were home, their families would feel their loss all over again.

No, I always keep the pets with me when I bring them back. I talk to them, and sometimes they understand me. I try to explain to them that they're dead, and it's time to move on. Sometimes it works. Other times, they just come to realize it on their own. Maybe the scents and tastes of the world feel wrong to them; maybe the sun doesn't warm their fur the way it used to; maybe the howls of the neighborhood dogs in the night don't call them to join in. Then they know, in the same way I know what to do when the Itch strikes, that they don't belong here anymore.

I've never had a pet of my own, but I've fostered plenty of dead ones. It's not so bad that they always have to leave. It feels right. I always see in their eyes the moment they understand, and I feel at peace along with them.

The shapes inside the bucket become more solid, more defined. I frown, my eyes still closed. It doesn't feel like fur under my fingers, though it's hard to tell through the mud. I feel out a limb, then another. A head; my fingers comb through silky hair. Maybe it's one of those long-haired dogs, the kind you have to bathe and brush every day.

But then my fingertips trace over eyes and a nose, and my own eyes fly open. The head is emerging from the bucket. Fingers poke out, and hands stretch up toward me. I grab the creature under the arms and haul it out, setting it down feet-first on the worktable.

There's no mistaking it: this time, I haven't brought back a household pet.

I've brought back a child.

CHAPTER TWO
Child

The child stands only a little taller than me, even on top of the table. They can't be older than three. As always happens when I first bring something back from the dead, I can't distinguish any features yet; the child's face and clothes and limbs are muddy, but if I ran water over them, there would only be more mud underneath—at least for now. The child stands there, blinking mud-filled eyes at me. They don't cry or laugh or try to run or reach for me. It always takes the animals I bring back a few hours at least to start developing their old personality, too.

I stare at the child and they stare back at me for what must be at least a minute. Well, I assume they're staring at me, because their muddy eyeballs are pointed my way.

I've never brought back a human being before. Of course, I knew it might be possible, but I always assumed it would feel different, that it would take some different sort of procedure. The child rose out of the mud no differently than dogs or deer or birds.

My head pounds, the headache more intense than usual. That's different, at least. I suppose bringing back a whole human being put more strain on me than I'm used to. Suddenly, I want nothing more than my bed. I usually leave the animals I bring back in the garden shed overnight, since they just stand around until the morning, anyway, but I can't leave a *child* out here.

I take the child under the armpits again and set them down on the floor; then I take their hand, switch off the bulb, and lead them out of the garden shed, locking the door behind us. The child makes no protest, shows no signs of wanting to go anywhere but where I lead them. I take us in through the laundry room and into the kitchen. Then I stop and look back; the child has left a trail of muddy footprints. I sigh, but my family will understand, and my head hurts too much to bother with cleaning up.

I lay some old towels on the couch and lift the child onto them. They lie down without protest, like a doll that only becomes animate when I push a button. They blink muddy eyes up at me, still without pupils or irises or whites, though a hint of eyelashes are coming through the mud. I drape another old towel over the child's body and tuck in the edges.

"Good night," I say.

The child doesn't answer.

I stare at them a moment longer. Where did this kid come from? What happened to them? Who are their parents? What am I supposed to do now?

My head pounds so hard my eyes water. I stumble into my room, climb into my bunk, and fall asleep as soon as my head hits the pillow. I have lots of jumbled dreams that I only remember in flashes when I wake. I'm pretty sure there was a little girl in most of them, dark-haired with pigtails and a little yellow dress.

When I open my eyes, my head doesn't hurt as much. Golden sunlight streams in through the curtains. I groan and stumble down the ladder; Sarah is already up, her bed made.

When I trudge into the living room, the child lies on her side like I left her, hands clasped together under her head. I started thinking of the child as *her* while I slept, though she still doesn't have any distinguishing features. No, that's not right; I crouch in front of her and peer closely at her face. The formless blob that was her hair is resolving into the pigtails I dreamed about, and I can see the shape of her nose and mouth more clearly now. It still doesn't feel quite real to me that I actually raised her from the dead.

I stand up and go into the kitchen. Only Mama and Grandma sit at the island counter, sipping coffee. The clock on the microwave tells me I've missed the first two periods of my first day of junior year, and I'm well on my way to missing the third.

Grandma smiles. "Good morning, Amy."

"Sarah couldn't wake you up," Mama tells me, "so we let you sleep. We figured last night took a lot out of you."

I blow out a breath and plop into a chair beside Grandma. My head doesn't hurt anymore, but it still hasn't gone back to normal. I feel as though someone played around with my brain, shuffling thoughts and memories so I don't quite know where to find everything; my skull feels tender when I run my hands through my hair. It's a little like after I come back from an episode in my therapist's office.

"It's a little girl," I say.

"Mm," Grandma replies, sipping her coffee. She and Mama seem unconcerned. "Bound to happen sooner or later."

They say I inherited Grandma's auburn hair and freckles, though on her, both faded with age. She wears her tissue-white hair long, tied into a braid, and the sag of her skin doesn't conceal the fine bones of her face, her high cheekbones, her bright blue eyes framed by thick lashes. She has a liveliness to her that makes her seem much younger, or maybe it's that she seems much more alive than younger people do. It makes her take up more space than you'd think with her slight frame.

I inherited my build from Mama. Unlike Grandma, Mama and I are both stocky. Thick-boned, round-faced, with plenty of meat on our frames, as Mama says. Mama's hair is dark and curly, like her daddy's; we both have Grandma's bright blue eyes, though.

"You knew I could bring back people?" I ask.

"We thought you might, one day," Mama admits.

"There's oatmeal. You'll have to make coffee."

I take a deep breath and gather my wits before getting up to gather my breakfast. I wash last night's mud off my hands in the kitchen sink; it browns the water as it flakes off and swirls into the drain.

"Do you know who she is?" Mama asks.

"Not yet." I don't look at her. I know who she's talking about.

Sometimes I know a pet's name right away, especially if it's a dog who's well-trained. You'd think a person, even a little one, would know their name better than a dog, but maybe it takes a person longer to come back all the way. It nags at me as I fix the coffee and warm my oatmeal in the microwave.

I'm not ready to ask until I sit back down with my breakfast. "Have you heard of . . . any little girls . . . dying lately?"

Mama shakes her head. She isn't as upset as I'd expect about a little girl dying, isn't as upset as I'm starting to get thinking about it. I've gotten used to pets and wild animals. This is different, though.

The more I think about the girl in my dream, laughing and swinging on the swings, blowing out her candles and playing in the sprinklers—I might be conjuring some of these things up in my imagination, I'm not sure—the more upset I get that this little girl didn't get more of a life, didn't get to grow up. But Mama and Grandma just sip their coffee thoughtfully.

My family doesn't look at death the way other families do. None of them are scared of it. Most of them aren't even sad at the thought, not even Aunt Betty, who cries at Christmas specials on TV. Not even Daddy, who doesn't have any of the Art—nothing ever seems to upset Daddy, though, really.

"Haven't heard anything," Grandma says. "We looked at the obituaries in today's paper. Nothing about a little girl. We have the papers from the last two weeks stacked in the laundry room. You should look through them just in case."

"Shouldn't you tell me to go to school?" I mutter through my oatmeal.

My eyes sting, but I don't want to cry in front of Grandma and Mama. Not that they'd criticize me for crying about death; it's just that I know they don't feel the same way. It makes me feel like there's something wrong with me.

"I'll drive you over there if you want to go." Mama pours herself and Grandma another cup of coffee from the pot I made and sits back down, unhurried. She's still in her nightdress and slippers.

That's another way our family isn't like other families: they don't think school is that important. If it were up to them, we wouldn't go at all. But Mama never finished high school, neither did Grandma or Aunt Betty, and Daddy works all day, so they can't homeschool us—not legally, anyway. Not that they'd teach us much if they *did* homeschool us. They think any knowledge worth knowing is what you seek out on your own.

I understand their point of view, but all my friends go to school, and my sisters, too—Maddie graduated high school a few years ago—so I've always gone. It's going to be kind of embarrassing, being late to my first day of junior year. It almost makes me want to pretend to be sick and skip today altogether, but that would put me behind right from the start.

After breakfast, I get dressed and gather my school things. Mama, who's thrown on a sundress and traded her slippers for sandals, joins me in the living room.

"You'll take care of her, won't you?" I ask, pausing at the couch to look down at the little girl.

Mama lays a hand on my shoulder. "Of course, Amy. Don't we take care of everyone you bring back?"

"A dog or cat is different."

The little girl's cheek is growing visible through the mud, along with the collar of her dress. It's the little yellow one I saw in my dreams.

"She'll be okay, Amy," Mama says as we slip out the front door and head down the overgrown gravel path to the driveway, where our beaten-down pickup truck resides. "Don't worry about her. It'll be nice having a little one around the house again. It's been so long."

Sure, it's been a long time since I, the youngest one, was three. But Mama's acting as though having a little *dead* girl in the house is the same as having a little *live* one. I drag my feet through the gravel.

"She might be scared," I say. "If something bad happened to her . . . "

Mama laughs. "I know how to take care of children, Amy. Come on."

Chapter Three

Toni

Mama smiles at me as we pull into the school parking lot. "Have a good first day, Amy." She seems so relaxed, not at all worried that I'm three hours late and brought a three-year-old child back from the dead last night. Sometimes I wish she *would* worry.

"Thanks," I mutter, and hop out of the truck.

Everyone, every single person, turns their heads to me when I walk into my chemistry class halfway through. I wish they'd all chosen today to be inexplicably uninterested in anything out of the ordinary. Like me, with bags under my eyes and a surly expression on my face, trudging into the classroom in the middle of the teacher's explanation of what to expect in the coming semester. I had Chem One with him last year, so he doesn't have to ask my name; he doesn't even seem surprised to see me coming in so late. I kind of wish he would.

"Hello, Amy." His smile is only a little exasperated. "Take a seat."

I hear a few snickers as I walk down the aisle, but I ignore everyone until I reach the empty seat next to my friend Jordan. She got a new haircut for the first day of class, a cute, medium-length bob that highlights the pretty curves of her face.

"Is everything okay?" she whispers as I pull out my chemistry textbook. "I waited to walk down to the bus stop with you, but then Sarah walked by without you and told me you weren't coming."

"Just overslept," I mumble.

"You didn't miss much," she confides. "Just the usual first-day-of-class stuff."

One of the boys a few rows in front of us, Darren, looks over his shoulder and smirks at me as though my late arrival to class is some kind of indecency worthy of gossip. I can't keep the scowl from my face, but I try not to look at him. My eyes fall instead on a girl in the fourth row, one of the only people in the classroom studiously taking notes. She has her hair buzzed almost down to her scalp—shorter than any other girl in school, I'm sure— emphasizing her long, elegant neck. I can't be certain, only seeing her profile, but I think I recognize her, though not from last year. She has long, long eyelashes, a thin, angular face with a wide nose, and flat cheeks that make her cheekbones stand out. She's not pretty, exactly, but she's striking. Her dark skin has cool undertones, nicely complemented by her blue blouse.

"Who's that?" I whisper to Jordan.

"Toni Davis. Remember her? She was in middle school with us, but then her family moved away or something."

Toni Davis. I remember. We were never friends, but we were friendly; we both grew up on Whaleback Hill. She always seemed to keep to herself back then, always hanging out in the library. I don't remember who she was friends with. She's sitting next to Norma, but Norma isn't paying any attention to her, too preoccupied passing a note to her friends across the aisle.

I try to focus on what the teacher, Mr. Simpson, is saying, but as soon as I manage to stop thinking about Toni Davis, I start thinking about the little girl on our couch back home. I wonder if anyone here knew her. Was she someone's sister? Niece? Neighbor? What happened to her? I don't want to look through the obituaries from the last few weeks stacked in the laundry room, but I will have to as soon as I get home. I can't stand not knowing who the little girl is.

After chemistry, I have English. Toni Davis is in that class, too, which surprises me because I remember she was in pre-AP English in middle school. The only friend I share my English class with is Adela. We sit at the back of the classroom.

"Jordan says you were late to chemistry," Adela says without preamble. "And you weren't in social studies."

"I overslept," I mumble.

Adela clucks her tongue and flips her long, black hair over her shoulder. "On the first day of class? Come on, Amy."

"Can we talk about something else?"

She rolls her eyes. "Fine. Guess who broke up this summer?"

"Who?" I ask without much interest.

"Peter and Jessica," she says dramatically.

"Weren't they homecoming king and queen last year?" In spite of myself, I feel a twinge of curiosity, like I'm watching a trashy reality show. Adela has a way of making banal gossip sound exciting.

"Yes, Amy. They *were*. And *now*, Jessica is single, and Peter—get this—Peter is dating Angela."

"Which one's Angela again?" I ask.

She huffs in exasperation. "You've known her since kindergarten, Amy. And last year, she was wearing glasses, and she was in the band. This year, she's wearing contact lenses, she straightened her hair, she quit band, and she's dating last year's homecoming king."

"Good for her, I guess."

Our teacher walks into the classroom and greets us. "Have a good summer?" she asks brightly.

We all mumble something that sounds affirmative.

"Well, you'll never believe what *I* did this summer." Ms. Banks puts her hands on her hips and launches into a story about a play she was cast in and the absolutely *awful* director who made everyone cry at least once every rehearsal.

"And of course, Toni Davis is back," Adela tells me as though Ms. Banks didn't interrupt our conversation. "But you already knew *that*, because she's in your chemistry class."

"How do you know these things?" I ask, my gaze falling to Toni again.

No one has joined her at her desk this time. She watches Ms. Banks as though she's lecturing about something that will appear on a test rather than recounting a pointless story about her summer.

"I pay attention, Amy."

"Do you know where she's been all these years?" I ask Adela.

She shrugs elegantly. "I've been trying to find out, but no one seems to know. You remember how her family disappeared all of a sudden? Some people said they went into witness protection. I guess that could be true if whoever they testified against went to jail and they're not in danger anymore. But I don't think that usually happens, does it? That people just move back?"

Without giving me time to speculate, she continues. "Some people said her father did something, and they went on the run from the law, but obviously *that* theory's out now that they're back. Gina thinks maybe Toni's grandmother was sick or something, and they went to take care of her, but she died or got better, so they're back. Whatever happened, they didn't get rid of their house, because they're in the same house they were in before, unless they bought it back, but that seems kind of unlikely. You know, the Sandersons moved in there for a while, but they could have been renting from the Davises if they still owned the house . . . "

Adela goes on for another few minutes. I'm strangely fascinated with the way Toni folds her hands on her desk, her slender wrists crossed, her back straight, her gaze unwavering. She was always studious, but I don't remember her being this serious. Did something bad happen to her and her family over these last few years?

Ms. Banks finally finishes her story and gets around to handing us the reading list for the semester. I scan it for anything interesting, but it's mostly the same old classics you'd expect—the kind of books that have never held my attention, and the reason I, unlike Toni Davis, have never tested into the higher-level English classes. I feel little sense of connection with the "litany of dead white men," as Jordan calls them. Even the occasional token female writer offers me little to feel excited about.

A title catches my eye: *Frankenstein* by Mary Shelley. Well, that will be moderately interesting, I suppose, to someone of my persuasion. A giggle bubbles out of my mouth, even though I feel more apprehensive than amused.

"What?" Adela asks me.

I shake my head. "Nothing."

CHAPTER FOUR
Speculation

At lunch, my friends and I occupy our usual table: Jordan, Adela, and Harper with their short, bleached-blond hair and baggy, faded t-shirt that exclaims "SAVE THE TURTLES!" Harper comments on my extreme lateness this morning. I give them the same excuse I used twice already about oversleeping, and when everyone keeps teasing me, I scowl until they stop.

None of our families have money to go on summer vacations, so we all spent the summer in town and don't have much to catch up on. Adela has more than enough school gossip to keep us satisfied throughout the meal, though. I heard a lot of it in English class, so I only half-listen.

I notice Toni sitting alone in a corner of the cafeteria, tucked away from the rest of the students. She doesn't look at anyone, her nose buried in a book, barely paying attention to her food. I can't help but wonder about her—about the past few years, about her seriousness. I dredge up a few more memories of her from middle school, and I'm sure she hasn't always been so self-contained, so lonely, so reserved. We've all changed since middle school, obviously. Almost everyone here has known each other since kindergarten, and I suppose the changes seem more gradual in everyone else, since I see them every day during the school year. Still . . .

When Adela mentions Toni, Harper glances over at her table and observes, "She doesn't look very happy."

"She's probably tired of everyone staring at her," Jordan notes. "Should we invite her over to sit with us?"

Harper looks skeptical, but Adela nearly bounces out of her seat, headed toward Toni's table.

Jordan grabs her arm. "Don't interrogate her, Adela, okay?"

"Who said I was going to?" Adela asks.

"History," I say.

Harper snickers, and Adela rolls her eyes.

"I can be tactful," she says.

She stalks over to Toni's table. Even more people in the cafeteria look in that direction now.

"Seriously, she's not a soap opera," I mutter, though I feel a twinge of guilt. I've been staring at Toni unabashedly, too.

Toni looks up as Adela approaches. Adela says something. Toni smiles and shakes her head, polite but not necessarily friendly. It's like there's a wall between them.

Adela returns alone, looking crestfallen. "She didn't want to come."

"Maybe she's overwhelmed," Jordan says. "It must suck to start at a new school where everyone else knows each other."

"She knows everybody," Adela counters.

Jordan shrugs. "Well, it's basically like she doesn't. It's been, what? Almost three years?"

"Or maybe she's been somewhere nicer than this and thinks she's better than us now," Harper grumbles.

Adela props her chin in her palm. "If she'd been somewhere fancy, why would she come back?"

"Maybe her parents won the lottery and spent all the money," Harper says. "Most people go bankrupt within a few years of winning the lottery."

"Maybe we shouldn't talk about her this much," I suggest. Everyone looks at me. "I mean, the whole school is gossiping about her. It's kind of . . . rude, isn't it?"

Adela rolls her eyes. "People are just curious, Amy. There's nothing wrong with that. If she'd just come talk with us, we could actually know what's up with her instead of speculating."

"Well, there's no *point* in speculating, is there?" It comes out snappier than I mean it to. Fortunately, Adela has thick skin, so she just shrugs and shakes her head. "Sorry," I add after a moment. "I was just thinking, I'd hate for people to talk if it was me."

"People are going to talk no matter what," Harper says with a sigh. "There's nothing better to do. Man, I can't believe we have two more years of this crap. First day of school isn't even over, and I'm already so *bored*."

"You could take AP classes if you're so bored," Jordan chides.

"No thanks," Harper says. "I don't think school has anything to teach me."

"You sound like my mom," I say. I'm grateful that we've moved on from the topic of Toni Davis.

"I love your mom," Adela says dreamily. "I wish *my* mom was that easygoing."

"That's one word for her, I guess," I say. I suddenly think of the little girl sleeping on our couch. Toni distracted me from that line of thought for a while, but now I feel my face crumple.

"You okay, Amy?" Harper asks.

I shake my head, my throat suddenly tight. Jordan is the only one I've ever told about my strange powers. They all know my family's different—that *I'm* different. They've seen the pets and other animals that come and go from our house; they've heard the rumors of my Aunt Betty sitting in graveyards, talking to ghosts every full moon, and of my mother's "almost" magical ability to ease the pain of the dying. They still accept me—all of them are outcasts, too, in one way or another—but we don't talk about it, which is mostly my choice. I can't explain to them what happened. I'm not even ready to tell Jordan about it.

Jordan gets up and sits on the bench beside me, putting her arm around my shoulders.

"Thanks," I mutter, leaning against her.

I want to cry, but as usual, my desire doesn't last more than a few seconds, as though a blanket of numbness is thrown over my emotions. In this case, it's kind of helpful. There's no worse place to cry than a school cafeteria. Toni might be relieved if I did, though—it would take some eyes off of her. I glance over at her table.

She's finishing her food without looking up from her book, her slender wrists graceful, her every movement careful and measured. Toni has secrets, too.

I wonder if they're anywhere near as strange as my own.

CHAPTER FIVE

Obituaries

Jordan and I climb into the back of the bus after school. I watch the milling of students through the window and spot Toni. I wonder if she'll come on our bus; we all live in the same neighborhood. But she walks over to a car and gets into the passenger seat. It drives off. Her parents must have come to get her.

The school bus leaves me and Jordan at the base of Whaleback Hill. It's a small neighborhood full of steep, winding roads, some of them impassable for anything larger than a pickup truck, and the school bus has never bothered trying to navigate it. We walk up the hill from the bus stop, Jordan telling me about some new music that was released today, me listening as usual. We come to a standstill in front of Toni's house without a word passing between us—both of us on instinct, it seems. We fall silent.

The Sandersons have kept it neat in the Davises' absence, the lawn trimmed, the paint fresh on the fence and the sides of the double-wide. The car that picked up Toni from school sits in the carport.

"Should we drop in and say hi?" Jordan asks.

"She didn't want to sit with us at lunch," I point out. "She probably doesn't want to say 'hi.'"

I really want to, though, and I can't entirely explain it.

Jordan shrugs, and we keep walking. My movements feel mechanical, and I sense myself peeling away from what my body is doing. It happens to me a lot, especially in the past year or so. Some times are worse than others, and I never know why. My therapist says I'm afraid of my feelings, and my mind does this to me to protect me. What am I afraid of now? My strange fascination with Toni? The anticipated agony of another school year? What I'll find when I get home?

"Are you okay?" Jordan asks. She can tell better than almost anyone else when this happens to me.

"Yeah." I force a smile, even though my mouth barely feels like my own. "Just wiped out." The cadence of my voice sounds wrong to my ears—and probably to Jordan's, too, but she doesn't say anything.

"See you later," she calls as we reach her house, and I turn to trudge up the last few hundred feet to mine.

Our family owns the property at the very top of the hill, right before the forest begins. Our front yard is much more overgrown than most of the others around it. Unlike Toni's yard or Jordan's, ours lives well outside of the bounds of *neat* and *tidy*. A snarl of flowers, bushes, and succulents, all larger and more vibrant than any others of their species (thanks to Maddie), scorn the restrictions of flowerbeds or rows. A beaten earth path winds its way to the front step.

I put a hand on the mailbox, which nestles in a brick pillar overgrown with flowering vines, and take several deep breaths. With my therapist's help, I've been learning how to handle these episodes when I feel distant from myself, outside of my body. I focus on my surroundings and try to find everything yellow:

Sunflowers.

The plush button centers of daisies.

Kitchen curtains through the window.

The tousle-haired pixie cut of dandelion heads.

Spots on the wings of a butterfly fluttering around the rose bush.

Stripes on the bumblebees buzzing in and out of tulips and hydrangeas.

The sun beaming down at me.

Then I focus on the feeling of my backpack straps digging into my shoulders, weighed down by textbooks. On the warmth of my muscles and the slight stickiness of sweat on my skin after climbing the winding roads of my neighborhood in the late summer sun. On the hot, rough brick under my hand.

Little by little, I find myself coming back into my body, into my thoughts, into my muted feelings. I feel more like a person with defined edges, with clear borders where the outside stops and I begin, though I still don't feel quite whole. I haven't felt quite whole in a long time.

I take another deep breath and walk up the path and through the front door. The couch where the little girl slept last night is empty, the old towels gone. The kitchen lures me toward it with the scent of fresh and drying herbs. Maddie and Grandma stand at the island counter, washing herbs in a giant metal bowl and sorting them to dry on baking sheets.

Maddie beams at me. She has Daddy's thick, blond hair, lightened to almost platinum by hours and hours in the sun, smooth skin darkened by the sun in contrast— no hint of freckles like mine. She looks a lot like Daddy, actually: broad, kind face; round, brown eyes; slender but deceptively strong hands. Pianist's hands, Mama calls them, though neither of them plays piano. Maddie's tall and curvy, too, the luckiest one in the family in that regard, even taller than Daddy. Daddy says that comes from his mom, but none of us ever met her.

"Amy!" Maddie calls, as if we haven't seen each other in ages. "How was your first day back at school?"

"It was fine. Where's the little girl?"

Before Maddie can answer, footsteps patter behind me like something out of a horror movie. I turn, my heart leaping into my chest, in time for a pair of little arms to fling around my knees. I blink down at the top of her head covered in tight, dark curls bunched into two messy pigtails. She's wearing the yellow dress, like in my dream. All the mud is gone, leaving nothing but cloth and hair and soft skin.

"You look like you've never seen a little kid before,"

Maddie laughs, walking over and scooping the little girl onto her hip.

"I've never seen a . . . well, not one like her." It seems rude to call her dead to her face.

The little girl smiles at me, dimples in her little round cheeks. She has soft, warm brown skin, huge eyes, and chubby arms and legs. She looks almost entirely alive; the only dead thing about her is the hint of vacancy in her eyes, the sense of not-quite-thereness. She reaches out her chubby hands for me, leaning away from Maddie's body so that my sister has to shift her weight to keep from dropping her.

Maddie laughs again. "She likes you already. Here, hold her. I have lots of herbs left to wash."

I don't want to hold her. I don't want to know if she feels alive. But she seems so determined that I give in and let Maddie hand her to me. Being the youngest, I don't have much experience holding children, but she fits nicely on my hip and snuggles up to my chest, which makes her easy to hold. I want to cry, and I can feel that blanket of numbness preparing to cast itself over me to prevent it. Maddie returns to her herbs.

"Where's your sister?" Grandma asks me.

"At the Y with her friends. Has the little girl said anything?"

"Not a peep," Grandma says. "Give her time. She'll talk when she's ready."

"If she even talked before," Maddie adds. "The Smiths, next door—their little boy didn't talk until he was almost five."

I suddenly want very much to be alone. Without a word, I walk into the laundry room, grab the stack of newspapers, and carry them and the little girl into the backyard. Since Maddie and Grandma are inside, the garden will be empty.

The little girl seems to have no desire to leave my arms. I sit on the roots of the old oak tree, the only tree that grows within our property, where the leaves will give us some shade, and let the little girl sit in my lap. She curls up against me. Does she really just like me? The

animals I bring back are often attached to me if they're
not desperate to go home. It's a lot easier to handle having
a canary or an old dog follow me around than this child
whose name I don't know yet.

I flip through the obituaries, starting with yesterday's
paper. It would take me a while to run out of things I'd
rather do than look at the names of dead people, but I
need to know this girl's name, where she comes from,
what happened to her. An animal without a name is wild
and free; a person without a name is just a ghost.

I read about how Margaret is survived by her loving
children, how Leanne's family would appreciate donations
to the local rescue shelter in lieu of flowers, and how
Tyronne battled cancer for fourteen years. I wonder how
many of these people could come back if I had the power
to bring them all, if I could control when the Itch strikes
and decide who to pull out of a bucket of mud. I wonder
how many of them would *want* to come back.

Most of them are old, but there's an eight-year-old boy
who was killed in a car crash, a young schoolteacher who
died of undisclosed causes, a twelve-year-old girl with
leukemia. No three-year-old girls—or two or four, in case
I'm wrong about her age.

Do people write obituaries for such young children?
I've never thought about it before. Maybe it's too painful.
Maybe everyone who needs to come to the funeral can
find out through the child's parents, since the child
hasn't had a chance to build up a network of friends and
acquaintances of their own.

I make it to the last page of the two weeks of obituaries
without finding a single clue about the identity of the
little girl. My fingers feel numb, and my mind is floating
somewhere eight feet above the ground, looking down at
my body like a helium balloon I let go of without noticing
and just keeps going up, up, up. I was so focused on the
task that I didn't realize the emotional toll it was taking on
me.

My therapist says dissociation is a defense mechanism,
a survival tactic. Death is the ultimate motivator for survival
tactics. I don't know if my brain is protecting me from the

threat of death or from the emotions that it conjures up, too huge to be contained within the bounds of my bones.

"Okay," a little voice says. "You okay."

I look down. The little girl is patting my cheek with her chubby hand. I focus on the sensation of her gentle, comforting touch, the sweet, soft sound of her voice. They are the first words she's said, as far as I know, since coming back. I know I don't look upset when I dissociate; I look numb. People who don't know the signs don't realize. My own family doesn't always realize, though my therapist has encouraged me to tell them so they can help me if I need it. But somehow, this little girl—this *dead* little girl—knows exactly how I'm feeling. Knows how to comfort me. Knows that I need comfort. I haven't spent much time around little kids, but I've heard some people say they can be more open to other people's emotions than adults. Of course, it might also be our connection. Every creature I bring back has a special link to me, the creator of their second, shadowy life.

Either way, the little girl helps me come back into myself, at least most of the way. When I feel more like a whole person, I pick her up and stand her on the ground in front of me, my eyes level with hers.

"Can you tell me your name?" I ask.

She just looks at me. She doesn't smile or speak or move. She doesn't even breathe. I guess my momentary distress triggered a response from her that's now lost. She still hasn't come back all the way. Or maybe she's dissociating, too. After all, to die at three . . . she probably has much more reason to want to leave her body than I do.

"It's okay," I tell her. "You don't have to tell me yet."

There are so many things I haven't told other people, even my family. I haven't told them how bad it's gotten—how the therapy helps, but not enough. I haven't told my friends, except Jordan, the truth about my strange skills or my family's rare cadre of talents. Who am I to tell someone else to spill their secrets?

I stand up and take the little girl's hand, and together, we walk back into the house.

CHAPTER SIX

Daddy

"Any luck?" Grandma asks as the little girl and I walk back into the kitchen.

I shake my head, tossing the two weeks' worth of newspapers and their useless obituaries back onto the dryer.

"Well, it's all right." Grandma bends over, smiling at the little girl. "You're more than welcome to stay with us as long as you need to."

The little girl holds onto my hand and stares back at Grandma with her round, brown eyes. Grandma doesn't seem offended or disturbed by her behavior, though from a live child, she probably would have demanded a "thank you, ma'am." She straightens and returns to sorting bunches of cilantro.

"Have you spoken to Aunt Betty?" Maddie asks, scooping washed herbs out of the big metal bowl. "She'll probably know what to do if anyone does."

"No. Is she up?"

"Not yet," Grandma says.

"Come on," I tell the little girl, and take her into the living room with me.

We sit on the couch and I turn on the TV, flipping to a kid's channel. I haven't seen this cartoon in a couple of years, and it gives me a pang of nostalgia, so I settle down to watch. Every now and then, the little girl lets out a giggle, but when I look at her, she's back to her blank stare. I guess it's not that different from how some kids look when they're watching TV.

A little after five, I hear Daddy's truck in the driveway. The smells of summer squash and beans have begun to drift from the kitchen, and I know that Maddie and Grandma have switched over to preparing supper.

The laundry room door opens, and I hear Daddy say, "Hello there, my little ray of sunshine."

The little girl and I have been sitting a few inches apart on the sofa. Now, she throws herself at me and flings her arms around my middle, burying her face in my side. I pat her back, startled.

"Hi, Daddy," Maddie says. "How was your day?"

"Oh, not bad," Daddy replies. "Hello, Martha."

"Hello, Bob," Grandma says. "Dinner will be ready in a few minutes. Your wife said she was going to be late."

Daddy steps into the living room, and the little girl holds me tighter until it's hard to breathe. My heart spikes with sudden fear, even though I've never been afraid at the sight of Daddy before. He's a little over average height, clean shaven, and with a round, jolly face. His blond hair, still thick as ever, is slicked to his forehead with sweat, the way it always is after a day of work in the summer. I take a deep breath to calm myself.

"Hello, Amy," he says, stopping and frowning slightly at my expression. "Are you all right?"

"Yeah, it's just . . . she's a little . . . I'm going to take her into my room to calm her down."

I scoop the little girl into my arms and hurry past Daddy, unwilling to meet his eyes for some reason. He doesn't question me. As the only normal person in a household full of women with strange talents, he rarely questions.

I take the girl into my room and close the door behind us, then set her on the floor and kneel in front of her, our eyes level. A moment ago, her body was taut with tension, but now as I hold her shoulders, the tension is gone. She stares at me, her eyes vacant, her face as expressive as a porcelain doll. It's almost like I imagined how she acted before.

It's not always beloved pets that I bring back. Sometimes, animals have the marks of beatings on their hides. Once their personalities come back, they usually hide under a bed, and often growl at anyone who gets near, except me. Those animals tend to be most afraid of Daddy, probably because it's more likely to have been a man who hit them when they were alive.

"Was . . . " I begin, gazing into the nameless little girl's blank brown eyes. "Was there a bad man who hurt you?"

The little girl just stares back.

"You can tell me. I promise I won't tell anyone you told me."

Still, nothing.

I'm shaking. Is there a man somewhere nearby who hurt this little girl? Who killed her? Is that why there's no obituary for her? Does anyone even know she's dead? My mind is spinning out dozens of possibilities, focusing on the most gruesome, the most terrifying. I try to breathe and steady myself so I won't frighten the girl, though she doesn't seem to notice my distress this time.

"It's okay," I tell her. "It's okay. You can talk when you're ready." I hug her, wrapping her tiny body in my arms. It's soothing to imagine I'm protecting her. A soothing lie. "It's okay. It's okay."

A knock comes at the door. "Supper's ready, Amy," Maddie calls.

"Okay."

I gather my strength and think for a moment before standing and crossing the small bedroom to the closet. I reach up to a cardboard box on the top shelf, where Sarah and I have stashed some of our childhood toys that we didn't want to get rid of. I set the box down on the floor in front of the little girl.

"I'm going to go have supper," I tell her. "Do you want to stay here and play with the toys?"

She blinks at me.

"It'll just be for a little while. Just stay here, okay?" I start toward the door, and the little girl follows me, ignoring the toys. "Stay," I tell her. I sound like I'm talking to a dog. "Please stay here. It won't be long." I reach for the doorknob, and she comes to stand beside me, holding onto the hem of my shorts. "You can't come!" I tell her, tears stinging my eyes. I feel trapped inside the room, inside my head. "Stay here. I promise, it's safe here."

Footsteps sound outside my door. "Is everything okay, Amy?" Maddie asks. "Can I come in?"

"Yeah."

Maddie opens the door and looks from me to the little girl, who's still holding onto the hem of my shorts.

"She was upset when she saw Daddy earlier," I tell Maddie, my voice choked. "I can't take her out there. But she won't let me leave."

Maddie reaches down and scoops the little girl up into her arms. She starts to carry her out of the room, but I catch her sleeve.

"Wait. She's scared. I think maybe there was a . . . a man . . . a bad man . . . " My eyes are tearing up again, and I can't explain what I mean.

"It's okay," Maddie tells me, patting my arm with her free hand, the little girl on her hip. "We'll take care of it."

Maddie carries the girl into the dining room, and I trail behind, terrified of what will happen when the girl sees Daddy again. I feel like some force is ripping apart my insides.

Daddy is sitting at his usual place at the table, across from Grandma and to the right of Mama's empty chair at the head. He looks up at Maddie and the little girl, smiling, but he doesn't stand up. I guess he does seem less intimidating when he's not looming over us, but the little girl still buries her face in Maddie's collarbone, trembling.

"Daddy, this is our guest," Maddie tells him.

"Nice to meet you," Daddy says in his warm, gentle voice.

"Sweetie, this is my daddy and Amy's daddy. He's a very nice man."

The little girl peeks at Daddy for a moment before hiding against Maddie's chest again. I'm afraid Daddy will be offended, but he just keeps smiling. As usual, he takes everything in stride.

"Now, you can go back to Amy's room and play by yourself for a little bit," Maddie tells the little girl, "or you can sit at the table with all of us. Either way is just fine, but you have to pick one."

"She can't," I protest.

"She can make up her own mind," Grandma says. "She's a big girl."

The little girl lifts her face from Maddie's chest, glances at Daddy, and reaches her chubby arms for me. Maddie smiles and hands her over. I stand there numbly for a moment, holding her on my hip, unsure of what to do next, terrified that everything is going to fall apart and that it will somehow be my fault. The girl still won't look at Daddy, but she's not shaking anymore.

"Here." Maddie indicates an old plastic booster seat strapped to a chair. There's a plastic plate and cup set there. I settle the girl in the booster seat and take the chair next to her.

Maddie serves us each some of the summer squash casserole, which smells delicious, and sits down next to Daddy. Sarah and Aunt Betty haven't made their appearance yet, but our family isn't in the habit of waiting around for people at mealtimes. Everyone tucks in. I watch the little girl to see what she'll do; the pets will sometimes eat scraps or kibble, though I don't think they need it to keep their mud-and-magic bodies alive. She grabs her plastic cup and puts it to her lips but sets it quickly back down.

"Lemonade," she demands.

Everyone looks at her. Then Maddie stands up and takes her cup into the kitchen, returning a moment later with the cup full of lemonade. The girl drinks it all down in a few swallows. Then she just sits there, ignoring her casserole but not seeming impatient to leave the table either. It's like she's herself in flashes.

We're halfway through the meal when the front door opens, and Sarah stalks in. She has Mama's dark hair and stocky frame, but the cadre of sports she's played ever since elementary school have made her more muscular than rotund like Mama and me. Outside, a car pulls away, carrying whatever friend or friends dropped her off; Sarah never has a shortage of friends, boyfriends, and/or acquaintances to ferry her places.

"You'll never believe what happened at the Y," she declares as she throws her book bag by the door and crosses the distance to the dining room table in a few strides.

Before we can learn what happened at the Y, Aunt Betty emerges from the kitchen, hair uncombed and eyes sleepy as usual. She's a less-there version of Mama, dark-haired and short like her sister but with sunken cheeks and not much flesh under the loose clothes she wears. She stops when she sees the little girl beside me and, without warning, her eyes overflow with tears.

"Oh, you poor thing," she cries. "What happened to you?"

CHAPTER SEVEN

Sister

"What do you mean, Aunt Betty?" I ask as my stomach drops, the casserole suddenly heavy in my gut.

Aunt Betty circles the table and crouches beside the little girl's booster seat, peering up at her with tearful eyes. "She's not all there, Amy. Did you not bring her back all the way?"

"I don't know," I reply. Did I do something wrong? Was it me? It makes a sick sort of sense—how could I expect to bring back a whole person when I'm not whole myself? If she's incomplete, if I messed up the process, it would explain why she still doesn't seem like herself almost twenty-four hours into her un-life.

Sarah sits beside Maddie, eyeing the little girl across the table. "Have you found out who she is yet?"

"Her name is missing," Aunt Betty says, smoothing back a lock of the girl's dark, curly hair. "She can't remember it. She won't be able to remember what happened to her either."

"Is it my fault?" I ask, already hearing the answer as an echo to my question.

Aunt Betty opens her mouth to respond, but Grandma interrupts, "Of course not. It's the first time you've brought back a person. You gave her as much of yourself as you were able without doing yourself harm."

"I did everything the Itch told me to do," I say, feeling like I'm justifying myself even though Grandma has already advocated for me. Her words don't exactly make me feel better. A mistake is still a mistake even if it happened because I couldn't do any better. Even if it happened because there's something wrong with me.

"Maybe she's too scared to come back all the way," Aunt Betty muses, her eyes still fixed on the girl's profile. The girl doesn't look her way, staring off into the distance as if to prove Aunt Betty's point. "Something so traumatic, so frightening . . . and she's so young. Maybe she wasn't put together strongly enough in the first place . . . yes, that might be it . . . "

"What are you talking about?" Sarah demands.

"Children are still developing their identities," Aunt Betty explains, stroking the girl's cheek. "It might make sense that they wouldn't be able to bring back all of themselves. If some recent trauma forced her to leave behind part of herself or divide herself, it would make it even harder."

"So it's not my fault?" I ask, confused.

"Maybe not," Aunt Betty says, never one to mince words.

"Of course not," Grandma repeats sternly.

"Wait, by leaving behind part of herself or dividing herself, do you mean she . . . " I'm embarrassed to say the word, so used to treating it as private and undesirable. "Dissociated?"

"Maybe," Aunt Betty says. "Maybe she suppressed some memories. Forgot on purpose. Or maybe you just aren't strong enough to bring back people yet."

"Why would I get the Itch to bring someone back if I wasn't strong enough? It's supposed to be innate knowledge, right? Wisdom?"

I desperately want something other than myself to blame, and at the same time, my mind is pounding certainty into me, telling me it can't be anything's fault but my own. Maddie frowns at me, seeming to mark the distress in my tone.

"Maybe her desire to come back overwhelmed your instincts," Aunt Betty suggests. "Or your souls resonated with each other in some way."

Through all this, the little girl is still staring off into space. It's like she's acting extra empty now that Aunt Betty is here to criticize me for it.

"Has her spirit spoken to you at all, Aunt Betty?" Maddie asks.

Aunt Betty shakes her head and closes her eyes. "It's too scattered and torn to speak. And the full moon is two weeks away. I'm just getting emotions. Fear . . . confusion . . . she wants her mother. And her sister."

"She had a sister?" I ask.

"Yes. An older one. About your age, I think."

I can't speak; my throat is too tight. *That's* why the girl is so attached to me. It isn't just that I brought her back to life—I remind her of the sister she lost. The sister who is probably out there somewhere, grieving in a way I can't even imagine. About my age . . . does she go to my school? Did I pass her in the halls today or sit in the same classroom? I'm now even more responsible for the little girl.

"The food is getting cold," Grandma says, breaking the short silence that followed Aunt Betty's pronouncement. "Betty, sit down and eat your casserole."

No one but Grandma can compel Aunt Betty to do anything, but whatever Grandma says is law to her, the same as it is for Mama. Aunt Betty sits at her place at the table the way a shadow settles over a patch of sunny grass, her gaze still fixed on the little girl.

I shiver, my appetite gone.

Chapter Eight

Scream

The little girl sleeps on an inflatable mattress in mine and Sarah's room that night, because she doesn't want to be in a different room from me. When I wake, she's sitting on the mattress, looking up at me. I remember a dream I was having. I think she was in it, but then it's gone, and I can't recall any of the details. I almost hoped she wouldn't be there when I woke. Almost? Maybe not *almost*.

"Hello," I say, the way you say hello to big spiders or wild animals to try to picture them more friendly in your mind.

She doesn't answer but watches as I climb down. Sarah is sitting on the edge of her bed, comparing two shirts she has splayed out on the bedspread. She nods towards the little girl.

"Creepy."

"She can't help it," I say, though Sarah is right.

"Well, I'm getting dressed in the bathroom." Sarah snatches up one of the shirts, along with the rest of her outfit, and stomps out of the room.

I eye the little girl's yellow dress and wonder if she'll need a change of clothes or a bath. It's not something I worry about with the pets or the wild animals. Do dead people develop body odor? Can they get rashes? Does their hair get greasy? I have no idea.

"Who knew you didn't even have to get teen pregnant to end up taking care of a baby?" I half-joke to myself, though it's not funny.

"I'm not a baby," the little girl pipes up, making me jump.

"No, you're not," I say slowly, careful not to seem overeager that she's talking. "You're a big girl."

"I'm three," she announces.

So I was right about her age. Does her sudden willingness to talk about herself mean she's getting more of herself back? Could Aunt Betty be wrong after all, and she just needed more time?

"And what's your name?" I ask, trying to sound light and casual, the way people sound when they ask that question of normal children. My heart pounds, waiting.

But she clams up as usual and stares at me with her wide, dark eyes. I turn my back on her and face my closet so she won't see my scowl and my teary eyes. Aunt Betty is never wrong about spirits.

I pick the usual sort of clothes, baggy and unremarkable—my high school-patterned camouflage. Sarah's doubly right: it feels weird to change in front of the girl. So I wait until Sarah comes back to put away her nightgown and hurry to occupy the bathroom before anyone else claims it. We have two bathrooms, but with seven people in the house, you need to act quick to use one, especially in the morning.

When I come out, I nearly trip over the girl, who stares up at me with that vacant expression of hers. My heart stumbles, and I can't meet her eyes. *Empty. Not all there. Just like me.*

I take her hand and lead her into the kitchen, where Daddy's halfway out the door with a piece of toast in his mouth. He waves at me jovially and mumbles something about having a good day around the piece of toast. The little girl shrinks against my side until Daddy's gone but betrays no other hint of emotion.

Grandma, Maddie, and Sarah are all at the kitchen table, eating eggs and bacon. I plop the little girl into the booster seat, which someone has moved into the kitchen, and gather my breakfast.

"She's not going to like it when you leave," Sarah

comments. "Every time I rolled over in the night, she was sitting there staring up at you." She pauses with a strip of bacon halfway to her mouth. "What if she's not a little girl at all? What if her body is possessed by a demon? Did you bring back a demon, Amy?"

"Don't be ridiculous," Grandma snaps. "There's no such thing as demons. And even if there were, your Aunt Betty would have sensed it right away."

"How do you know she would have sensed it if there's no such thing as demons?" Sarah asks.

"She's not a demon," I say, sitting so heavily in my chair that I slosh my coffee onto the table. Not a demon, just broken. Maddie passes me a towel to mop up the spill in that efficient way of hers, as if she's notified the instant something needs her attention.

"Well, she's creepy." Sarah crunches on her bacon.

"Don't listen to Sarah," Maddie tells the little girl. "She's just being silly. You know you're welcome in our house, and you can stay as long as you like."

Sarah snorts but doesn't contradict Maddie. The little girl stares back at Maddie, giving no indication that she heard or understood. I'm eager to go to school and get away from her for a few hours, though I feel guilty thinking about it. She's attached to me because she misses her sister. She's probably scared—at least the part of her that's in there. Who knows what happened to her? But Sarah's right, and I need a break.

Sarah and I finish breakfast and gather our school things. As we head toward the front door, the little girl gets down from her booster seat and totters over to stand beside me.

Maddie joins us and scoops her up. "Amy has to go to school. She'll be back before you know it."

The little girl reaches her chubby arms toward me. It's weird, that gesture coupled with her expressionless face. I can't suppress a shudder and turn away from her, shouldering my book bag.

A horrible noise assaults my ears. Beside me, Sarah claps her hands over her own ears, her expression scandalized. I look back at the little girl, whose face has reddened as though she has a severe sunburn. Her eyes are squeezed shut, tears already falling from them, and her mouth is opened so wide I can see her tonsils. She pauses for breath and my eardrums crackle; then she lets out another awful scream that rattles my brain.

"Go!" Maddie yells over the racket. "She might calm down if she realizes she can't get you to stay!"

I don't have to be told twice. Sarah and I duck our heads and dash out of the house, slamming the front door behind us. The little girl's cries get muffled, but not by much; the walls of the double-wide aren't exactly soundproof. We hurry down the garden path to the street.

"Oh my God." Sarah shakes her head, her eyes wide. "You never did that when you were a baby."

"How would you remember?" I ask. Sarah's only one year older than me.

"I'd remember."

I let it go. Sarah can pick up an idea and run with it forever, no matter how ridiculous her arguments get.

We follow the steep, switchback road down through Whaleback Hill, the early morning sun baking familiar smells out of the asphalt and the grass and the siding of the houses we pass. I wonder if the little girl's family lives in one of those houses, if they're mourning her, if they even know what happened to her.

"Hey!" Jordan calls. She's standing on the sidewalk outside her house, her book bag hung over one shoulder. She hurries to fall into step with us. "On time today?"

I scowl, and Jordan laughs lightly. She's in a good mood. Sarah moves a few steps ahead of us as if to signal that she doesn't belong with us. Or maybe she's giving us the chance to talk; maybe I'm just cynical.

"Adela wants us all to hang out after school," Jordan says. "Are you available?"

Sarah glances over her shoulder at us. I wonder if she's thinking about the little girl who doesn't want to leave my side and who will probably be anxiously awaiting my return. Who knows if Maddie will even be able to calm her down? Dead things can be awfully stuck in their ways.

"Sure," I say.

The longer I delay my return to that house, the better for me.

CHAPTER NINE

Invitation

I'm taking my history textbook from my locker when I notice Toni Davis across the hallway. She's pinning pictures to the inside of her locker door with a kind of mathematical precision. I find my gaze caught by her again, the graceful curve of her wrists and the elegant lines of her neck. I wonder if she did ballet in middle school or maybe while she was away.

Two of the school's most aggressively straight guys swagger down the hallway, and I look back at my locker, not wanting to catch their eyes. Vic and Darren. I prefer to avoid interacting with them at all costs.

"Hey. Toni, right?" Vic asks.

I glance up, the fall of my auburn hair partially concealing the scene across the hallway. Toni turns from her locker, surprised as if no one has addressed her in weeks.

"Hi," she says.

"Remember me? I'm Vic, and this is Darren."

"Yeah. Nice to see you again." She has a deep voice for a girl, elegant and precise to go with the way she carries herself.

"So, we're having a back-to-school party on Friday night." Vic leans against the locker next to Toni's, his hands in his pockets. He has a bit of stubble on his chin, and he doesn't have the sense to realize that it makes him look stupid rather than cool.

"Okay," Toni allows.

"Anyway, it's a party at my house. A pool party. You should come. I'd like to see you there."

I gag internally. I eye Toni to see if she's falling for Vic's incredibly weak game. She has her back turned to me, facing her locker. Her body is straight, not leaning towards or away from Vic, not giving me any indication of her attitude toward him.

"Thank you, Vic," Toni says. "I'll consider it."

"Okay, great." Vic sounds as though he's taking her consideration as a definite yes. He doesn't even have the self-awareness not to look smug. "It'll be a good time. Here, put my number in your phone and call me so I'll have your number."

It's a good strategy; Toni won't have the chance to give him a fake number that way. Not that I know if she would have given him a fake number. I fiddle with the strap of my book bag while they go through their exchange. When Vic is finally done, he and Darren swagger off down the hallway. Darren catches sight of me and slams my locker door closed as he passes.

"Hey, dyke."

I stand here, shaking with anger and maybe something else. Some part of me is peeling away from the rest, but I stuff the feeling away; sometimes if I ignore an episode, it will resolve itself on its own. I glance back at Toni and catch her eyes for the first time. Hers are dark, wide, and unreadable. I jerk my gaze away and yank my locker back open to finish arranging my things before storming off to history.

It doesn't help to ignore the dissociation. By the time I reach my classroom, I'm floating, everyone around me transformed into ghosts . . . or maybe I'm the ghost. Either way, I'm certain we would pass through each other if I walked straight toward them.

Time slips away, and my body somehow navigates itself through the intervening hour and a half until lunch.

I find myself in the cafeteria, holding a tray I have no memory of allowing the lunch lady to plop edibles onto. I turn toward my friends' usual table, but then catch sight of Toni at her lonely table in the corner. My feet pilot me toward her. When she looks up at me, catching my eyes for the second time that day, I'm committed to talking to her. Another part of me has made the decision for the part of me that has to deal with it.

"Yes?" Toni asks.

"I don't know if you remember me," I tell her. "We were in middle school together. I'm Amy."

"Right," Toni says with a polite smile.

"I didn't mean to listen in earlier, but I heard Vic and Darren inviting you to their party." My throat and mouth are dry, and I'm afraid I'll choke on my words if I don't get them all out in time. "I just wanted to let you know that they're assholes. Vic especially. He'll do anything to get in . . . to get in a girl's pants."

Toni frowns slightly. She has her elbow propped on the table, her hand curved downward like the branch of a weeping willow, and her fork perched between her index and middle fingers like a loosely held pencil. It really is as though every movement she makes is part of some carefully choreographed dance. Is it as natural as it seems or a performance? What would someone have to do to train themselves to seem like everything they do is naturally deliberate and measured?

"Sorry again," I mumble, though I've forgotten what I'm apologizing for. Maybe for bringing my bungling self into her graceful radius.

"It's okay. Thank you." Her eyes search mine. She wears minimal makeup, mostly foundation and concealer, it seems, with maybe a touch of eye shadow. It's much classier than anything I could ever manage. I usually skip the makeup entirely to match my baggy, inconspicuous outfits.

"Sure. I just didn't want you to get mixed up with them. Unless you—"

"It's okay. I wasn't going to . . . go to the party, anyway." Her shoulder tucks in a little, and her chin dips toward it, the first uncertain movement I've seen her make. It's accompanied by a small smile.

"Oh." I stand there with my tray, wondering if I'm slouching. "Um, my friends are getting together this afternoon if you want to come." I realize she might not know who my friends are, so I gesture clumsily toward them.

Toni lays her free hand on the back of her fork-holding hand. I have the feeling a door is closing in my face; I only now realize how open her body language was before, in contrast with its current state. "I have a lot to unpack. We just moved in."

"Oh," I say again. "Well . . . see you." I start to turn away from her.

"Thank you . . . for the warning."

I can't tell if my smile looks like a grimace. I throw in a nod to emphasize it and hurry back to my friends' table. They all stare at me as if I've been doing backflips in the middle of the cafeteria.

"What?" I demand.

"Why were you talking to Toni Davis?" Adela asks. She has her long, black hair gathered into a ponytail today. The part of her hair that lays against her skull is like a beetle carapace, shiny and smooth.

"I was being friendly."

"You're never friendly," Harper observes.

I scowl. "Excuse me?"

"You never talk to strangers," Jordan says.

"I don't have any strangers to talk to in this stupid town, do I?" I jab at my food with my fork too forcefully to collect any of the soft, unidentifiable substance.

"Why are you so angry?" Adela asks, flicking her ponytail off her shoulder to swing like a banner behind her.

"I'm not angry." Am I? The dissociation has faded enough for me to be aware of my surroundings and my body as more than watercolors in the distance, but my mind remains locked away behind an impenetrably blank canvas. I don't even know why I went to talk to Toni Davis. If I'm angry, I can't explain it.

"What were you talking about?" Jordan asks in her pacifying tone.

"Vic and Darren. They were inviting her to their party earlier. I warned her that they were assholes."

"The legendary back-to-school bash," Adela sighs, propping her chin on the back of her hand. "We'll never get invited."

"That was nice of you," Jordan tells me.

Was it nice? Was it right of Toni to thank me for the warning? What was my motivation? I can't remember much of anything up until I was standing at her table, so I can't analyze my decision to walk up to her. Did I want her to know about Vic and Darren for her own sake or because I want to keep her from being accepted into the fold of school society I'll never fit into? Is she like a picture I want to hang on my wall, detached from the world, always available for my observation?

I'm inventing motivations, trying to think the worst of myself. That's what my therapist would tell me. When my mind is a void, I cast stones into it, trying to fill it with something—anything—that fits my distorted concept of myself.

"Amy?" Jordan asks. Her hand is on my arm, though I can't remember her putting it there. Adela and Harper have fallen into some discussion, moving on from the novelty of my friendliness toward Toni.

"I'm okay," I say. "I'm just distracted."

"I noticed. Everything okay at home?"

The little girl pops into my mind, her face red and her mouth wide with an ear-splitting scream. I wince at the memory, as if my eardrums are doing a rerun.

"Yeah. Just the usual." The words come out automatically. I don't want to talk about home, or the girl, or how I've decided to neglect her in favor of hanging out with my friends. It's not my responsibility. I didn't ask to bring her back from the grave. I have enough problems as it is.

"Okay," Jordan says dubiously. "Remember you can talk to me, okay?"

"Thanks, Jordan."

I glance at Toni once again, as if she's a sinkhole continuously tugging on my gaze. She's walled herself off from the world again, eating with the same deliberation she does everything. I'm suddenly sure it's an act. How could I ever have thought differently?

CHAPTER TEN

Summer Smile

None of us have cars or money for an Uber, so after school, we walk the ten blocks to Glendock Park. It's not a very impressive park, but it has about a square mile of forest with unkempt trails that no one uses except for delinquent teens like us.

The bowels of the school hallways have finally regurgitated us, leaving us covered with the bilious stain of homework, as Harper said once. It's a great word, *bilious*. I find myself muttering it under my breath.

"What was that?" Jordan asks, walking beside me.

"Nothing," I say. I'm already feeling a little giddy, and we haven't even started smoking. Maybe it's the relief of leaving behind the stares of my classmates and the confines of my classrooms. Like being in a rat maze with scientists leaning over us, watching our every move. I think Jordan made that comparison once before.

Adela leads the way into the forest, skipping a few steps. "Come on, guys!"

"You're such a dork sometimes," Harper says.

"She's just usually better at hiding it," Jordan adds.

Adela scowls over her shoulder at them both. "Excuse me, I thought *I* was the one with the treasure." She pats her pocket.

"Aye aye, Captain," Harper says, snapping a salute.

"Ugh." Adela rolls her eyes and stalks forward over the skeletal fingers of roots and through downtrodden ferns until she locates our usual moss-covered log. She hops up onto it and pulls a textbook from her book bag, placing it on her knees as a workspace. The rest of us amble over and take our seats as Adela spreads out a strip of tobacco paper, lays down a few pinches of weed, and rolls with practiced efficiency. Harper hands her a lighter.

I drum my fingers on the log under me, feeling the soft pliancy of rain and dew-soaked wood. I haven't felt this excited in days, maybe weeks. It's so good to have friends and weed.

"Too bad Toni Davis didn't come," Adela says, flicking Harper's lighter. "I'd *pay* to see her when she's high."

Adela's words are like nails in my skull, erasing the giddiness I felt a moment ago at the freedom of the forest. It's like I'm a sieve—happiness occasionally fills me, only to drain away before I can even think of how to retain it. All at once, I want to be alone and far away from what's happening.

"I saw Josh today," Jordan tells Harper. "Are you two still dating?"

"Kind of." Harper takes the blunt from Adela and inhales, their cheeks hollowing. "We're casual. You know. Non-exclusive."

"I don't think I could handle that," Adela muses. "My mom says when I get a boyfriend I'll probably smother him and chase him away."

Jordan and Harper snort.

Adela shrugs and puts an arm around Harper's neck. "Who needs a man, anyway?"

I feel weary and miles away from my friends. How can they feel so comforting one moment, so alienating the next? They're not doing anything wrong—it's me who always grows so distant. It seems like it would be so easy to laugh with them, to join the conversation, but it's like lifting hundred-pound weights. I wish I hadn't come.

But then I would have had to go home to the little dead girl and look into her dead eyes. Maybe there's just no place where I can find peace. I tell myself to stop being so dramatic, which is what people have told me or implied every time I voice thoughts like that. I wonder what it was like when my mind didn't feel like a battleground. I can hardly remember, or even know for sure if it ever happened.

I've lost track of the conversation. Adela is talking about more school gossip, I think; I recognize the inflections of her voice. I force myself to listen. At least it might take me out of my head.

" . . . still hasn't come back to school. I wonder if she's afraid to show her face now that she and Peter broke up."

Jordan hands me the joint and I take it mechanically, going through the motions of breathing the smoke into my lungs, holding it, releasing it, tapping off the ash onto the wet forest floor.

"Who are you talking about?" I ask. My voice sounds like a stranger's, or like my own recorded and played back to me.

Adela is scrolling through her phone and doesn't answer. For a moment, I think she's ignoring me, or maybe that I only imagined speaking. Everything feels so unreal. But then she announces, "She hasn't posted anything since Peter broke up with her. Her last post is a picture of the two of them. Look at this and tell me she's not heartbroken." She hands the phone to Harper, who hands it to Jordan, who hands it to me.

The screen shows a picture of a familiar girl and boy, though I might have had trouble remembering their names if Adela hadn't told me. They're both our age, attractive; Peter has his hair cut into a fade, which accents his high cheekbones and strong jaw; the girl has her springy curls in a bun, her eyes huge and bright with her broad, summer smile. They both wear swimsuits and have their arms around each other. The filter on the picture smooths every blemish and imperfection, brightens all the colors beyond belief, like a brochure for young love.

"Peter and Jessica," Adela sighs. "The hot item at the end of last year."

"What happened to them?" I ask, my eyes fixed on Jessica for some reason, as though she's waving to catch my attention.

"I *told* you, Amy," Adela says. "Peter left her for Angela, who used to be in the—"

"Band, right, I remember."

Something's really bothering me about Jessica. I don't think we've ever interacted, at least no more than two people who have gone to the same school since kindergarten are forced to interact, but I feel as though we must have spoken, and she must have told me something vitally important, and I must have forgotten. This fog in my brain makes it so hard to think, to parse familiarity and alienness.

Adela leans past the others to take her phone back from me. "I'm telling you, Jessica is so heartbroken, she hasn't come back to school."

"Her stepdad's so strict, though," Jordan says. "I don't think he'd let her stay home from school over something like that."

"Fine, but you have to admit, the timing—"

I gasp, and everyone turns to stare at me. My fingertips are growing numb, and I know I'm not getting enough oxygen, or maybe too much—I can't remember which one—but I can barely spare them a thought.

"What's wrong, Amy?" Jordan asks.

I've realized what bothered me about Jessica's picture. She looks just like . . . well, not *just* like . . . it's the eyes, maybe . . . But I'm certain, the way I am when I wake in the night and know I must go into the garden shed to raise some new dead thing from the earth.

My voice sounds cobwebby to my ears, as if it's been stowed in an attic for too long. "Jessica . . . does she have a little sister?"

CHAPTER ELEVEN

Holly

"Are you sure you're okay, Amy?" Jordan asks.

I blink. I didn't realize we were standing on the sidewalk in front of my house. Jordan must have walked up here with me to keep an eye on me, but I don't remember a good part of the journey home. I know we rode the city bus, and I know we had to walk most of the way because public transportation in this town is terrible, and I know Adela and Harper argued a lot, but it's as if it were all a movie I'm remembering and not a set of experiences I had. I can't even remember what I was thinking all that time or if I thought at all.

"Wait!" a voice calls. Maddie.

I turn, and from the back garden, a small shape emerges, running full-tilt toward me. My heart pounds, and I freeze like in one of those dreams where you can't move. Jordan will see.

"Who . . . ?" Jordan begins.

The little girl pounds down the front garden path and launches herself into my arms. I catch her, barely, and hold her to me with shaking arms. I can't look at Jordan. I can't face her. I don't want her to be involved in this.

Maddie appears, huffing and puffing. She has dirt stains on her forehead, her fingers blackened with fresh soil, her hair damp with sweat. She puts her hands on her knees, bent over. "Sorry," she gasps. "I thought I was keeping her busy with the potatoes, but she must have heard you coming."

"It's okay," I say numbly.

"Who's this?" Jordan asks.

The little girl turns toward her, her chubby arms still clasped around my neck. I can't see what Jordan sees, but I can imagine it: the girl's vacant stare. Jordan recoils, her face paling.

"What's wrong with her?" she asks.

"She's dead," I say.

Jordan meets my eyes. Understanding settles over her face. Incredible. How can she understand?

"That's why you've been distracted ever since school started," she says.

I nod, not knowing what else to say.

"Who is she?" Jordan asks. This time, the question carries a lot more.

My eyes sting. "Jess—" I choke on the name.

Tears stream down my cheeks, though I feel distant from the emotion that produced them, already floating away from my body, from the sticky warmth of the summer sun. I try to force myself to feel as much of it as I can. Sorrow grounds me a little—I'm alive, I feel. It's okay to feel sad and upset. Jordan's kind eyes give me permission.

"Jessica's sister," I whisper.

Maddie straightens, frowning down at me, but I'm focused on Jordan.

Jordan inhales. "Oh, God. That's why Jessica hasn't been . . . and when you saw her picture . . . "

"That's when I realized," I whisper. "I didn't know who the girl was until this afternoon."

"Why don't we go inside?" Maddie asks.

Suddenly aware of all the possible eyes on us— though at least our house is somewhat apart from our neighbors'—I nod. Jordan and I follow Maddie inside. The little girl rests quietly in my arms, still holding onto my neck, almost choking me. I sit on the couch, and Jordan sits beside me. She puts a hand on my knee, and I realize how much I need the contact.

"Does Jessica go to your school?" Maddie asks. She's standing over us. There's something in her eyes I barely recognize, a warmth and a fierceness. It feels comforting and motherly, a world apart from her usual easygoing, sunny demeanor.

"Yes," I say.

"Should we tell her?" Jordan asks. "Tell the family, I mean?"

I realize my arms are shaking, and I relax my hold on the little girl. Jessica's sister. "I . . . I don't know. It's usually a bad idea to let pets . . . but this is . . . "

"Different," Jordan says, nodding. "Yeah, no kidding."

I look up at Maddie. "If I died . . . would you want to see me?"

Jordan flinches away from the question, but Maddie doesn't, of course. Her expression doesn't change. "I would leave it up to you, but I'm not like most people."

I nod. It's a testament to the seriousness of the situation that Maddie acknowledges our family's strangeness. My family usually acts as though other people are the strange ones, as though our way of looking at death is the normal way.

I look at Jordan. "Jordan, if your brother . . . if . . . would you . . . "

Jordan shakes her head. "I have no idea." She goes a little paler. "God, I have no idea."

Her uncertainty comforts me. It feels like it's okay to not know. I've been beating myself up because I don't know how to deal with this, because it should be instinctive. But this isn't a certain situation. There are no certainties in death.

"Should we call the police?" Jordan asks.

"What would we tell them?" I ask dully.

My family never involves *outside authorities* in our life or our business—not medical professionals, not teachers, and certainly not the police. It took a lot for them to even consider sending me to a therapist. We know no one who's confident in their own expertise would stoop to believing our fairy tales, and usually, we don't need anyone else. It would be nice to turn this over to the police, but it's not exactly standard procedure to interview dead people.

"I'll go make some tea," Maddie says and leaves for the kitchen.

Jordan and I sit quietly for a moment. In the silence, I remember Adela's voice telling me the little girl's name. I asked her what it was, and of course, Adela knew.

I look down at the little girl sitting peacefully in my lap and brace myself. "Holly?" I ask.

CHAPTER TWELVE

Numb

The little girl doesn't react at first, and for a second, I think maybe I got it wrong. Maybe she's not Jessica's sister. She didn't react to Jessica's name a minute ago, after all.

"Howee," she murmurs, almost inaudible. "Howee."

My eyes overflow, and I hold her tight against me. "Holly. What happened to you?"

She doesn't answer, of course.

"Do you remember your sister?" Jordan asks. "Jessica?" It seems she has the same thought as me.

From Holly, nothing. She just stares off into the distance, moving her lips inaudibly as though still trying out the shape of her name.

"Holly," I insist. "That's your name, right? You're three years old. Your sister's name—"

"Jessie," Holly pipes up. "Jessie?" She blinks and squints at me as if she can't see me clearly. "Jessie?"

"I'm not Jessie, Holly. I'm Amy. Remember?"

Holly's lower lip trembles, and her eyebrows start to go red again, like they did this morning before she started screaming at me for trying to leave.

"Jessie?" she wails, tugging at my shirt with her small fist.

I try to remain calm, but I can feel my grip on her

tightening again. I don't want her to scream at me. I don't want her to reject me for not being her sister even though just this morning I wanted to get away from her. Have I gotten used to being needed despite how much I've resented it today?

"It's okay, Holly," I say. The lie tastes rotten in my mouth, and I'm sure it sounds rotten to her.

Holly looks up at me, and my breath hitches. For the first time, her eyes look alive; they sparkle, they catch the light in a new way, their pupils focused on me, and I know that she's seeing me—not the ghost of her sister—for the first time.

She squeezes her eyes shut, tilts her head back, and screams. But it's different than this morning. This morning, she seemed both angry and incomplete, her screams belied by the vacancy in her eyes. Her cries now tear at my heart. I feel the emotions vibrating in my flesh: fear, confusion, loneliness. She wants her sister, and I'm a poor replacement.

Along with the emotions, I get a nose-full of scents, stronger than any I've smelled since the night I brought her back to life. Lemonade, cookie dough, warm laundry, a flowery perfume, and at the same time, garden earth, the metallic water from the garden spout, and a faint hint of decay. She's at once more alive and more dead than she's been since she came back.

I rock her back and forth, holding her to me and crying into her hair. "It's okay. Shh, Holly, it's okay."

She doesn't pay attention to the lie but keeps screaming.

"Maybe we should—" Jordan begins, raising her voice to be heard over the racket.

Before she can finish, Holly squirms out of my grasp. Her little sandaled feet thump to the floor, and she scurries away. Jordan and I don't have time to react—she reaches the door to Maddie's room, stands on tiptoe, and turns the knob. The door swings open, and she dashes inside.

"Jessie?"

Maddie comes back into the living room with two mugs of tea. "What's going—"

Holly rushes out of Maddie's room and scurries over to mine and Sarah's. Again, she reaches up on tiptoe, opens the door, and rushes inside.

"Jessie?!"

"She remembers," I tell Maddie. My words come out garbled; my tongue's going numb. My whole *face* is going numb.

Jordan grabs my arm. "Breathe, Amy," she says, and I realize I haven't been.

Maddie sets the tea mugs on the coffee table and heads after Holly. The little girl nearly collides with her as she bursts out of my room and runs over to the bathroom.

"Jessie?!"

"She's not here, sweetie," Maddie says. How can she sound so calm? I'm struggling to even get enough oxygen.

Evidently, Holly doesn't listen to Maddie either. Maddie doesn't force the issue, but instead follows quietly as Holly rushes off into the kitchen.

"She remembers," I whisper. "She remembered Jessica—Jessie. Do you think she remembers . . . how it happened?"

Jordan pulls me into a hug. "Just breathe, Amy. You have to breathe or you're no help to her."

I conjure up my therapist's office, imagine her telling me to steady my inhales and exhales. Four counts in, four counts hold, four counts out, four counts hold. It becomes a rhythm, and gradually, feeling returns to my face and my fingers. Holly is still running around; I can hear her little footsteps.

"She was scared of my dad," I tell Jordan quietly. "Last night, she freaked out when he came in. You said something about Jessica's stepfather being really strict?"

"Oh, no, Amy." Jordan shakes her head. "Strict is one thing. He wouldn't . . . hurt his daughter."

"How do you know?" I ask.

Jordan doesn't answer. I assume she doesn't *have* an answer. Then she says, "We should tell Jessie. Tomorrow afternoon, if she doesn't come to school again, we can go to her house. Talk to her."

"Do you think she'll tell us anything?" I ask.

"It's better than speculating."

"Okay." I hate the idea so much my chest hurts, but Jordan's probably right. What other option do we have?

Jordan hesitates again. "Do you think we should tell Harper and Adela?"

"There's no way Adela won't tell the whole school," I say.

"This isn't gossip, Amy—this is serious. She won't take it lightly."

I fall quiet for a moment, feeling bad for speaking ill of Adela. Of course she wouldn't *actually* tell the whole school. She has more sense than that.

The back door slams. Holly must have gone to look for her sister in the backyard.

"Let's not get them into this yet," I say finally. "I don't want to scare them."

I can sense Jordan's reservations in the stiffness of her body, but she doesn't object. This is my secret, my world. I squeeze my eyes shut for a moment against an overwhelming rush of emotions. I want so badly to be as ignorant as my friends, to stop death from prowling after me wherever I go.

Then the familiar lack of feeling rushes in as the emotions fade into nothing—still there, wherever I stash everything I can't allow myself to feel. I know it's coming back to bite me someday, but I'm grateful for this partial numbness right now.

It's keeping me in one piece.

CHAPTER THIRTEEN

Innocent

"What's going on?"

My Aunt Betty glides into the living room like a ghost, her nightgown floating around her. Jordan jerks in surprise even though she's met Aunt Betty before; Aunt Betty has that effect on people.

"The little girl remembered," I tell my aunt. "I realized who she was, and I said her name, and she remembered. And now she's . . . " I gesture weakly toward the back door.

"Looking for her sister," Aunt Betty says in a faraway voice.

She doesn't seem to notice Jordan is here. Her eyes are fixed on the old wallpaper on the other side of the living room. I wouldn't be surprised if she doesn't even realize *I'm* here in the strictest sense. She turns on her heel and glides back out.

"What . . . um . . . " Jordan swallows. "Your aunt speaks to, um, ghosts, right?"

"Yeah. Dead people in general. She hasn't been able to get anything out of Holly, though." I clench and unclench my hands, trying to ground myself in the movement, in the physical sensation. "She said Holly wasn't all there and wouldn't be able to remember her name. She said I did something . . . or something went wrong when Holly came back."

"Wrong?" Jordan asks.

It's strange to see Jordan out of her depth. We've only talked about this necromancy stuff a couple times before. At school, and in most areas of life, Jordan is so sure. Not that she thinks she knows everything, but she trusts her ability to figure it out or find answers. When it comes to death and the strange ways my family interacts with it, though, Jordan is . . . well, innocent.

"I've never . . . " I sigh. I'm trying to pull my thoughts together enough to give a coherent explanation. "I've never brought back a person before. So it's either my inexperience or the trauma of what happened to her. Or just that she's so young and doesn't have a fully formed identity. Basically, there are a few reasons why . . . " My mind is wandering far from my mouth, conjuring up scenarios. What might have happened to Holly. How Jessica might react to seeing her little sister, who she knows is dead.

Though . . . does she? What if Holly is considered missing, and her family doesn't realize what happened?

Voices come from the kitchen, and several sets of footsteps draw closer. None of them is Holly's light-footed patter. Jordan and I turn as Mama comes in carrying Holly in her arms; the little girl is limp as a doll, her eyes closed. Mama smiles at us as she passes on her way to my bedroom. Maddie and Aunt Betty follow her into the living room, and Maddie sits down in the armchair while Aunt Betty goes to stand by the TV, ignoring all of us.

A moment later, Mama returns from my bedroom, her arms empty. She comes to sit on the couch beside me and rests a warm hand on my back.

"How are you, Amy? You've had a hard afternoon."

For the first time, I have a twinge of guilt about how I started the afternoon—smoking weed in the forest with my friends rather than coming home to Holly. I wonder if I still smell like weed. Not that my family would care if I did; it probably wouldn't even occur to them to be mad about something like that, though I've always hid my smoking from them as a matter of principle.

"I'm fine," I say. "You put Holly to sleep?"

Mama keeps rubbing my back, an almost hypnotic sensation. "I didn't have any other clients today, so I came home early and found Maddie chasing little Holly around the garden. I thought she needed some rest."

"I didn't realize you could do that with . . . reanimated people," I say. Mama's clients are near death, which seems to me very different than *back from the grave*.

"Neither did I," Mama says lightly. "I've never had the opportunity to try. Now, you girls both look tired. Why don't you do something else for a while? Watch a little television or play a card game. We have Uno."

"Card game?" Jordan asks, as if struggling to remember what that is. I sympathize with her—my family's ability to switch between discussions of death and the mundane even throws me off-balance.

"Get your mind off this whole business," Mama says, as if that explains everything.

"She has something to tell her sister," Aunt Betty says suddenly. She's swaying where she stands, still not looking at any of us. "It's urgent, but she doesn't know how to say it in words. She's too young."

"Is it about what happened to her?" Jordan asks meekly. I'm surprised she conjured up the courage to address Aunt Betty directly, especially about something she's so unsure about.

Aunt Betty shakes her head slowly, but it doesn't seem like a denial. After a moment, Mama says, "That's enough for now. Betty, why don't we talk about this somewhere else? You girls drink your tea before it gets cold." Mama rises, takes Betty's arm firmly, and steers her out of the living room.

My eyes go to the mugs of tea Maddie brought us, to the steam still curling off the surface. Mama's right. I need a break from thinking about this before I'm forced to fall back even more on my defense mechanisms, as my therapist calls them.

Jordan and I pick up our mugs and sip in silence. Maddie turns on the TV, changes the channel to a nature show where a soothing-voiced British man is talking about fish, and leaves us alone. Neither of us says anything. On the screen, silver herrings zip by like dimes catching the sunlight. Deep-sea creatures nibble on debris that floats to the ocean floor. Squids fan out their bioluminescent trimmings.

We'll figure out what to do. Like Jordan suggested, we can talk to Jessica tomorrow. Right now, I think we're both trying to forget—if only for a little while.

CHAPTER FOURTEEN

Bus Stop

Jordan spends the night at my house, taking Sarah's bottom bunk—it didn't take much convincing to get Sarah to stay over with one of her many friends. Holly sleeps on the inflatable mattress like the night before. She hasn't woken up since Mama soothed her, which I'm grateful for.

When my alarm rings, I blink myself awake and look over the edge of my bunk at the mattress. Holly is sitting up and holding two dolls she must have taken from the cardboard box full of old toys that I offered her a couple of days ago. She's not playing with them, though; she's just holding them, one in each hand, facing each other as if they're having a silent conversation. She's staring at them both with unblinking intensity. Maybe she's waiting for them to start talking to each other.

I climb down from my bed. Jordan's stretching and yawning. Holly doesn't react to either of us, which is just as well for me. I don't want her to start screaming again because I'm not her sister.

"Sleep well?" Jordan asks sleepily.

"I guess so." Memories of dark and muddled dreams circle through my head, but I can't remember any specifics. "You?"

"I dreamed that we talked to Jessica about Holly, but

67

in the middle of it, she started rotting away." Jordan's eyebrows crease. She looks like she's remembering the dream as she recounts it. "Jessica was dead, too. She just crumpled in front of us."

My heart fumbles in my chest. Could it be that that's why Jessica hasn't . . . No. I can't worry about that now. Brush teeth, wash face, get dressed. I can do those things.

Jordan and I get ready for school and eat a silent breakfast with Mama, Grandma, and Maddie. Daddy left for work even earlier than usual today. Jordan and I check in on Holly before we leave and find her still sitting there with the two dolls.

"Goodbye, Holly," Jordan says uncertainly.

To my relief, Holly doesn't seem to hear her.

We're about to leave to catch the bus when Mama comes up to us. "You girls will stay out of trouble, won't you?"

I don't know how to answer. Mama never says anything like that. Stay out of trouble? What does she mean? Don't bring any other dead girls back to life? Don't go vigilante and try to get justice for Holly's death?

"Yes, ma'am." Jordan's much more used to taking instructions from parents. It occurs to me that what Mama said is pretty parental, which only adds to the strangeness of it.

"Haven't you told me death isn't anything to be afraid of?" I ask.

"Death is one thing," Mama says calmly. "Family trouble is another. You never know how other people handle death in the family, especially with a young child. You never know who might be upset if you pry into their business."

A shiver trickles down my spine, though I'm sure she didn't mean it ominously. She's not suggesting someone murdered Holly and might come after us if we try to find out what happened. That's just my brain thinking up the worst possible scenario.

"We'll be careful," I promise.

Jordan and I head out into the humid morning. It's overcast, promising afternoon showers. We walk in silence down the switchback road toward the bus stop. It feels strange to be accompanied like this, to not be the only one too distracted by what's going on in my head to have a conversation. Jordan looks pale in the summer sunlight, like a transplant from winterland.

About halfway down Whaleback Hill, we hear raised voices coming out of an open front door. It's not unusual to overhear domestic disputes in a neighbor's house—in this neighborhood of double-wides, most walls are thin enough that you can hear arguments even if the door is closed. I tend to ignore it as best I can, figuring people leave my family alone to do whatever it is we do, so we might as well not mind anyone else's business, either. But something draws my attention to this house. Sitting in the driveway is the blue car I saw Toni Davis get into on the first day of school. This is her house.

" . . . not an invalid, Mom. I can go to school on my own." That voice is Toni's. It's so strange to hear her lose her cool. There's no guardedness in her tone, just exasperation and the sort of careless familiarity you have with the people you've lived with all your life.

As we get closer, I see Toni standing on the threshold, holding the door open. She's half-turned to look behind her, her book bag hanging off one shoulder. She's wearing a short-sleeve blouse, and I notice for the first time how thin her arms are.

"If you'll just wait ten minutes," a woman calls from inside the house.

"You can't keep being late to work. I'll see you later." Toni stalks down the front steps, slamming the door behind her. She spots us and freezes. I realize that Jordan and I have come to a halt, too, both engrossed in Toni's conversation with her mom.

"Hi," Jordan says. "Sorry to intrude."

I'm so glad to have her with me to say the appropriate thing. My mouth is too dry for speech—or maybe it's just my brain that's dry.

"It's okay. We were the ones broadcasting to the whole neighborhood." Toni makes a concerted effort to wipe the annoyance off her face, replacing it with the cool, unruffled expression she always wears at school.

I *knew* it was an act.

"We're all heading for the bus stop, right?" Jordan asks. "Want to walk with us?"

Toni's lips part, and she takes a moment to answer. "Okay." She crosses the neat yard and joins us on the sidewalk. Like robots sputtering into motion, we all start walking downhill together.

My thoughts are scattered, and it takes me a moment to remember what I was thinking about before we saw Toni. Jessica. Holly. Death. Murder. It seems a little absurd now in the bright morning light with kitschy garden decorations all around. I wish it would stay that way— ridiculous, unlikely, maybe all a misunderstanding.

"Is there any chance you're named after Toni Morrison?" Jordan asks. The question feels jarring to me, but I suppose it's just friendly conversation.

"What?" Toni asks, which tells me she was caught off- guard by the question, too. "Oh, yeah. My parents are big fans."

"That's awesome," Jordan says. "*The Bluest Eye* is one of my favorite books of all time. I'm Jordan, by the way. I don't know if you remember me."

"Yes, I remember. I've actually never read any of her books all the way through." Toni says this as though the words surprise her in slipping out of her mouth. "I told my parents I did, though."

Jordan laughs, and the sound seems to loosen something between the three of us. I could be imagining it, but I think Toni's shoulders relax.

"That's fair," Jordan says.

"What . . . what do you two do for fun?" Toni asks.

It's such an awkward question that I giggle nervously. I try to stifle it, and it turns into a snort. Toni and Jordan both look at me; Toni then looks down at her feet. Did she realize I was laughing at her? I didn't mean to. It's not even that funny, looking back.

"Well, you know I like reading," Jordan says. I'm so grateful to her for resuming the conversation as if I didn't interrupt. "I love music, too. I've been waiting all summer to go to a show this Friday. Discarded Infernal. Have you heard of them?"

"No, I don't think so," Toni says.

"They're sort of old-school heavy rock," Jordan explains. "Really cool sound."

Toni nods, then looks at me. My stomach drops. Her eyes are dark and inscrutable, a part of her usual mask. "What about you, Amy?"

What do I do for fun? I don't have a good answer like Jordan. All I do most days is watch TV and smoke pot with my friends when we have it. Occasionally raise something from the dead. Except for that last part, I'm not very interesting. I wish I drew or painted or did pottery, or maybe played the guitar. I used to think I wanted to be a vet until I realized how hard it is to get into veterinary school. When I was younger, I would spend hours in the forest behind our house, hunting for bugs and searching for small animals. I haven't really been passionate about anything in years, it feels like.

"I'm going with Jordan to the concert on Friday," I find myself saying. "You should come, too."

From behind Toni's back, Jordan frowns at me. She asked me to go about a month ago. I've never been to a rock concert before, and I was worried there would be a lot of noise and smell and bodies pressed together; I didn't think I could handle it, so I said no. Now I'm apparently going after all, thanks to my big mouth. I don't even know how much it costs. Will I be able to pay for it?

"Oh." Toni glances at Jordan, who hitches on a smile to cover for me. "Maybe. I have to ask my parents."

We're almost at the bus station. My palms are sweating at my sides. I wonder if I have sweat stains on my baggy T-shirt. Why didn't I dress more nicely today? I don't even think my socks match.

"What are you into, Toni?" Jordan asks.

Toni frowns distantly. "I don't really know."

I'm confused. Why did Toni give the answer I was thinking of for myself? Is she really as lame as I am?

"Well, you should come to the concert if you're interested," Jordan tells her.

"I'll ask my mom," Toni repeats with a small smile.

When we arrive at the bus stop, the bus is visible

only a couple of blocks away. We stand there in silence, waiting, and I wonder how the other kids on the bus will see us. Toni in her immaculate, short-sleeve blouse, her sandals sparkling white, her book bag slung gracefully over her shoulder. Me next to her in an oversized T-shirt, sweatpants, and fraying backpack, my shoes scuffed, and one shoelace untied. It's like we were each standing on a different tectonic plate and the two plates crashed together, shoving us side-by-side.

I glance at Toni out of the corner of my eye. I desperately want to say something to her, but I don't know what or why. Soon we'll all be whisked away into the bowels of school and talking to her will be much more intimidating, and I've barely spoken to her this whole walk—Jordan has carried the conversation. *Where have you been for the past two years? Why did you come back? Why are you so mysterious? What secrets are you hiding?* None of those questions really seem appropriate.

Then I hear myself saying, as if from far away, "I can bring the dead back to life."

Chapter Fifteen

Silent

Jordan gasps. My face flames; if it gets any hotter, my hair will catch on fire. Toni stands between us, slender and poised, looking at me with a blank expression.

I can bring the dead back to life. Am I possessed? Did some other Amy take over my body for a moment only to vanish and leave me to deal with the consequences of her words? I wait for a reaction on Toni's face—disdain? Fear? Annoyance? But all I get is a crease between her eyebrows.

The school bus pulls up, and we all climb aboard. Jordan and I head toward the back, as usual, and Toni sits a few rows ahead of us. As I sit heavily in my seat, I realize we didn't say goodbye, didn't conclude the conversation. My outburst was the final note. Well, I know how to make an impression, apparently—just not the right kind.

"What was that?" Jordan hisses.

"I don't know why I said that. It just came out."

"You haven't even told our friends, and you randomly tell a person you barely know?"

"It's not like she'll believe me," I snap. "She'll just think I'm crazy or stupid and never talk to me again." I feel as though my organs shift downward as I speak, as though my insides are trying to drop out of the bottom of the bus and spill all over the asphalt. Did I really just sabotage any

73

possible friendship I could have had with Toni by being a complete weirdo?

We ride to school in silence. By the time we arrive, I've turned over the conversation so many times in my head that I've started to invent even worse details to flesh out my memory.

Jordan and I get out in the school parking lot and make our way to our lockers, me dragging my feet. As we navigate the hallways, I notice a knot of loud people. I'm anxious to avoid them, but a familiar head of frizzy hair in the center of the crowd catches my attention. I stop in the middle of the hallway. Jordan halts next to me, eyes going to my face and then to the gathering right ahead of us. She grabs my arm as she realizes what's happening, too.

Jessica's come back to school.

"He's such an idiot," one of the girls is telling Jessica. "He doesn't know what he lost. Angela . . . ugh, she's such a skank. They deserve each other."

For a moment, I have no idea what the girl is talking about—it's almost like she's speaking another language. Then I remember Adela's gossip about Jessica and Peter breaking up and Peter starting to date Angela instead. It seems so insignificant, so indecent to even pretend it matters with Holly dead; I watch Jessica for a reaction, but she just turns her back to her friends and rummages through her locker.

"I don't even care," she mutters. "I'm over him."

"Yeah, girl," another of Jessica's friends says. "Who needs a jerk like him anyway?"

"What are *you* looking at?" snaps a third friend, her gaze falling on us and her expression turning sour.

"Nothing," Jordan says and grabs my arm, pulling me along. As we move out of earshot of Jessica's friends, she tells me quietly, "We'll wait until she's alone and talk to her then."

But every time I see Jessica throughout the day, she's accompanied by at least two other girls. Her expression is serene, or maybe it's just blank, like mine is when I'm numb. She keeps her eyes on the floor and doesn't seem affected or interested by anything around her, least of all her chattering friends—though none of them appear to notice.

"You two are quiet today," Harper observes when we're all gathered in gym class. The four of us and two other girls make up a volleyball team, but only the two other girls are actually playing.

I tear my gaze away from Jessica, who's playing with her friends in the adjacent court. At the same time, Jordan looks away from the empty bleachers as though coming back down to earth. I wonder if I have the same look of confusion as she does, as if she's struggling to remember how to act like a normal person.

"I'm offended you had a sleepover without us," Harper drawls. "Weren't we going to all get together to mourn the start of the school year?"

Adela isn't paying attention to the game, facing completely the wrong direction as she stares with rapt attention at Jessica's court. I hadn't noticed she was focused in that direction, too, but I should have realized she would be eager to know how Jessica is dealing with her breakup with Peter. She must be disappointed that Jessica isn't showing any signs of . . . well, anything.

"Sorry," I mumble since Harper probably expects a response. "We were studying together, and it got late."

"Is that why you didn't turn in your math homework this morning?" Harper asks me archly. "Because you were up *studying* so late?"

"Yes, we're having a secret romance," Jordan replies without the slightest hint of embarrassment as my cheeks warm.

Jordan is straight, as far as I know, and I've never had a crush on her—well, maybe a tiny one in middle school—but it still feels weird to joke about it. I've always been anxious for my friends not to think I think of them *that* way.

Harper rolls their eyes.

Adela tears her eyes away from Jessica. "Jordan and Amy are having an affair?"

"No, jeez," I mutter.

"Has anyone heard—" Adela begins.

The volleyball sails toward Harper's head. Harper bats it away, and it bounces out of the court—there are several groans. Harper is unaffected. "No, Adela. None of us knows any extra gossip about Jessica because we all have lives."

Adela sighs. "I want to talk to her, but it's like she has an armed escort."

"Leave the girl alone," Harper says. "She missed the first two days of class because of the breakup. She obviously needs space."

Adela shakes her head. "Everyone wants the opportunity to bad-mouth their ex. It's cathartic."

Jordan shoots me a look. I can tell she doesn't like staying silent about the whole thing with Jessica. Maybe it's easier for me because I just feel like the others are talking about a completely different person, a different world from the one where Holly was screaming for her sister. It's the first time I've felt that dissociation might actually work in my favor.

The gym teacher, a blond, sallow-faced woman in her mid-twenties, ambles over to us. "You girls could put in a little more effort." Her tone isn't very convincing.

"I'm not a girl," Harper snaps.

The gym teacher shakes her head and exhales. She has dark circles under her eyes; I heard someone say she recently had her first kid. "Participation is half your grade. Think about that, okay?" She wanders over to another team.

Harper shrugs. "Like she'll fail us. She doesn't want to deal with us again next year."

I glance at Jessica, who's putting a lot more effort into her game than we are. Maybe it's better that Jordan and I haven't had a chance to talk to her at school. She's obviously just trying to get through the day, like we are. We'll have to try to catch her at home.

Chapter Sixteen

Truth

In a whispered bathroom conversation, Jordan and I figured out that our bus route takes us past Five-Star grocery, which is a few blocks from Jessica's house. If we get off near the grocery store, we should be able to walk there. We don't know Jessica's address, but we know she lives near Darren, Straight Guy Vic's best friend. Jordan's dad took her by Darren's house to collect payment for some plumbing work he did for them, and she saw Jessica's mom across the street.

"I hope Darren's not there," I mutter as we climb onto the bus.

"If he messes with us, I'll remind him that I've heard his mom call him 'sweet pumpkin pie.'"

I snort, my spirits lifting somewhat.

We sit in the back of the bus as usual. My stomach flips over—Toni Davis is coming down the aisle, and she catches my eye. We both avert our gazes, and I assume she's going to avoid me like any normal person would.

"Can I sit here?" Toni asks, indicating the empty seat Jordan and I left between us since no one else ever sits in the back.

"It's bumpy," I choke out.

"Pardon?"

"You can feel the metal frame through the cushion," Jordan supplies. "That's why we avoid it."

"I don't care." Toni slips her book bag off her shoulder and settles herself onto the bumpy seat. She stares at something out the window and doesn't say anything more as the bus idles and the rest of the kids file in. I know I'm staring at her, but I can't make myself stop. What is she doing here, with us? Didn't I scare her away with my outburst about being able to raise the dead?

The bus grumbles into gear and rolls away from the school building. Chatter from the other rows overlaps and becomes white noise, and I'm still staring at Toni. *Look away. Look away now. What's wrong with you? Now she's going to think you're a creep on top of being a weirdo.*

"You weren't lying, were you?" Toni asks, turning to face me. Her eyebrows are pulled together, but it's hard to interpret her expression.

From behind Toni's back, Jordan's own eyebrows shoot up. She swipes her hand across her neck. I'm sure she's trying to order me not to tell Toni anything else, but the gesture's kind of funny considering it's death we're talking about.

"No," I reply, to which Jordan gestures more frantically, shaking her head and cutting the air with one hand in a diagonal motion of *I won't allow this.*

But now that the secret's out, now that Toni's asking me to my face, I can't bring myself to lie to her.

Toni takes in a measured breath and folds her hands together on her lap. She sits straighter than the seatback, her shoulders squared. She gazes at her hands for a moment, then turns her dark eyes back to me. I swallow.

"How does it work?" She sounds curious, not skeptical or amused the way most people would react. Maybe she's one of those people who believe in ghosts and psychics. It's not what I would have expected, but I'll take it.

"I get an Itch, usually in the middle of the night. It's like an instinct. I go out to my garden shed and mix together soil and water and knead it into mud. Then I pull their bodies out of the mud."

Jordan has stopped gesturing and just leans back in

her seat, resigned and resentful. I'm sure she's thinking about how I'm telling all this to a stranger before I've told the rest of our friends.

"You bring back people?" Toni asks.

"Usually pets and wild animals." I'm about to tell her about Holly, but I bite down on the impulse. Better not to lay it all out at once. Better not to involve her too much.

Toni nods thoughtfully. "So they're just alive again?"

"Not really. They usually last a few days or weeks until they've accepted their death and move on."

"Like ghosts."

"Sort of. Ghosts are imprints people leave behind; according to my aunt Betty, they're not actually people's spirits. Their spirits have moved on. The ones I bring back, they're whole spirits in a physical body. I don't really know why some spirits become ghosts and others choose me to bring them back, but . . . " I'm talking too much. I close my mouth.

Toni frowns. "Spirits choose you? So you can't choose who comes back?"

My stomach twists. So that's why Toni's so interested in my abilities? She wants me to bring back someone she's lost? Mama warned me about that risk, but I've never had to deal with it until now, because I've never told anyone outside my family except Jordan.

"No, they decide. Not me."

To my relief, Toni doesn't seem disappointed or angry, though as always, it's hard to tell what she's thinking. She doesn't storm off or insist, in any case.

"So you believe me?" I ask. "About the whole thing?"

"I'm . . . considering it."

I nod. It's more than I expected this morning—a lot more. I didn't think she'd ever talk to me again. I glance at Jordan, who has her arms crossed and is staring out her window.

"You knew about all this?" Toni asks Jordan.

"Yeah, Amy told me last year. Hey, Amy, we have to get off soon."

I look out; we're getting close to the Five-Star grocery. I would give anything not to have to talk to Jessica, to just stay on the bus with Toni. We could all walk home from the bus stop together. We could hang out and talk about anything—books, music, our families, school—I don't really care what.

"Where are you going?" Toni asks.

"To a friend's house," Jordan says, at the same time as I say, "To the store."

Toni blinks.

"To the store, then a friend's house," Jordan amends.

"Oh, okay."

"Amy, do you have your note?" Jordan asks, starting to stand.

I dig in my backpack for the principal's note. Jordan and I both had to forge our parents' signatures to show the principal we were allowed to get off the bus at a different stop from our usual one. Fortunately, we're both pretty good at imitating our parents' handwriting since we've had practice.

The bus nears our stop, and Jordan stands up, shouldering her book bag.

"Well . . . bye," I mumble.

"Bye," Toni replies.

Jordan and I show our notes to the bus driver, who nods and lets us off about a block from the Five Star grocery store, at one of the regular drop-offs. The other student who got off with us walks away without a glance.

"Ow!" I exclaim when Jordan slaps me in the shoulder. "Why—"

"Why did you *tell* her?"

"It was an accident, okay? It just slipped out!"

"This morning, yeah, but what about just now?"

"What was I supposed to do? Lie to her?"

"You do it to your friends all the time." Jordan looks away from me. "I never thought you'd tell someone just to impress them."

I start shaking, though I can't tell what emotion is causing my reaction. A few passersby glance at us; standing on the sidewalk isn't the best place for this conversation.

"First of all, if one of our friends asked me directly, I'd tell them the truth." My voice is quiet, alien to my ears.

"And second, I didn't tell Toni to impress her."

"Why'd you tell her, then?"

I open my mouth for an angry retort, but my mind is suddenly blank. Why did I tell her? How can I explain to Jordan that half of what I do is a mystery to me? She won't believe me. Maybe she's right—maybe the part of me that took over this morning at the bus stop just wanted to seem more interesting, less like the pathetic pit of blankness that I am.

I turn my back on Jordan and take several deep breaths, squeezing my arms with my hands like my therapist taught me. My face is going numb again.

"Let's just go," I snap.

Jordan is quiet for a moment. I can feel her eyes on me, probably resenting me, probably judging. Then she starts off, leading the way toward Jessica's house.

CHAPTER SEVENTEEN
Classmates

It's a lot farther to Jessica's house than we thought. Halfway there, it starts to drizzle; neither of us has raincoats or jackets, so we just hurry along through the quiet neighborhood. All the houses are old, and many are run-down, though the yards are generally well-kept. It's hard to tell if this area is nicer than Whaleback Hill. It certainly must have been back when the houses were new.

Jordan and I haven't spoken since our argument near the bus stop. Is she still angry at me for being honest with Toni? *I'm* not going to apologize first.

Just as the drizzle is turning into rain, and I'm about to ask Jordan if she's sure that Jessica's place is this way, she stops in front of a house with a wraparound porch decked out with a two-person swing and a rocking chair. "I think this is it."

I look up and down the street. Raindrops plop into puddles, disturbing their surfaces into overlapping circles. No one's outside, and the block is eerily quiet.

"Are you sure?" I ask.

"That's Darren's over there."

Jordan indicates a larger, shabbier house across the street with a broken washing machine in the front yard. I don't know if I've ever imagined Darren's house before, but if I did, that wasn't what I pictured. Something about it is intensely sad, though I refuse to feel sorry for someone like him. I can still picture him slamming my locker shut in front of me.

"I'm pretty sure this is Jessica's," Jordan says. "We might as well knock."

My feet seem to grow roots, planting me in the spot. I didn't think about this initial awkwardness. How are we going to bring up the subject with Jessica? Will she even talk to us? We've barely exchanged a word before, though we've been in school together practically all our lives.

Jordan looks at me and sighs; my face must show my anxiety. "I'll talk first. But you have to be the one who deals with the whole Holly thing."

I nod. Of course, that's my responsibility. As long as Jordan gets us in the house and in front of Jessica, I'll figure out the rest. Anyone else in my family would be better at this than me, but somehow, I'll have to manage.

We walk along a stone path and climb creaky steps to the front door. I run my fingers through my wet hair, relieved to be out of the rain and wishing for the second time today that I took better care of my appearance.

Jordan knocks on the cloudy glass panes of the front door. Then she notices the doorbell and jabs the button. We wait. We wait some more. Rain patters on the porch roof and slides off the edge like a beaded curtain, making the few flowers planted along the porch dance frantically. Jordan rings the doorbell again. I don't have a watch or a phone, so I can't confirm that we wait there ten minutes, but it feels like it. Jordan rings the doorbell twice more.

Finally, footsteps come from the other side of the door, and a shadowy shape emerges against the clouded glass. The person clears their throat before opening the door part way, revealing their face. She looks enough like Jessica that I decide it must be her grandmother.

"We don't want to buy anything," the woman says.

"We're from Jessica's school," Jordan explains. "We stopped by to see her."

"Oh." The woman hesitates. "That's nice of you."

"Is Jessica home?" Jordan presses.

"Yes. Just a moment." The door closes and footsteps recede; the shadow on the glass grows blurrier and then vanishes from view.

"She's not happy to see us," Jordan mutters.

"No kidding." I shift my weight from one foot to the other, and the floorboards creak under me. "I guess it makes sense. They're . . . mourning."

I've never experienced mourning firsthand. My grandpa died when I was a baby, and anyway, I doubt my family would give me a reference for how normal families behave in grief. I've seen plenty of other strangers grieving, though, especially when Mama used to take me to visit her clients.

"No one seems to know about Holly at school," Jordan says. "I guess they're keeping things private. I wonder . . . "

Footsteps approach the door, and it squeals open again. Jessica's grandma peers out at us. "Jessica isn't feeling up to having visitors. You girls will have to come back another day."

My heart stumbles. I never imagined that we'd be turned away without even being able to speak to Jessica, but I guess I should have anticipated the possibility. Of course she doesn't want to speak with two classmates she barely knows. Suddenly, our plan seems childish.

I'm about to turn tail and flee like a frightened dog, but Jordan is digging around in her backpack. She pulls out a stack of her neat school notes.

"Could we just come in to give her the homework from the first two days?" Jordan's voice is polite and earnest, just the kind of thing that endears her to adults no matter the situation. "I know she doesn't want to fall behind. It'll just take a minute. She asked me to bring these to her."

Jordan's grandma looks down at the stack of papers, then up at Jordan, then over at me. I try to give her my best innocent smile and blend into Jordan's aura of scholastic responsibility. I don't think I've taken a single note all week.

"What did you say your name was?" Jessica's grandma asks Jordan.

"Jordan Nguyen."

"I remember you." The ghost of a smile haunts the woman's face. "From a field trip back when you were all in elementary school, I think. Maybe a history museum or something."

"Oh, yeah! You were one of the chaperones, weren't you?"

I recognize a certain hollowness in Jordan's smile and tone that tells me she's lying, but other people rarely catch her in a lie, not even teachers who've known her for years. Jordan doesn't remember the field trip. Not that it matters.

Jessica's grandma nods and opens the door wider. "Come in, girls. Jessica's in her room. I'll show you where that is."

We step into the foyer. Its white tiled floor, cream walls, and cream-carpeted staircase make it seem spacious and bright, even though all the curtains are drawn and there are only a couple of lamps on. An archway leads to a living room full of half-packed or half-unpacked boxes, furnished with more light-colored furniture.

I can see the woman who let us in more clearly now, and I realize I made a mistake in judging her age. She's thin, the bones of her hands tracing a clear profile under her skin, but the lines of her face are from care, not age. Her close-cropped hair is black with only a hint of gray, and her warm brown skin is clear and barely wrinkled. She must be Jessica's mom, then, not her grandma. Her eyes are sunken and nervous, like those of our sleep-deprived gym teacher. Now that we're inside, she doesn't look at us; her gaze darts around the room, even avoiding Jordan, who she seemed so taken with a moment ago.

"Well, follow me, girls."

Jessica's mom heads toward the stairs and we follow, our footsteps clicking on the tile and then padding on the carpeted stairs. At the top of the stairs, we head along an indoor balcony to a door decorated with flower decals. They must have been put up a while ago because they seem childish for a sixteen-year-old. Jessica's mom pauses at the door, and I wait for her to open it, but after a moment, she continues to the next door along the balcony. Not Jessica's room, then.

As I pass the flowery door, goosebumps erupt all over my body, and I feel smooth mud in my hands, between my fingers. Holly's half-living, half-dead scent saturates my nostrils. Baby shampoo, fabric softener, sunshine on a warm deck; damp earth, rotting plants, dust. I lose track of my limbs for a moment, and my mind goes so blank I can't tell if I'm conscious.

"Amy?" Jordan asks, grabbing my arm.

I blink and breathe. I'm alive, I'm awake, I'm here. Jessica's mom turns back to look at me. I can't tell if she's concerned or impatient.

"I'm fine. Just dizzy."

Jessica's mom knocks on the second door, this one with a plaque on it that says Welcome in fancy cursive. It kind of reminds me of Harper's house, which their mom has decorated with all sorts of plaques that have stock inspirational phrases or simply single words like *Believe* or *Wine*.

"What?" calls a voice from inside the room.

"Your friends want to give you the homework from the days you missed."

There's a pause. "I told you to say I'm not feeling well."

"You don't want to fall behind on your first week, do you, honey?"

Another pause. I get the feeling that this conversation would go a lot different if we weren't here; Jessica's voice when she said she wasn't feeling well had a hint of desperation, as if begging her mom to send us away without having to say it out loud.

But today at school, Jessica was working hard not to show emotion to her friends. I guess that's what makes her say, "Fine. Come in."

Chapter Eighteen

Fury

Jessica's mom opens the door, and Jordan and I step inside. Inspirational posters paper Jessica's walls, featuring everything from athletes to famous historical figures to cute animals, each accompanied by phrases like *Reach for the stars!* or *Anyone can be a hero*. Jessica sits on her bed on top of a mussed bedspread. She lowers her phone, looks up at us, and frowns. She obviously expected to see her friends.

"What do you want?" she demands. She clearly feels no need to be civil with us.

Jordan and I both look back at the doorway. Jessica's mom has left. Jordan closes the door softly.

"We just want to talk to you." Jordan looks at me expectantly.

I look around the room, searching for the right way to do this. I wish I were better at small talk, at getting people to relax and warm up to me. Mama does that with her clients. When I was little, I used to visit clients with her sometimes until she realized it was the reason I was having nightmares and crying inconsolably at kindergarten. I remember the exhausted faces of family members and the feeling of intruding on something incredibly private, like walking in on someone in the shower.

But Mama never seemed uncomfortable, and she always slipped into the scene as though she belonged there, as though she were a missing puzzle piece that completed the picture. She would talk to the family and carve out little pockets of normalcy amid the grief and despair. Sometimes she would even make someone laugh, and their face would transform with the realization that life was still happening, even in a space that brushed up against humanity's deepest, most unknowable fear. If the dying person were lucid enough, Mama would talk to them, too. Often the family members behaved as though their dying loved one was a fragile, insubstantial creature, but Mama would treat them the way she did any other person. All that was before she even used her abilities; I think half of her magic is just in her capacity to make people, dying and grieving, feel like they're still welcome in the world.

But of course, I don't have that talent. I can't put people at ease because I'm never at ease myself, not around death or loss, not even in everyday life. Jessica is staring at me, waiting for me to speak.

"Are you moving?" I ask. "I saw the boxes—"

"No." She doesn't elaborate. I can see she's not going to give me an inch.

There's nothing I know to do other than get to the point. I clear my throat. "Jessica . . . we know about Holly."

Instantly, I realize I made a mistake. Jessica's cheeks redden, and her face contorts in fury. With a jolt, I notice her eyebrows are reddening, too—just like Holly's.

"Get out," she rasps.

"Please listen to me," I plead. "I want to help you."

"Get *out*!"

"Jessica," Jordan says. "How did you get that bruise?"

Jessica turns her face away, but not before I realize Jordan is right—a faint bruise discolors her temple and cheekbone. She must have covered it up with makeup at school because I've been looking at her all day and never noticed it until now.

"That's none of your business. I don't care what you have to say—just leave."

"Jessica," I say desperately, "someone hurt Holly. You know that, right? You know there's something suspicious about—"

Jessica raises her gaze to me. Her eyes are overflowing, but her expression is still furious. "I know about your family. I know your aunt supposedly talks to ghosts, and your sister says she can predict the future or whatever the hell. I don't need your help. I don't want a message from beyond. I want you to get out of my house, or I'm calling the police."

She and I are both shaking like the two tongs of a tuning fork. Something as deep and unsayable as the urge to defy death courses through my shivering body. I want to run over to her and throw my arms around her. I want to breathe in her scent. I know exactly the smell of her shampoo, the smooth texture of her skin, the reassuring feeling of her arms around me. I'm so scared, and she's the only one who can help me.

"Please don't be mad, Jessie," I whisper, and I hear Holly in the cadence and pitch of my voice.

A shadow of confused recognition darts across Jessica's face, but then it's gone, and there's nothing but her fury. She picks up her phone, dials, and shows us the screen: 911.

"It's okay," Jordan assures her, a veneer of calm over her voice even though I know she's freaking out, too. "We'll leave. Just . . . if you know something, tell someone. It actually might be a good idea to call the police."

Jordan grabs my arm and steers me out of the room. Jessica's livid gaze follows us out. It's a relief to close the door and escape the pressure of her anger.

We stand outside Jessica's room for a moment. I can't move, and Jordan seems unable to help me. The corpse-hush of the white and beige house weighs on my ears. There's not a single noise: no clock ticking, no birds singing outside, no pots clanking or microwave beeping or dogs barking. I can't even hear the rain. Has it stopped, or does this house just swallow up the sound?

"Come on," Jordan murmurs finally. "Let's get out of here."

CHAPTER NINETEEN

Bruise

Jordan and I slip out of Jessica's quiet house and walk about half a block before stopping and just sitting down on the curb. Neither of us speaks for a few minutes. The rain has stopped, and the sun is out for the first time since the morning. Kids play in a yard across the street, laughing and running around in some mysterious game that's not quite tag and not quite hide-and-seek. With a jolt, I spot Darren taking out the trash, but he doesn't look our way and heads back into his house. A few cars roll by, and birds gather on power lines, squawking and bullying each other for what I guess are the best spots.

"Well, that was terrible," Jordan says finally.

"I'm sorry. It's my fault."

"No, it's okay. You did your best." Jordan laughs humorlessly. "I don't even know what I was expecting. Why would she open up to us? As far as she knows, we have no idea what we're talking about. We're just two almost-strangers who lied our way into her house and asked her about her dead sister."

"When you say it like that, it sounds like a really terrible plan."

Jordan laughs again, this time more genuinely, and I join her. It relieves a bit of the tension and guilt I feel.

"Maybe we should have talked to her mom instead," I muse. "She seemed to like you."

"I'm sure bringing up her dead daughter would really endear me to her."

I snort, and we fall into giggles that have an edge of hysteria to them. I'm suddenly exhausted, and all I want is to go home to take a nap. But going home means facing Holly again, and that cuts off my giggling. I can't help but feel like we failed her.

"You saw the bruise on Jessica's face, right?" Jordan asks.

"Yeah."

"I can't think of anything that could give her a bruise like that except . . . you know. Someone hitting her."

I scratch the back of my neck. "Do you think it has anything to do with what happened to Holly?"

Jordan shrugs. "It's possible."

"There's that whole thing with how Holly was scared of my dad," I remind her. "She could be scared of the man who killed her and hit Jessica."

"It doesn't necessarily mean there's one man who did both things. Seeing someone hit her sister would traumatize her on its own. She might have died from something else entirely."

"What are the chances, though?" I shiver. "There's still Jessica's stepdad."

"Yeah," Jordan admits. "I mean, the most likely people to hit Jessica are probably her parents. Or her boyfriend."

"Peter?" Could he have something to do with this? Is it a coincidence that he and Jessica broke up the same summer Holly died? Maybe. Jessica might have just dumped him because she couldn't deal with a relationship on top of her grief. I wish we had a timeline for when all these things happened; that might help us sort out how they're related.

"I know you said you didn't want to, Amy, but maybe we should talk to the police. We don't have to tell them about Holly coming back or anything—we could just say we're Jessica's friends, and we're worried about her."

I bite my lip. I guess I have an instinctive mistrust of the police because my mind immediately jumps to everything that could go wrong: they could catch us in a lie; they could tell us to mind our own business; they could get suspicious and question us until we reveal everything we know and then send us to a psychiatric ward for believing we can speak to the dead.

"Jessica and her family have no reason to talk to us," Jordan prods. "They're required to talk to the police."

"Maybe they already have. Maybe the police have already found the murderer and locked him up."

"Oh, no way, Amy. You think a child murder investigation—an *arrest*—could happen in this town without everyone hearing about it?"

"Yeah, okay. You're right." I pick up a pebble from the sidewalk beside me and throw it across the street. It hits a trash can with a pitiful clink.

Jordan looks up at the clear sky. "The police must think it was a natural death or an accident or something. To be fair, we don't really know for sure it wasn't."

"I guess not."

Jordan eyes me sideways.

"What?" I ask.

"You sort of . . . channeled Holly back there."

The image of Holly's flowery bedroom door flashes through my memory. And of course, there were those last words I said to Jessica that came out of somewhere that didn't feel entirely like me. *Please don't be mad, Jessie.* She recognized Holly's voice, I think, or half-recognized it but dismissed the thought. I remember, too, how much I wanted to go over to her and put my arms around her. That impulse definitely didn't come from me. I'm not the type to go around hugging people I barely know.

"The things I bring back are kind of connected to me. They usually trust me, even the wild animals. Sometimes, I can feel their emotions, especially if they're really scared. I've felt what Holly's feeling a couple of times. But it never went this far before."

Jordan shakes her head. "I know you told me about this thing last year, but I'm still getting used to it."

"That's okay. I know it's . . . weird."

I suddenly think of Toni Davis and how quickly she believed me. For some reason, I want to tell her everything that's happened the last few days. I guiltily force my thoughts back to the current conversation; I know Jordan would get mad at me again if she knew I wanted to confide in Toni before our friends. It's selfish of me, really, to want to get anyone else involved.

"I'm sorry I pulled you into all this," I tell Jordan.

"Don't be silly." Jordan slaps my shoulder lightly. "I'm your friend. I wouldn't want you to go through this alone."

I clench my hands, the fleshy sides of my fists digging into the grainy texture of the asphalt by my legs. I'm not being fair to her. She's trusted me a lot—I should return the favor.

"Okay," I say.

"Okay what?"

"Let's go to the police."

CHAPTER TWENTY

Station

Our town's police station is tucked away between the public restrooms and the old library, which is now some kind of government building. It's a long walk and a crowded ride on the city bus to get there. It's not raining anymore, but the air feels like a wet blanket wrapped around us, and by the time we get to the station, we're soaked again.

We walk into the building, down a hallway past the entrance to the public restrooms and enter through a double glass door. I decide the police station was once part of the library, too, because its ceilings soar overhead much higher than necessary, dwarfing the assortment of cubicles on the main floor. Twin staircases lead to the open second floor, which has been partitioned into offices with walls that look suspiciously like those of a double-wide.

All around the perimeter of the main floor, where I guess they once had bookshelves, there are filing cabinets, bare walls, a few plaques and framed photos, and a break room. Well, more of a break alcove since it's not walled off. A hush lies over the station, I guess as a leftover from its time as part of the library.

There are only two or three people among the cubicles, and Jordan and I stand by the entrance for a few minutes, waiting for one of them to notice us. There's a front desk nearby, but no one is sitting at it.

Finally, a young woman barely older than us—maybe just out of high school—bounces in through the front door of the station, carrying several coffee cups. She pauses, looking down from her long, lean height. She's wearing a bright floral dress that comes down to her mid-thighs, and she has really nice legs. I blush and try not to stare.

"Hi there. Did you girls need something?" She has the kind of loud, unrestrained personality that makes me fold into myself. Even Jordan, who usually holds her own, seems diminished in her presence.

"We, um, wanted to talk to someone," Jordan says.

"Bless your little hearts. How long have you been standing here like little mice? Come on, follow me."

She leads us to the closest occupied cubicle, her long, golden ponytail swinging behind her. The cubicle is taken up by a large man with a comb-over, who looks up and grins at the young woman.

"Here you are, George. Two creams, syrup, no sugar." She hands him a cup. "Do you have time to talk to these little mice?"

"Sure. Sit down, ladies." George takes a sip of his coffee.

The young woman heads off to deliver the other coffees. There's only one chair in front of George's desk, so Jordan and I hesitate.

George gestures at the empty cubicle beside his. "Pull up that chair."

Jordan grabs the chair, and we both sit facing George across a desk cluttered with papers, open file folders, a couple of writing pads approaching the end of their paper supply, and a scattering of pens and pencils. He gathers some of the papers and folders into piles, but it doesn't help much.

"So. How can I help you girls?" George has friendly blue eyes and a broad, unconcerned smile across his tanned face.

Jordan and I exchange a look. I decide I've relied a lot on her to do the talking today, so I face George and say, "We think there's been a murder."

George takes another sip of his coffee. "What makes you say that, darling?"

Jordan stiffens beside me, and I charge ahead before she starts lecturing him about appropriate ways to refer to women. "One of our friends, Jessica . . . um . . . Jessica Myers. Her little sister, Holly . . . "

George finally sobers up and nods. "Holly Myers. Yes, awful tragedy."

"Are you investigating her death?" I ask.

"What's your name, sweetheart?"

"Amy."

"All right, listen, Amy. Holly's death was an accident. I know it's sad, but that's all there is to it. Accidents happen, and sometimes it's hard to accept, especially when it's someone so young."

"How do you know it was an accident?" I ask.

"We looked into it. The case has been closed since last Tuesday."

It's the first indication I have about when Holly died. Sometime before last Tuesday, which was eight days ago. Depending on how long the police investigated it—and I have the feeling it wasn't very long—she's been dead for two weeks or so. Maybe less.

I consider the evidence we have, if we can even call it that. Holly is afraid of my father. My Aunt Betty thinks something traumatic may have happened to her, causing her to forget her identity until I spoke her name. Then there's Jessica's bruised face, which may or may not be related. The last one is the only thing I could tell this policeman, but it feels wrong to do it without Jessica's knowledge. Would I be helping her if I spoke up or just causing her more pain? Do I have the right to reveal a secret she covers up with makeup? Do I have the responsibility to tell someone in case Jessica's too scared or ashamed to tell anybody?

"How did Holly die?" I ask.

George shakes his head. "I want to respect the family's privacy. They didn't want us to make an announcement or tell any journalists. They need to be able to mourn in peace."

Holly needs to be able to rest in peace. I don't say anything; I think we've reached the end of the line with George. This is what I was afraid of, what my family warned me against. But I came here for Jordan, because this is what she understands about the world, what she's known her whole life that she should do in situations like this. I glance at her. She's staring at George and looking like she's going to be sick.

George sighs. "Look, if you have something to tell me, I can make a report." He waits for a moment. Neither of us answers. "Why don't you go out and enjoy the sunshine, girls? I know death is hard to accept, but unfortunately, it happens. The best thing you can do for your friend is to just be her friend. This is a hard time for her and her family, and I'm sure she appreciates your concern."

If only he knew that Jessica kicked us out of her house an hour ago. I start to stand.

"Did you interview Jessica?" Jordan asks, making me pause.

"Of course. We interviewed the whole family."

"She didn't tell you anything?"

"Nothing that made us think her sister was murdered or anything like that, sweetheart."

"We think someone hurt her. Hurt Jessica."

"Hurt her how, honey?"

"Can you please stop talking to me like that?" Jordan snaps. I wince; I've been waiting for her to have that reaction. Some of the friendliness in George's face shuts off. "Did she tell you if someone hurt her physically? Hit her?"

"I think it's time for you young ladies to leave," George announces. "That's enough nosiness."

"We're not being nosy." Jordan's voice rises in pitch and volume. A couple of other policemen look our way. "We're worried about Jessica, and I'm tired of you not taking us seriously. How can you be so sure Holly's death was an accident? Jessica has bruises all over the side of her face. What if the same thing happens to her that happened to Holly? What if she dies because of your incompetence?"

There's nothing at all friendly in George's expression

anymore. I'm perched on the edge of my seat, ready to bolt.

"I don't want to have to do anything drastic here, girls. Why don't you leave nice and quiet?"

I jump to my feet and grab Jordan's arm. "We will," I squeak. Jordan resists me for a moment, glaring at George. Practically everyone in the police station is watching us now; I blush furiously.

Jordan finally relents and lets me drag her out of there. The weight of all those stares follows us out.

CHAPTER TWENTY-ONE

Come Clean

"You could have had my back in there," Jordan snaps at me. "I can't believe you let him talk to us like that."

I don't answer. We're walking around the tiny downtown area without paying attention to where we're going, each trying to cool down. I'm annoyed at Jordan for having an outburst, but I know how she feels. Even though I knew ahead of time that talking to the police wouldn't be any help, I'm still frustrated by the reality of it.

"What if it really was an accident?" Jordan asks quietly after a pause. "What if we're just sticking our noses where they don't belong?"

"Where *do* noses belong?" I ask without thinking.

Jordan snorts and gives me a gentle shove. "On your face, dummy."

I smile. I managed to lighten the mood by accident—at least a little bit. For a moment, I only think about the sunshine, how lucky I am to feel it, and the origin of idioms.

"Jordan? Amy?"

We both turn. Adela and Harper are crossing the street toward us, carrying ice cream cones. Jordan and I exchange an uncomfortable look—how are we going to handle this? The other two join us, and we gather on the sidewalk.

"What are you doing here?" Adela asks. "I haven't seen you downtown in ages, Amy."

"You two aren't *actually* having an affair, are you?" Harper drawls.

Adela's eyes widen. "Oh my God, are you?"

Jordan looks at me again and then down at her shoes. I realize she's not going to help me out. She must be tired of lying for me. Now that I think about it, she's done that a lot today. She helped dispel curiosity about why she'd slept over at my house, then she faked her mother's signature on that note to the principal, then she got us into Jessica's house by tricking Jessica's mom, and then she helped me obscure the truth in our conversation with Jessica. I've put too much of a burden on her. Not to mention that yesterday, she came face-to-face with death for the first time and has been supporting me ever since instead of justifiably falling to pieces.

"We just came from the police station," I tell Harper and Adela. Jordan looks up; Adela's eyebrows raise, and Harper frowns, waiting for me to elaborate. I lower my voice, even though I doubt anyone can hear us. As usual on a weekday afternoon, downtown is pretty dead. "Don't tell anyone, okay? But Jessica's little sister, Holly, is dead."

Adela and Harper stare at me, both going a little pale.

"How do you know?" Adela asks. The ice cream is dripping onto her fingers, but she doesn't pay attention to it. "Did . . . did you see something? Is that why you were—" She gestures in the direction of the police station.

"No," I assure her.

I take a deep breath. It's hard to believe I'm doing this, here, now, in the middle of a sunlit street. Part of me thinks I'm dreaming, and my limbs start to float away. I try to focus on my feet planted on the sidewalk in my scuffed shoes, Harper and Adela's startled faces, the smell of barbecue from a nearby restaurant. I'm really here, really doing this.

"You know how my aunt hangs out in graveyards and talks to ghosts?" I ask.

"Did she speak to Holly's ghost?" Harper asks. I can't tell how skeptical they are.

"No. It's . . . my aunt isn't the only necromancer in my

family. I'm one, too."

Adela's face clears. "I knew it! I always knew you had some kind of psychic powers, Amy. You have that energy. My mom thinks so, too."

Harper and Jordan both shoot Adela a bemused look.

"Well, my powers aren't exactly psychic," I hedge. "They're more . . . hands-on."

"What, can you raise the dead?" Harper asks, in the tone of someone who knows their question is absurd.

"Um . . . sort of. I mean, yes."

Everyone falls silent for a few seconds. Was it a mistake to tell them? What was I thinking? But unlike when I blurted out the truth to Toni this morning, there's a feeling of relief weirdly mingled with the worry. Whatever else happens, at least I've come clean with my friends.

"Are you serious, Amy?" Harper asks.

"She's telling the truth," Jordan affirms. Her support warms my belly; this time, I feel like I've earned it.

Harper and Adela stare at Jordan, then at me again.

"So . . . you're saying you brought Holly back to life?" Adela asks. "Then, she's not dead anymore?"

"No, she's still dead. When I bring things back, they're not really alive. They're sort of on the border between life and death."

"She's a zombie?" Adela yelps.

Jordan sighs. "No. She's kind of like a corporeal ghost."

"Well, not really—" I begin.

"They don't need to know all the technical stuff, Amy."

Even though my Aunt Betty would be scandalized at me for allowing the spread of misinformation about death, I relent. "Okay, yes, kind of like a corporeal ghost."

"Prove it," Adela demands. "I want to see her. Where is she? Is she being questioned by the police?"

"Of course not. The police wouldn't believe me. She's at my house."

"Why were you at the police station, then?" Harper asks.

I huff out a breath. "Trying to convince them to investigate her death. It didn't work. They think it's an accident."

"It's not?" Adela asks, paling still further.

"I don't know. Come on, let's go catch the bus at the bank."

"Are we going back to your house?" Jordan asks.

"Yes." It's strange how confident I feel. I don't know if it's from finally telling the truth or from finally being able to talk about the one thing I know more about than any of my friends. Maybe it's both. "Yes, whoever wants to come, we're going to my house."

CHAPTER TWENTY-TWO
No Telling

The four of us—me, Jordan, Adela, and Harper—are sitting on the floor of my bedroom. Holly nestles quietly in my arms, ignoring everyone else. At first, I was worried about how she would handle meeting so many new people, but I'm not even sure she noticed.

Adela and Harper are staring at her with mingled looks of fascination, disbelief, and horror; Jordan just looks a little ill. I told her she could go home and rest, but I didn't really expect her to accept. We both want to see how our friends react.

So far, they're speechless. Even Harper, who loves little kids, hasn't tried to interact with Holly. Neither of them have asked anything since we arrived, either, though they bombarded me with questions on the way here.

"What do you think?" I ask after the silence has stretched on for several minutes.

"Is it true?" Adela asks. "Is she really . . . "

"Yeah."

Adela shakes her head, her eyes still fixed on Holly. "How did she . . . you know? How did it happen?"

"I don't know. That's what Jordan and I were trying to find out. The police are convinced it was an accident."

"Should we be talking about this in front of her?" Harper asks. "Won't she get upset?"

"Yeah, probably better not to get too into it," I agree.

"So she's still in there?" Harper asks. "She has feelings and stuff? Does she talk?"

"Sometimes. And yes, she definitely has feelings, even if they're different from before." I shift Holly in my lap, prying her arm from around my neck so I can look at her properly. "Hi, Holly. How are you doing? Did you have a good day?"

She gazes blankly up at me and doesn't respond.

"These are my friends." I gesture to the others. "Want to say hi? You met Jordan yesterday, remember? And that's Adela and Harper."

Holly keeps looking at me, not even glancing at the others. I don't know why I even bothered; I guess I want to try to make this feel as normal as possible for my friends.

Telling Holly that we saw her sister today is out of the question. I don't want her to have another meltdown. But maybe there's something I can ask her about that feels less risky.

"I saw the door to your bedroom today, Holly. I love the flowers you have on it. Remember those flowers?"

A crease appears on Holly's forehead. "Fowers?"

Adela and Harper give a start of surprise at hearing her voice for the first time.

"Yeah. They were really pretty."

"Pwetty fowers." Holly's frown deepens. "Pwetty fowers?"

"Yeah," I repeat encouragingly. "Do you remember them?"

Holly thinks for a moment. "Home? We go home now?"

My heart aches. Why did I bring up the stupid flowers? But I have to get her to remember somehow, don't I? How can I help her deal with her death if I don't know what happened? How can I make sure there's not some killer roaming loose?

"Soon," I lie. "We'll go home soon."

"Oh, my God." Tears are falling down Adela's face. "This is so horrible. How can you stand it, Amy?"

Barely, I think. Out loud, I say, "I know it's upsetting. You don't have to stay here if you don't want to."

No one moves. I try not to let my relief show. They finally all know the truth about me, and they're not running away. Maybe they want to, but they're not—at least not yet. I don't even know how long I've waited for this to happen and dreaded the worst outcome.

"We go home now?" Holly insists.

"Not yet," I tell her.

"*Can* she go home?" Harper asks.

"Shh," Adela tells them. "Remember what Amy said. Let's not talk in front of her."

"Holly, can you tell me what happened to you?" I ask. "Please, I need to know. What happened to you before you met me? Do you remember that?"

"Home?" Holly's face crumples. "Jessie?"

There's nothing for it—I'm just going to have to brave another meltdown.

"This could be bad," I warn the others. Jordan, who of course has already experienced the bad, scoots away from me. "Holly," I say as calmly as I can, "I need you to tell me what happened. Jessie needs to know what happened."

I brace myself for Holly to start screaming, but she doesn't. She looks at me for a moment, her lower lip trembling, and then says, "No."

"No what?" I ask.

"No telling. I'm not telling. I want Jessie."

I glance at Jordan, who looks torn between relief and confusion. This is new—and definitely unexpected.

"Why won't you tell me, Holly?" I ask.

She shakes her head adamantly. "Jessie said no telling. Daddy's going to get mad. Daddy . . . " She frowns as though suddenly confused. "Daddy?" Her eyes overflow with tears and the dreaded thing happens: she tilts her head back and lets out an inhuman, eardrum-shattering scream.

"What's she doing?" Adela yells over the noise. She and the other two have their hands over their ears. I, the closest, have my arms occupied trying to comfort Holly, so there's nothing I can do but grimace and bear the pain.

"I used to babysit a kid who would do this," Harper shouts. "You just have to wait for them to get over it."

"You just listen to this?" I yell back. Holly writhes in my lap, trying to get out.

"Let her go," Harper orders.

I don't try to argue but do as they say. Holly squirms out of my lap and runs out of my bedroom.

"She did the same thing yesterday," Jordan groans. We hear Holly screaming as she runs through the house, looking for Jessica. "Why did you have to bring up her sister again?"

"How else are we going to find out what happened to her?" I ask, getting to my feet. I shouldn't let Holly run around unsupervised; it's not like she can injure herself, but what if she tries to go home? "Jessica won't talk to us, and the police won't listen."

"I'll go with you," Harper offers, scrambling to their feet as I head toward the door.

We leave the others in my room and follow Holly's screams into the kitchen, where we find her tugging on the door to my parents' bedroom, wailing. We don't try to stop her; we just watch. It's incredible how much calmer I am than when this same thing happened yesterday. Maybe I'm getting used to it. Maybe I even expected it. Maybe having all my friends here, accepting this side of my life, makes it feel more normal. Of course, there's also the chance that I'm dissociating just enough to function, but I can't tell.

"This again?" Grandma asks, trudging in from the backyard.

"Sorry, Grandma."

"Hello, Harper." Grandma takes off her muddy galoshes and leaves them in the laundry room. "I see Amy's initiated you into this whole business."

"Uh, yeah." Harper glances at me, then at Holly, who bursts out of my parents' bedroom and into Grandma and Aunt Betty's. "So, it's, uh . . . " Harper laughs nervously. "Actually true? All of it?"

"Unless Amy told you we can all fly."

"No, ma'am," Harper replies.

Holly runs back into the kitchen and rushes past Grandma into the laundry room.

"You couldn't have waited until your mother was home, at least?" Grandma asks me. "Now, who knows when she'll calm down?"

"Your mom's good with kids?" Harper asks me as we follow the little girl into the backyard.

"No. I mean, yes. But the main thing is that she can soothe the dying. Or in Holly's case, the dead."

Holly dashes through the garden, ignoring the paths and trampling through the plant beds. I wince; Maddie and Grandma won't be happy about that.

"Wow," Harper says. "Damn. Does everyone in your family—"

"Hang on."

Holly is heaving on the door to the garden shed with all her might. This one's padlocked, so she won't get it open, but it's the last door she can try. I don't know where she'll go next. Harper and I hurry to catch up with Holly. The racket of her rattling the old garden shed door makes her screaming even more unbearable.

"Jessie!" she wails.

My calm is eroding, and I don't know how much more of this I can stand. I can't blame her for wanting her sister, but I can't help her if she's like this. If only Jessica knew how desperately her sister wanted to see her—and if only Jessica understood that seeing Holly doesn't mean she's really alive.

I glance at the old faucet on the side of the shed and remember the night I brought Holly back. An idea strikes me, and I rush forward. I grab the key to the padlock from under the conch shell and reach to unlock it, but Holly refuses to budge.

"Can you get her out of the way?" I ask Harper.

They nod and grab Holly under the armpits, lifting the little girl into the air. Holly's sandaled feet kick at anything and everything, and she twists and jerks, trying to get out of Harper's grasp. Before I lose my chance, I jab the key into the padlock and open the door.

"Okay, let her go."

Harper tries to set Holly on the floor, but the dead girl lurches out of their hands and hits the packed earth with a thud. Holly runs into the shed, looking around frantically.

"Jessie?!"

"Jessie's not here, Holly," I tell her. I pull the bucket out from under the work table and show Holly. "Remember this?"

"I want Jessie!"

"I know you do." I crouch in front of Holly and hold the bucket out to her. "Look at this, Holly. This is where I pulled you out. Remember that?"

Holly pauses her cries and takes a tentative step toward the bucket, peering inside.

"I mixed dirt and water and made mud," I tell her. "And then I pulled you out of it."

"Mud?" Holly asks, her voice pitched more normally, though there's an edge to it as though she might go back to screaming any second.

"Yeah. Do you want to make some mud in here?"

"Amy, I don't think she's—" Harper begins.

Holly nods, making Harper cut short. I nod in return and put my hand on Holly's shoulder.

CHAPTER TWENTY-THREE
Bucket

Holly helps me fill the old bucket with fresh soil—she spills almost as much dirt as ends up in the bucket, but I'm not worried about that—and follows me as I carry a watering can outside to fill it from the faucet. The familiar ritual almost puts me in a trance. I wonder if it's having a similar effect on Holly, who hasn't made a sound since she agreed to help me.

Since Holly is too short to reach the worktable, I leave the bucket on the floor and let Holly water the soil. She stares down into the dirt as the water swirls on top of it, creating rivulets of blackened water and sinkholes of moisture.

Harper watches the procedure. "Is this really how you do it?"

"Yeah, more or less."

"So could you . . . pull a dead person out of there right now?"

"No. It only works if I get the Itch first. The instinct. And Holly's the only human being I've ever brought back." I've explained all this already, but I'm trying to be patient with my friends. All things considered, they're taking it really well.

The water drains out of Holly's watering can and she stands there with it tilted forward, staring at the mud as though waiting for it to speak to her. I wait for a moment to see if she'll do anything else. When she doesn't, I take the watering can gently from her and grasp her hands in mine. I lower our hands into the mud and show her how to knead it into an even mixture. There's absolutely no expression on her face, but her hands pick up the mixing motion. After a few repetitions, I leave her to continue on her own. I stay crouched beside her and watch.

"Holly . . . you know, don't you?" I ask. "That you're not alive anymore?"

She doesn't answer but keeps kneading the mud. Harper kneels down on her other side, staring into the bucket, too.

"Jessie's still alive," I continue. "That's why you can't see her. Maybe later, if we can convince her . . . but first, we need to know what happened to you. Can you tell us?"

Still no answer. I wait. She's up to her elbows in mud now.

"Jessie told you not to tell anyone, huh?" I prod. "Well, I talked to her today, and she said it's okay to tell me."

Harper shoots me a disapproving look. Now that the words are out of my mouth, I feel bad, but I don't know any other way to get Holly to talk. I try to think that Jessica would want people to know the truth, but I'm kidding myself. I have no idea what Jessica wants. She must have had a reason to order Holly not to tell anyone. Concern for Holly's safety? For her own? There's no way to know.

"No telling," Holly murmurs without looking up from the mud. "No telling, Howee."

I sigh. I feel too guilty about lying to insist anymore. Instead, Harper and I just watch for a few minutes as Holly continues to mix the mud, leaning further and further into the bucket.

Suddenly, Harper lunges toward Holly as though to grab her, but they're too late. The bucket tips over, and Holly goes in head-first as mud spills all over the floor of the garden shed. Harper and I both let out loud four-letter words.

Just then, the door opens. "Amy, is everything—"

Maddie stops short as she takes in the mess. "Oh, dear."

"Sorry!" I exclaim as Harper and I rush to fish Holly out of the mud and right the bucket before all the mud escapes. "I'll clean it up."

Maddie sighs. "No, it's okay. Holly will need a bath. I'll let you do that, and I'll clean up in here." She looks the three of us over. We're all covered in black mud, worse than Maddie after the most intense gardening days. "You two will probably need showers, too."

Harper and I nod. I carry Holly out of the shed, and we head back to the house, trying to brush the worst of the mud out of Holly's hair and dress.

"Does Maddie have any sort of death powers?" Harper asks, glancing over their shoulder.

"She can manipulate the life cycle of plants," I respond automatically. "She can keep them from dying or even resurrect them if they die. She can also talk to dirt."

"Talk to *dirt*?"

"Dirt is basically made of dead things. It's where we're all headed, too."

Harper shakes their head as we step into the laundry room, wiping our feet on the mat—not that it helps much.

"Your family is nuts, Amy. I thought *my* mom was weird."

"Your mom's still pretty weird."

Everyone else is in the kitchen, sitting around the island counter: Jordan, Adela, and Grandma. Grandma's made tea. They all exclaim when they see us.

"What happened?" Adela demands.

"Is Holly—" Jordan begins.

Grandma points at my parents' bedroom door. "Use that bathroom. I don't want mud all over the house."

"We're fine," Harper tells the others as we cross the kitchen to the master bedroom. "Holly just decided to take a swim in a bucket full of mud."

It's good to see Harper's back to their usual snarky self. Maybe the shock's wearing off. The other two exchange looks; Jordan then stands up, and Adela follows her lead. They troop after us through my parents' bedroom and into the master bathroom.

Jordan plugs the drain in the bathtub and runs the

water, testing it for warmth. Harper uses a washcloth to wipe mud off their arms while Adela sits cross-legged on the rug beside her. I stand there holding Holly and waiting for the tub to fill, both of us dripping small clods of mud onto the tile with plops like little sighs.

"At least she calmed down," Adela notes, rubbing her head. "My ears are still ringing."

"Did she say anything else?" Jordan asks.

"Amy showed her how she came back to life," Harper says. "She seemed to listen. But she wouldn't tell us anything."

"Jessica told her not to," I say.

"But that was when Holly was alive," Adela protests. "Nothing can hurt Holly anymore, can it?"

"No, but it can hurt Jessica," I say. "We'll have to take it slow. At least we learned a few things today."

Jordan shuts off the faucet. "Water's ready."

I set Holly down beside the tub. "Want to, um, take off your dress, Holly?" Now that we're all in here, it seems super awkward for us all to watch her bathe, even if she is only a toddler.

"Here, I'll do it." Harper has finished wiping off the mud and takes over. I let them, gratefully, and sit on the floor next to Adela.

"Now what?" Adela asks.

"No idea," I say. I've run out of steam. I don't even know if I'll have the energy to get up off the floor.

We're all silent for a few minutes; the only sound in the bathroom is the water splashing as Harper uses a fresh washcloth to bathe the little girl.

"You don't think we should let her family see her?" Adela asks.

"No," Jordan replies before I even open my mouth. I look up at her; she hasn't seemed sure about that before now. "They're trying to mourn her. If they see her like this, they'll think she's alive, but when they realize she's not, it'll be like losing her again."

"Okay, that makes sense." Adela wets another washcloth and starts absently wiping the mud off my arms.

"I can do that," I mumble.

"Oh, shush."

I close my eyes and allow myself to feel the soothing sensation. I'm small; it's me in the bathtub. I smell baby shampoo and taste soap suds. Jessica is kneeling beside the bathtub, holding a towel over her face and then dropping it. The sudden appearance of her smile sends me into fits of giggles that echo against the tile and the glass shower door.

I open my eyes again, and the vision is lost. It's so strange to see my friends sitting around me, unchanged, unaware.

No matter how much they know, they don't belong in my world.

CHAPTER TWENTY-FOUR

Blank

Harper is drying Holly off while Adela combs her curly hair when the door bursts open.

"You're still in here?" Sarah demands. "Dad is showering in the other bathroom, and I'm about to burst."

"We're almost done," Adela assures her.

Sarah puts a hand on her hip and waits, tapping one foot.

"Hang on." Harper pauses to stare at my sister. "What death power do *you* have, Sarah?"

All my friends look at Sarah with interest.

Sarah sighs and rolls her eyes. "You wouldn't believe me."

"We're hanging out with a dead girl," Jordan points out. Last year, when I told her about me and my family, I left out Sarah's powers.

Sarah scowls at me. "I'm not taking responsibility if they get upset."

"I know," I say tiredly.

My sister turns back to my friends and crosses her arms as if to ward off any further questions. "I can tell how people will die. Not when or where, just the cause. And before you ask," she continues as Harper and Adela open their mouths to speak, "the answer is no. I'm not telling any of you how you're going to die."

"You know, though?" Adela asks. "How all of us—"

"I've known for years. I can tell the moment I meet someone. Well, can and do. I don't really get to choose. And the answer is still no," she adds, cutting off Adela before she can say anything more.

"How many people's deaths have you seen that happened the way you thought they would?" Harper asks.

"Ha, I told you you wouldn't believe me."

"I'm just curious," Harper protests.

"I have no idea. I don't keep track. A lot."

"And it's always exactly how you thought?" Jordan asks.

"Yep."

"Do you know how *you're* going to die?" Harper asks.

There are a few gasps. Everyone in the bathroom falls silent, waiting for her answer.

Sarah shrugs. "Of course I do. Heart attack. That's why I stay healthy, to make sure it happens as late as possible."

"That's horrible," Adela says.

"Not really. It's you people I don't understand. You always want to know, but you always hate being told. You start obsessing about your death instead of enjoying your life, or you don't believe me and never talk to me again."

Jordan shakes her head. "Okay, we won't ask, then."

Adela looks down at Holly, who hasn't reacted at all to the conversation. "Hold on. Can't you tell how Holly died?"

"I never met her when she was alive. I see the future, not the past. Now can you please get out of here before I pee myself?"

Harper wraps Holly in a towel and hoists her onto their hip. Then we all leave the bathroom. Sarah slams the door behind us.

"Does she have any other clothes?" Harper asks as they set the little towel-cocooned girl on a kitchen chair. Adela has Holly's yellow dress, which is still stained with mud.

"No," I reply. "She came back wearing that."

"So you've had her in the same clothes for three days?" Harper demands.

I sigh and rest my elbows on the counter. My shirt clings to my skin with sweat and mud and humidity. Adela wiped the mud off my skin, but I still need a shower.

"She's not alive, Harper," I say. "She doesn't eat or go to the bathroom. She probably doesn't sweat, either. She can wear one of my shirts; there's a bunch of clean clothes in the laundry room."

Harper heads over to find something for Holly to wear. Adela is staring at the muddy yellow dress, frowning.

"What's wrong?" I ask her.

"Oh," Adela says with a start, looking up guiltily. "Oh, no. I'm fine. I was just thinking . . . how this is such a big part of your life, Amy. How . . . normal it seems. But I don't . . . I can't . . . " She trails off and looks down, her expression still guilty.

"It's okay," I tell her. The kitchen suddenly feels crowded. I wish I could lie down and close my eyes. "I know it's not normal to most people, believe me."

"I can't believe you never told us," Adela says.

I look away, my claustrophobia increasing. I open the window above the sink, hoping some fresh air will help. The scent of Maddie's flowers whisks across my face, heavy with the heat of summer and the moisture of the recent rain. I try to tether myself to that scent.

"I mean, I understand why you didn't," Adela adds quickly. "And I'm glad you told us now. It must have been so weird, though, walking around with this secret life. Does the normal world seem kind of . . . I don't know, trivial? Like school and all that? You must have thought we were all so silly and shallow, not knowing anything about all this to do with death—"

"Adela," I snap, rounding on her. She blinks at me, and I realize how harsh I sounded. "Sorry. But can we just not talk for a minute?"

"Are you okay?" Adela asks.

"Yeah, I just need to . . . " I amble out of the kitchen, unaware of what my body is about to do until it happens. Out of the corner of my eye, I see Jordan and Harper exchanging a look, probably a concerned one, but I can't collect my thoughts enough to wonder or care what they're thinking.

I walk over to the living room couch. My calves hit the cushion, and then I'm sitting, my limbs unresponsive. I stay there for an uncountable amount of time, knowing I must exist but uncertain of how, exactly, I do.

Jordan appears without the others. "Amy, you okay?"

I shake my head slowly. I'm only aware of this because the room is moving back and forth. Is Amy even my name? It seems unconnected to me. I don't want to disappoint Jordan, but I can't figure out what's the thing that would disappoint her or how to fix it.

"Do you want to be alone?" Jordan asks.

Alone. That sounds better. At least then I won't have to worry about disappointing anyone or experiencing the confusion of people speaking a name I'm not sure belongs to me.

"Okay," I say, slow and unsure of how the word will sound until it falls from my mouth. Something's off about my answer, but I can't remember the question to match them up. I squeeze my eyes shut, wishing everything would stop.

Time passes. I drift in and out of awareness, sometimes lost in swirling, disjointed thoughts, sometimes noticing some event around me. Mama appears at one point and asks if I want dinner, but I can't remember how I respond. I become aware of arms around my neck, of a small nose pressed against my skin like it's checking my pulse, asking if I'm still alive.

Then I'm lying in my bed with no memory of climbing the ladder to my bunk. There's sunlight on the ceiling, a sheet of it rolled out through the slot above the closed blinds. My arm is asleep, and my fingers tingly-numb. I look down; Holly lies curled against my side like a ball of tiny humanity, wearing one of my baggy, unremarkable shirts. I should get my arm out from under her, but I can't make my body move.

The door opens, and Sarah walks in, freshly showered and changed. She frowns up at me.

"Aren't you getting up? We have to be at the bus stop in twenty minutes."

I stare at her. I know I should answer, but there are no words in my head. There's a blank wall where access to things like movement, speech, and an awareness of my own thoughts should be.

"Okay." Sarah shrugs. "Stay here if you want to. It's not like you'll miss anything."

I blink and the room is empty. I don't remember when Sarah left. There's a knock at the door.

"Come in," my voice says.

Mama enters, her eyebrows making a V above her troubled eyes. She stands next to my bed, looking up at my face. "Are you not feeling well, Amy?"

"I don't know," my voice says.

Mama puts a hand on my forehead. I barely feel it; it's as though some textureless, colorless barrier exists between me and the world to go along with the one between me and myself.

"You don't seem sick," Mama says.

My voice doesn't answer on its own, and I don't know how to make it.

"Do you want me to let you rest?" she asks.

"Okay," my voice says.

"I don't have any clients this morning, so I'll be here if you need me." With one last worried look, she leaves the room.

My eyes are latched to the space where Mama stood, her words echoing in my head without attaching to any meaning. Just sounds I should recognize. But like everything else I should recognize—my thoughts, my immobile body, my own identity—they're locked away behind that blank wall.

CHAPTER TWENTY-FIVE
Echo

Why did this happen to me?

Yesterday afternoon, I told my friends the truth about me. I felt confident. They accepted me, my full picture, for the first time. But then . . . what? Was my confidence a lie to myself? Did everything that happened yesterday sap my energy while I wasn't paying attention until I was past my limit by the time I noticed? Sometimes it's hard to know how I feel, how much is too much, when I'll react in all the ways that frustrate me.

Since I'm able to think about all these things, I must be a little more aware and awake. I blink at the empty room, at the golden motes of dust drifting in bars of light that emanate between the blinds. What time is it? Is it time for school? No—Sarah told me we had to leave, but I didn't react. She must have left without me, probably hours ago. Mama came in here too, didn't she? What did she say? My head pounds, and I stop trying to force myself to pull together coherence from the wisps of my consciousness.

I look down at my side and jolt with surprise. Holly is sitting up, staring at me solemn-faced. No, not solemn; it's her usual blank expression, her dead-girl expression, her not-of-this-world expression. We watch each other for a moment. My body is welded to the bed, and she's still as a doll on a shelf; it's almost like we're kindred.

The door opens, and Mama comes in with her phone. She holds it out to me.

"It's Mary," she tells me.

I frown slightly at her. Mary? My therapist?

"You said you wanted to talk to her."

"I did?" I ask.

Mama's eyebrows form their V again. "You don't remember, sweetie?"

Sweetie? When was the last time she called me that? I'm still confused, but I decide not to worry her any more and just take the phone. The plastic case is smooth and warm, but I feel it as though it's muffled from my touch through several layers of gloves.

"Hello?" I say. My voice sounds like it's a recording of me being played back, uncanny and grating.

"Hello, Amy." Mary's voice is calm, a soothing counterpoint to Mama's concern. "Can you tell me how you're doing?"

I try to make words come out, but if there is an answer in my head, it scatters between my brain and my mouth. I have to give her some kind of answer, though. "No."

"That's okay," Mary says. "Are you in your body right now?"

"No," I reply before I can doubt myself, worry about what she wants to hear. What Mama wants to hear. Through the open door, I see her sitting on the couch. Listening in? I'm not sure.

"That's okay, Amy," Mary tells me. "Good for you for noticing. Can you tell me five things you can see right now?"

Blank. My thoughts—blank. I can see lots of things, but I can't make myself narrow in on any objects I can name. It's like everything around me is a flat backdrop painted different colors rather than distinct, three-dimensional bodies.

"Amy?" Mary asks.

"The light," I say. "Through the blinds. Mattress—there's a mattress on the floor. The closet door is open. Sarah left her jacket—jacket on the chair. How many is that?" I glance to my side, where Holly still sits upright, staring down at me. "Holly. She's watching me."

"Great," Mary says. She doesn't ask who Holly is or sound worried at my scattered speech. That's one of the best things about her, how she acts like what's happening to me is normal, or at least solvable. "Now, can you tell me four things you can touch?"

I clench one hand on the sheet, the other on the phone. I try to feel the textures, to notice how they imprint themselves on my fingers. "Sheet. Phone." I cast about me for anything else. My body is *not* floating in nothingness. There have to be other things I can touch. "The elastic on my shorts. Holly . . . " I look down at my arm and realize for the first time that Holly has her hand on it. "Holly's hand."

"Good job, Amy. Now, can you tell me three things you can hear?"

I close my eyes to concentrate, but the darkness traps me inside the walls that cut me off from the world, so I open them again.

"Someone's mowing the grass," I whisper. "The TV is talking. I mean . . . voices on the TV. Maddie's singing out in the garden." I become aware of those things as I name them, and they're like lifelines to reality.

"You're doing so well, Amy. We're almost there. How about two things you can smell?"

The scent saturates my nose as soon as she speaks, as if it were waiting for permission to invade. It's Holly's death-scent: garden soil, rusted metal, still water. This time, I don't notice any of the smells I associate with the living Holly. I guess she's feeling particularly dead right now—which, now that I think about it, might be affecting me through our emotional connection.

"All right," Mary says after I describe the smells. "What's one thing you taste?"

I run my tongue over the inside of my mouth and almost gag. I don't think I brushed my teeth last night. "Ugh. Bad breath."

Mary laughs gently. "Good. It sounds like you're a little more present. How do you feel?"

"Better," I say. I manage to sit up without having to think about it . . . or maybe *because* I don't think about it. Holly keeps watching me with her empty eyes. "Thank you, Mary."

"It's no problem. Do you want to talk?"

"I'm okay. I think I want to talk to my mom."

"That sounds great. I'll see you this Saturday, okay?"

"See you then." I hang up and gather Holly in my arms before climbing down from my bed. Mama looks up as I walk into the living room.

"It's good to see you up."

"Mama—" Before I'm even aware of my feelings, tears are spilling down my cheeks. Mama jumps to her feet and puts her arms around me and Holly. I lean against her chest and close my eyes, sobbing.

I tell her about everything that happened yesterday. How Jordan and I talked to Jessica and got kicked out of her house. How we went to the police and got dismissed. How I decided to spill all my secrets to my friends. How I tried to get Holly to talk about what happened to her but instead set her off again. How I convinced her she was dead.

By the time I finish, Mama has sat me down beside her on the couch. Holly perches on the coffee table, watching me emptily. Mama pets my hair. It chases away the cold and reminds me that I have a body and that my body is safe. When did she and I start drifting apart, and how did it happen? Somehow, I've convinced myself that I'm all alone in this house, with no one to rely on among my family. I lean into her touch.

"They accepted me," I say, my voice still shaking with tears. "My friends. They accepted all the weirdness and the scary stuff. They weren't mad at me for lying to them. Why am I so upset?"

"Maybe you built it up for so long that you were convinced it was going to go poorly," Mama suggests. "So when it didn't, you didn't know how to react."

"Maybe."

What she describes doesn't sound like a very reasonable response to what happened, but I guess feelings aren't reasonable. It also sounds like too simple an explanation to be the full truth. But what matters most is that Mama doesn't think I'm as incomprehensible as I do. I make some kind of sense to her, and that reassures me that maybe one day, I'll make sense to myself.

I lean against her shoulder and let her pull me close. Holly is still watching us like a robot waiting for some unknown command to activate.

"Has she been like that ever since yesterday afternoon?" I ask.

Mama nods. "As far as I know, yes."

"Is she echoing me, or am I echoing her?"

"You know better than I do."

I shake my head. A few more tears trickle down my face. "Why does everyone expect me to know things? I don't understand any of this. I have no idea what's wrong with her, what happened to her, what to do next."

Mama gives me a squeeze. "I'm sorry, Amy. I misspoke. You don't have to know. It isn't always about knowing."

"Can you try to talk to her?" I plead. *Fix it, Mama.* It's like I'm a little kid again, handing her a broken toy.

"Why don't we let Holly be for now? I think you and she will each know when you're ready to talk. You don't rush the Itch when it tells you to reverse death, do you? You don't force the animals you bring back to move on before they're ready, right?"

"But it's different. She's . . ."

"I know you're worried because you identify with her sister, and you want to give her closure. But something you have to understand, Amy, is that we have no power over the living. You can't mend the hole a loved one left behind."

Something inside me shrinks away from Mama's words, rebellious. It isn't just because of Jessica that I want to find out how Holly died. It's because of Holly, too. Because she needs to rest in peace. But she's right—I've never been impatient with pets or wild animals when they take time to come to terms with their death; maybe I'm being harsh with Holly, with myself. Why is everything so muddled? I want a clear answer to at least one of the questions pounding in my brain.

"I think I really did convince her that she's dead," I mutter, realizing that Holly hasn't blinked in several minutes. "Maybe now she'll never talk again."

"She's still here. She would have left the world completely if she didn't have anything else to say. She'll talk again when she's ready."

Where does Mama get all that patience from? I sigh.

"Do you know her parents?" I ask.

"A little. Your daddy knows them better. They spoke a bit when he was building that expansion to the courthouse."

"Is Holly's dad in construction, too?"

"No, he's a judge."

I sit upright. Mama's arms fall from my shoulders. "Holly's father is a judge?"

"Yes, that's what I said."

That would explain their nice, big house—nice and big by this town's standards, anyway. But more than that ... could it explain why the police ruled Holly's death an accident so quickly? Or why they were so diligent about keeping it out of the news?

Maybe I'm jumping to conclusions. Maybe I want this to be bigger than it is. But something Holly said yesterday comes back to me.

Jessie said no telling. Daddy's going to get mad.

I rub my eyes, hard, trying to force the thoughts out of my head. I can feel myself starting to slip away again. It's all too much for me. Mama's right—I'm not ready to deal with this. But will I ever be ready?

Just then, a knock comes at the door. Mama lays a hand on my knee in reassurance before heading over to answer. I curl into a ball on the sofa, hoping whoever it is will leave soon.

"Hello," Mama greets the visitor.

"Hi. Is Amy here?" I don't recognize the voice; the speaker stands out of sight.

Mama turns to me. "Amy?"

It's almost as tough to unfold myself from the couch and walk over to the door as it was to get out of bed. I join Mama at the door and blink in surprise at the girl standing on the front step.

CHAPTER TWENTY-SIX
Private

"You didn't come to school today," Toni Davis says.

"No, I didn't feel well." I stare at her, confused.

What is she doing here, at my house? She looks out of place on our front step, her spotless jeans and unwrinkled white blouse a stark contrast with the overgrown flowers of our front yard. At the same time, something about her—her slender arms, the way she stands on the balls of her feet, her wide eyes—suggest she might blow away in a gust of wind. She's not wearing her book bag. School must have let out a while ago.

Mama looks from Toni to me before leaving without a word. I want to ask her to stay, but that would be weird even considering how weird Toni probably already thinks I am. I bite my lip and shift my weight from one foot to another, not quite meeting Toni's gaze.

"Um . . ." I begin.

"Can we talk?" Toni asks.

"Oh. Okay."

"In private?"

"Oh," I say again. "Sure." The only real option is my bedroom, and the thought of Toni Davis standing among my messy possessions makes my stomach clench. "Um, this way."

I lead her through the living room. Toni Davis is in my house. Toni Davis wants to talk to me. Toni Davis wants to talk to me *in private*. What's going on? I'm not secure enough in my connection to reality to process this.

Holly, still sitting on the coffee table, stares at us as we walk by—I forgot she was here. Toni eyes her curiously but doesn't ask anything. For once, Holly doesn't want to stick to me like a burr. Maybe it's because she's deader than usual. Her vacant eyes follow us until I close my bedroom door behind Toni.

Sarah made her bed this morning, but of course, I didn't. There are clothes draped over the desk chair and books and papers piled on the desk. The sheets nestle in a Holly-shaped nest on the inflatable mattress where she's been sleeping, our old toys strewn about where Holly left them. I cross my arms as though to shield myself from caring about what Toni thinks of the room. I realize I still have mud on my shirt and caked to my skin in patches; I never showered after yesterday's mishap. My face burns hot enough to bake the mud into clay. Why couldn't Toni have showed up a little later, after I'd gathered the strength to get clean?

Toni barely glances at her surroundings but stands in the middle of the room with her ballerina's posture. She seems to be chewing on the inside of her mouth, her jaw tense. I wait for her to speak first, even after the extended silence ratchets up the awkwardness.

"What happens after you die?" Toni asks finally as though she's spilling the last dregs of soda in a bottle that had to tilt all the way to release them.

I stare at her for a moment. "I have no idea."

"You can raise the dead, but you've never asked them what they saw?"

"I told you, it's mostly pets and wild animals I bring back. They're not really talkative."

I wish I hadn't added that last part; Toni doesn't seem like she's in the mood for sarcasm. There's only one explanation for why she showed up to my house uninvited, unannounced, when we barely know each other: she's desperate.

"Do you want to sit down?" I ask, gesturing to the desk chair.

Toni shakes her head tightly. "You said it's *mostly* animals. Does that mean you've also brought back people? People who aren't ready to move on?"

I take a deep breath. "Only one so far. And she's a little kid, so I doubt she could explain what she saw even if she understood it. She didn't even seem to accept she was dead at first." I'm aware of the decision to say all this, but it also feels as though someone else is saying it for me. I must be living in a whole new reality where everyone knows my secrets. I might as well hang up flyers around the school.

Toni stiffens, then looks at the bedroom door behind me. "That little girl out there?"

"Uh, yeah." I hesitate. "Toni . . . did you lose someone?"

She trembles, poised on the edge of something. She doesn't meet my eyes. "Yes. My . . . my girlfriend."

I stare. A rushing sound fills my ears. That's why she asked me all those questions yesterday on the bus. That's why she believed me. She loved someone who died.

And she likes girls.

It's terrible of me to care about that right now, but . . .

"I'm sorry for your loss," I find myself saying.

"I know you can't bring her back. That's not what I'm asking. I just want to know what happens."

Part of me wants to blurt out a promise that I'll do the impossible to bring back her girlfriend even though I've never been able to intentionally trigger the Itch, and I have no idea where she died—probably not in this town, since Toni only recently moved back—and I'm almost certain I can only bring back those who died relatively nearby. I keep my mouth shut, thankfully.

"I want to talk to her," Toni says, pointing toward the living room. Toward Holly.

"I don't think that's—"

"Please, Amy." Her eyes are even larger than usual in her thin face.

How will Holly react to queries about the afterlife? A few minutes ago, I agreed with Mama that we should let her be for a while, until she's ready to talk. The past few days, I've been bombarding her with questions, and it's only made her more and more erratic. But how can I deny Toni when she's standing here begging me, when a possible source of answers is just in the other room?

"Okay, but you need to be gentle." I can't believe I'm doing this—I need to go through with it before I change my mind. "She gets upset when I ask her how she died. She misses her sister, who's still alive and can't see her, so don't bring that up. Actually, it's better not to bring up her family or her old life at all."

Toni nods. She doesn't ask why Holly can't see her family. It's bizarre to have an almost-stranger accept my authority so easily; I'm not used to being listened to.

"If she starts to get upset, don't press her. It takes a lot to calm her down."

"I won't," Toni promises.

I take another deep breath and count to ten before releasing it. I hope I don't regret this. But even more than that, I realize, I hope Toni doesn't regret it. I don't know how much she can handle. She looks so brittle, as though her perfect posture is evidence of how thin she's stretched.

I open my bedroom door and lead Toni into the living room.

CHAPTER TWENTY-SEVEN

Afterlife

Toni, Holly, and I sit on the roots of the old oak tree in my backyard. A short way off, Grandma and Maddie are weeding the garden and chatting like birds calling back and forth. A breeze tosses the leaves overhead, brushing shadows over Toni's face.

"Holly," she tries again. "I just want to know what it's like. What happens."

Holly is stiff and cold in my lap. She doesn't cling to me, doesn't look at Toni, doesn't react to her words.

"She hasn't been like this before," I say apologetically. "She usually does something."

Toni clenches her hands into fists on her knees. "Is it my fault?"

"No, she was starting to get . . . vacant before you came." I glance at the garden shed. Maddie and Grandma have the door open so they can come and go with tools and bags of soil or fertilizer. "Yesterday, she was freaking out, so I showed her how I brought her back to life. I think that made her realize she was actually dead, so now she's . . ."

I look back at Toni and lose track of what I was saying. She's so close that I can smell her fruity soap, pick out the birthmarks on her jaw and above her right eyebrow. I could reach over and rest my fingers on her knuckles.

Unlike my friends, Toni doesn't ask any other questions about Holly. She squeezes her eyes shut, and a shudder travels through her body.

"I'm sorry," I say.

Toni doesn't answer but sits there with her hands clenched and her eyes closed. I turn my attention to Maddie and Grandma again, trying to give her privacy. Why did I agree to let her talk to Holly? I should have known she wouldn't be satisfied. Holly didn't come back to tell the living what's on the other side; she came back because she wanted her sister so badly. Getting an answer out of her about anything, let alone something as huge as the afterlife, was always going to be like pulling teeth with your bare hands.

"Let's go for a walk," I say. Those words must have come out of the air because I can't remember the thoughts that led me to say them.

Toni's long eyelashes flutter, and her eyes open. She frowns at Holly. "Please, I just need to know what happened to you after you died. What does it feel like? What does it look like? Are there any sounds or smells? Is there a white light or whatever?"

Holly's head turns slightly for the first time. Toni's eyes widen a hair, but she remains intent on capturing the answer. I feel a change in Holly. I can't tell if it's a subtle shift in her posture, which I can sense through our contact, or something emotional that I can sense through our connection. Either way, something Toni said affected Holly. It only takes a small shift to tip a glass of water off the edge of a table.

But seconds pass, and Holly still doesn't speak. Toni's shoulders sag, and she crosses her wrists in her lap, bowing her head. My eyes sting with tears of frustration, but I blink them away.

"Come on," I say. "Want to take a walk?"

I slide Holly off my lap and onto the roots of the oak tree, then get to my feet. Toni looks up at me, her expression closed off and tired. I hold out my hand to her. After one last glance at Holly, Toni takes my hand and lets me pull her to her feet. Her hand is soft and delicate, her pulse beating warmly against my fingers. Standing, she ends up a lot closer to me than she's ever been before. She's a few inches taller than me, which means her eyelashes lie low over her eyes as she looks down at me. The fruity scent of her soap intensifies, and her body heat seeps into my skin.

Hoping the heat doesn't show in my cheeks, I let go of her and take a step back. "Holly, we'll be gone for a few minutes. Stay here, okay?" I doubt she'll leave this spot in her current state, but it wouldn't feel right to just abandon her like she's a doll that I can expect to find where I left it.

Toni and I leave the backyard, cross the empty car park, and wander along the sidewalk. Toni has her hands in her pockets and her gaze on the ground. I try to walk in a straight line and keep my arms from swinging too much so I won't knock into her.

"I'm sorry," I say again. I bite my lip to keep myself from spilling a bunch of excuses.

Toni shakes her head slowly. "I don't know what I expected. I shouldn't have bothered you."

"No, it's okay. I'm glad you came."

She snorts, not daintily. "Why?"

I rub my nose with the back of my hand, trying to conceal my blush. My elbow brushes her arm, and an apology gathers on my tongue. I keep it back.

"I've been having a hard day," I say instead. "I get kind of locked inside my head sometimes. It's good to talk to someone else."

Toni considers my words. "I know the feeling."

We walk in silence down the meandering sidewalk, neither in a hurry nor with a destination in mind. I'm replaying every interaction Toni and I have had over the past few days—not that there were that many, though I've thought about each of them so many times that it feels like we've had dozens of encounters. It's the first time we've been alone together, the first time there hasn't been anyone or anything else to drive the conversation. The closest thing was when I went to her table in the cafeteria to warn her about Vic and Darren. Even then, we had the watchful eyes of my friends and people at the neighboring tables, and I had a goal that told me what to say.

Be cool, I tell myself. Which is, of course, the ideal way to be cool—ordering yourself to do it. *Be cool*, I try again. *Pretend you're talking to your friends*. I don't need an objective or someone else around to have a normal conversation with them. I already know Toni and I have things in common: we both like girls, we're both outcasts, we both get trapped inside our heads sometimes, neither of us really has a life. We're both frustrated by the irresoluteness of death. Right? Oh, God. I have to stop thinking about it, or I'll never be able to open my mouth.

"Where have you been these past couple of years?" I ask.

Was that a bad question to start out with? What if her family really was in witness protection or her father really did go on the run from the law?

"Oh," Toni says, her voice breathier and tireder than ever. "All over the place. Cuba. Thailand. The Swiss Alps."

I didn't expect that answer. No one I know has even been to another country, let alone the other side of the world. Except Adela and her mom, who came from Honduras when Adela was a baby, but they were moving here, not traveling.

"Were your parents traveling for work?" I ask, though I can't imagine a job someone in this town would have that would require them to travel to the Swiss Alps.

"No." Downward-curved lines frame Toni's mouth and crinkle her forehead. She looks a lot older than she's ever seemed to me. "We were going to different clinics. They got more and more out there as my parents got more desperate. The last one had me examining my whole lineage to exorcise the trauma of my ancestors. There was a whole lot to go through. But hey, I'm still here, so maybe that's what did it."

I stare at Toni, then I make myself stop staring. "Oh. Um . . . so you were . . . sick?"

"Terminally ill." She says it so calmly, though she's obviously troubled.

"Is it hard to talk about? You don't have to—"

"No, it's okay." She shrugs. "No one else at school has bothered to ask. I guess they'd rather make up a bunch of rumors."

"Yeah." And me and my friends were helping spread some of those rumors. Great.

"You can tell your friends if you want," she tells me. "That way maybe what really happened will start spreading, and I won't have to tell everyone myself."

"Aren't you worried people will start asking you tons of questions?"

"People don't generally like to talk about terminal illness. This lady at the grocery store who used to be so nosy asked where we'd been, and when I told her, she just said, 'bless your heart' and that's about it."

I think about all those deathbed visits I used to do with Mama, how isolated the families were from the world around them. A lot of them seemed starved for someone to talk to and would unload on Mama about all sorts of things, from their grief to the bills to funeral arrangements to how difficult it was to go to work every day. And even the families didn't always know how to talk to their dying loved ones.

I think, also, about the silence in Jessica's house—the emptiness, the deadness of the space between the walls. Her mother's face, so weathered with pain that I thought she was Jessica's grandma at first.

Death is silent, like Holly, but so are the people around it.

"My family isn't shy about death at all," I confide. "They act like it's no big deal. Just part of life—which it obviously is. Right? Sometimes it bothers me. Actually, a lot of the time it bothers me. I guess I'm not as comfortable with it as they are."

I force myself to stop talking. I have no idea if I'm making sense or if I'm shoving my foot down my throat.

"Thank you for saying that."

I peer at Toni out of the corner of my eyes. She's staring at her feet as she walks, but some of the lines have smoothed from her face. She still looks older than she is, and exhausted, but she thanked me.

"Which part?" I ask, unable to contain myself.

Toni huffs out a laugh. My eyes glue themselves to her shoulder, half-bared by her blouse, and the way it moves with her laughter.

"I don't know," she says. "Being honest, I guess."

"No problem." I grin, though I don't know why. Then a weight slings itself across my ribcage as I realize something. "Your girlfriend . . . did you meet her at one of those clinics?"

Toni nods. "Yeah. She was sick, too. She had late-stage cancer."

I remember that Toni still hasn't told me what her own terminal illness was. The way she said that last bit makes me think *she* didn't have cancer. I don't want to interrupt her to ask, though.

"She was nuts. She used to escape from the clinic in the middle of the night and run around naked even when she'd been so sick earlier that day she couldn't sit up in bed. She would . . . she was really sweet. She would be embarrassed that I told you that."

"I won't tell anyone," I promise.

Toni shoots me a warm smile. It's the first time she's actually smiled at me. My chest swells, and my heart skips a beat.

Toni Davis smiled at me.

CHAPTER TWENTY-EIGHT

Disaster

I'm not sure how long Toni and I have been gone on our walk. We went up into the forest a bit, along the trails I used to wander as a kid. We walked slowly, our footsteps more a matter of habit than intentional transportation. We talked about a few different things, most of them unimportant, and the feet and the minutes melted away. Now, Toni and I are heading up the front path of my house, but I can't remember when we decided to turn back; it's like a dream where you show up at your destination regardless of the path you take.

The door bursts open, and Maddie and Sarah run out to meet us. Maddie looks worried; Sarah, annoyed.

"She's not—" Maddie's eyes scan us quickly, and she deflates. "She's not with you."

A cold weight settles in my belly. "Who?"

"Holly," Maddie says. "She's gone."

"What? I left her in the backyard, right where you and Grandma could see her!"

"Sweetie, you didn't tell us," Maddie says with obvious exasperation. "You just disappeared. We didn't realize you'd left Holly behind."

My fingertips tingle—the first warning sign that I'm hyperventilating. I can't hear my breathing yet. That means I can still get it under control. But part of me is thinking I deserve to have a panic attack, deserve to feel the consequences of my stupidity. I can't believe I was so happy chatting with Toni a few minutes ago. I should have known something would go wrong.

No. Holly didn't disappear because some cosmic balance had to even out or because I had to be punished. She disappeared because I left her without telling anyone to look after her or even taking her inside where it might be harder for her to wander off. This is one hundred percent my fault.

"How long has she been gone?" Toni asks.

"We just realized a few minutes ago," Maddie says, "but I haven't seen her since you were sitting with her earlier."

"She can't go that far by herself, and it's not like she'll get hurt," Sarah says. "We'll find her. Calm down."

"This is serious, Sarah," Maddie snaps. "Other people don't know what she is. She could get lost."

Sarah's lips part in surprise. I can't blame her—Maddie almost never loses her temper.

Maddie turns to us. "You were coming downhill, right? So, Holly probably didn't go up that way."

"She's trying to get home," I whisper. "That's the only place she'd want to go." The numbness has settled in on my fingers and is creeping up through my hands.

"Well, she probably doesn't know how to get there, so we should look for her in every direction," Maddie says.

The door opens again, and Mama and Grandma emerge, serious-faced. They look us over as if checking to see if we have Holly tucked away somewhere. Then they join us. I wait for them to scold me. I'm sure Grandma will have lots to say to me about being irresponsible and childish. How I shouldn't be trusted with my power.

But Grandma only says, "Well, let's all head downhill. She'd go toward where she can see other houses."

We start off in a clump down the sidewalk. I can't feel my feet, only the impact of the concrete through my legs. Our house is on the main road that winds its way up Whaleback Hill. The road has the name of some man, maybe a general or something, but everyone just calls it

Whaleback Road. Lower down, there are side-streets. I guess we'll have to split up when we get to those.

"You don't have to come," I mutter to Toni.

"It's okay. I feel kind of responsible."

I snort. "Don't. This is all me."

Toni touches my elbow, which makes my skin tingle in an entirely different way from how I'm losing feeling in my hands. "It's okay, Amy. We'll find her."

Her reassurance is a lot more effective than Sarah's. I actually feel the numbness subside in my hands, which means I'm getting my breathing under control and my body is receiving a more normal amount of oxygen. If I can stave off this panic attack, if I can focus on finding Holly instead of blaming myself, maybe we can avoid disaster.

Grandma, Mama, and Sarah each split off from our group as we come to different intersections. Per Grandma's instructions, if anyone finds Holly, they should bring her home and wait for everyone else to get back. Only Mama and Toni have cell phones, so we'll have to do our best to notify who we can.

Maddie, Toni, and I walk in silence down Whaleback Road, our heads rotating back and forth as we try to take in every possible spot where a little girl might be. I eye the houses, wondering if we should knock on doors to ask if anyone's seen Holly or taken her home to get her out of the street. But there's no time. If the worst happens and we don't find her before we get to the foot of the hill, I guess we can start talking to neighbors. There's no way Holly could have walked further than the foot of the hill, is there? The creatures I bring back have the same general physical abilities they did when they were alive. I've never seen Holly run faster than you'd expect for a toddler, and Toni and I haven't been gone *that* long. I guess she could have—

I have no idea what I trip on, but I'm falling before I can recover my balance. My knee strikes the sidewalk with a flash of sharp pain that takes my breath away. Maddie whirls to see what happened, and Toni crouches beside me, her delicate hand on my shoulder.

"I'm okay," I gasp. "Just tripped."

Toni helps me stand, but when I put weight on my knee, another flash of pain as strong as the first makes me cry out. Maddie grabs my arm, and she and Toni lower me so I can sit on the sidewalk. My heart is pounding, and my breath is ragged, but at least my knee only throbs dully when I don't try to stand on it.

"You should keep going," I say. "Find Holly."

From down the street, a man calls out to us, "Everything okay, ladies?"

"Just a little accident," Maddie calls back.

The man approaches. I recognize him, but I can't connect him with a name. For me, that's the case with most people who live on Whaleback Hill. He's older—retired, maybe—and plump, his skin tanned and lined by a lifetime of outdoor work. He reaches us, panting a little from the hill, and looks down at me in concern. I wish he had minded his own business.

"She can't stand?" the man asks. "Think that knee's broken?"

"No," I say quickly. "It's fine."

"Need me to call an ambulance?"

I shake my head. "No, no, I'm fine." I look at Maddie and Toni. "Keep going, please."

"It would be the second time this hour I've called 911," the man muses. He's obviously one of those people who likes to hear himself talk.

"Why did you call 911 the first time?" Maddie with polite concern.

"Sandra and I saw a little girl walking down the street all by herself. I wasn't sure, but Sandra said she didn't recognize her. Didn't think she was from around here. Police sent an officer up, and Sandra rode to the station with the little girl to keep her company and make sure she was safe."

Everything within me is frozen. I wonder if my heart has stopped. The throb in my knee is stretched to a single, sustained note. I stare up at the man in horror, knowing there are dozens of awful scenarios waiting to present themselves to me as soon as my brain starts running again.

"Oh?" Maddie says, her voice higher than usual.

The man nods. "Must have gotten lost, poor thing. Can't imagine—"

"My house is right down there," Toni says, pointing. The man's eyebrows go up at the interruption, but Toni doesn't seem concerned. "Mom should be back from work by now. She can drive us."

"Go," I whisper. "Hurry."

Toni nods, stands, and sprints away.

CHAPTER TWENTY-NINE

Power

Toni's mom wants to take me to the hospital when she finds out I can't stand up. She's a tall, slender woman a lot like Toni in an immaculate button-up and sensible high heels.

"We can go later," I say desperately. "We just need to go to the police station. *Now*."

Maddie casts me a look. Is she going to scold me for being rude to someone I just met? I don't have room inside me to care. But Maddie doesn't say anything. Maybe she's too worried to focus on politeness, either.

Toni's mom sighs. "All right, then."

Toni and Maddie help me into the back of the car, and Toni climbs in the passenger seat beside her mom. They begin a muttered argument in the front. It's not hard to tune them out; their conversation is low on my list of priorities. I'm not sure what Toni told her mom to get her to drive us downtown with no notice, but I don't have to worry about it. I don't have to worry about Mama and Grandma and Sarah, either, since Toni called Mama's cell phone to let her know what's going on.

"Any better?" Maddie asks me.

"What? Oh, yeah." The pain in my knee hasn't really changed—no better or worse—but I barely notice it. It's also a low priority for me right now.

As we ride down Whaleback Hill, I have the time and lack of distraction to think through every terrible possibility. Obviously, the police will recognize Holly; they're not incompetent enough that they won't remember the face of a little girl whose death they investigated a few weeks ago. But what if they can't accept it? What if they assume she must be some girl who's mysteriously identical to Holly? That might be easier for them to understand than a girl they know was dead moving around and talking. Honestly, that's the best-case scenario, because if they think Holly is some other girl, they won't jump to calling her family.

Her family . . . oh, God.

If the police rationalize Holly's mysterious reappearance, if they prioritize informing her family over figuring out how she could be alive . . . this could be catastrophic.

I remember the silence in Jessica's house. The pain in her and her mom's faces. Seeing Holly, seemingly alive, and having to—sooner or later—deal with her death a second time is something so horrible, I can't even contemplate it without starting to peel away from my body. I can't believe I ever considered letting Jessica see Holly or telling her what happened. There's no way it can bring her or her mom anything but pain.

Because Holly isn't alive anymore, and she never will be again, no matter how it might sometimes seem. I used the concept of a corporeal ghost to explain to my friends what my power can do, but there's something much more cruel about the way Holly haunts the world of the living. She's enough a part of it to actually convince her family that her death never happened. If she were a ghost, they wouldn't be able to hold her, smell her, comb her hair— all those things that root themselves most deeply in a person's memories and reawaken them most clearly. Holly has the ability to do so much more damage than a ghost ever could.

"Maddie?" I ask quietly as Toni turns on the radio, filling the car with a mournful R&B tune. "Why do I have this power?" My throat is so tight I barely get the words out.

Maddie looks down at me for a moment. A crease forms between her golden eyebrows. In that instant, she seems so far away from me: tall, beautiful, sure of herself and her place in life, all the things I'll never be. Or maybe I'm the one who's far away from her, a changeling that doesn't belong in the world she seems so comfortable in. Maddie, like the rest of my family, is at peace with death. They all see beauty in it, or at least rightness, when all I can see is senseless monstrosity.

"People don't have powers for a reason, Amy," Maddie says finally, turning to look ahead. "At least, I don't think they do. Some people are good at singing or basketball or math. It's not *because* of anything; it's because people all have different strengths."

"That's not what I mean," I half-sob. I grab Maddie's hand and squeeze it as though I'm going to go flying out of the car if I don't hold on. "What is it *for*? What good does it do?"

Maddie's eyes drop to her lap. Why isn't she looking at me? She doesn't answer.

"What good do *any* of our powers do?" I insist. "Even Mama—hers just makes dying easier, but should we have to accept death at all? Couldn't she have a power like yours only for people? Couldn't she keep death away?"

"I don't keep death away, Amy."

"You make plants live longer. That's the same thing."

Maddie shakes her head slowly. "You know about root systems, right?"

I'm not in the mood for this detour. I assume she's going to give me some vague, metaphysical explanation for her power, and right now, I don't give a damn about plants or root systems.

"I was asking about my power," I say, even though I'm the one who brought up hers. "What good does *my* power do?"

Maddie ignores me. "Plants are connected through their root systems. They communicate with each other about danger, environmental factors, and nutrients. They're not just a collection of individual plants; they share the same soil, the same bacteria, the same water."

I squeeze my palms against the sides of my face. Maddie grabs my shoulder, drawing my focus back to her. Her eyes are soft, but her mouth makes a firm line.

"I don't keep individual plants from dying, Amy. I influence the life cycle of the whole garden. I borrow life and realign it. That way, each kind of plant can express itself as fully as possible. Grow bigger, brighter, more fragrant than it ever could alone. A dozen tomato plants lend me their vitality to make one tomato vine fulfill its potential."

I never fully understood the scope or mechanics of Maddie's power. Most other days, I would be intrigued by this new information—information I never bothered to find out before. But right now, it's all I can do not to scream at Maddie to stop talking about plants.

"I'm asking—"

"I know what you're asking. You're not listening to the answer. Our powers are different, but—"

"They're not different, they're opposites!" My voice is rising enough for Toni and her mom to hear me, but I can't make myself calm down. "You give life. *Real* life. What I give is fake and . . . and poisonous. It hasn't helped Holly, and it's going to be torture for her family."

"Dealing with death is never easy or straightforward. You don't know how this will end or how people will be affected. I could choose not to use my power, suppress it, and let my garden grow on its own. The plants would live, and even thrive, but something inside me tells me it's worth doing. I trust my instincts. I follow what the plants, their root systems, and the soil want me to do. So far, you've been listening to the creatures who want to come back to life."

"No one wants to die," I mutter. "Everyone would come back if they could. That doesn't mean they should."

"I agree that not everyone should come back to life. But I disagree that everyone wants to. Most people are scared of dying—and yet, most people accept it when it comes. You used to go with Mama on her deathbed visits."

"Yeah," I say defensively, as if she's accusing me of something.

"So did I when I was little, before you were born. Do you think any of those people would want to come back after what they went through?"

I fall silent. I didn't know Maddie used to go on those visits with Mama. Maddie was probably much better company than I was.

Toni's mom is driving into the downtown area; we'll be at the police station soon. R&B still plays from the radio, hopefully keeping most of our conversation private. I'm already ashamed of my outburst.

"No," I admit, trying to make my voice calmer. "But how do you know Holly coming back will do any good?"

"I don't know that it will. That's what I've been trying to say. It's not about knowing the outcome—it's about trusting the process. I believe that there's all sorts of messy decisions and uncertainties in life and death. That's why I trust my instincts and the impulses I feel coming from my garden. In the future, you can decide if you don't want to keep using your power, but now that you're in this position, I think the best thing you can do is trust."

"Trust Holly?" I ask.

But what sticks out to me about what Maddie said is the part about death being full of uncertainties. How can she accept that? Does she really just follow her instincts, trust the process or whatever and live with it?

"Trust Holly," Maddie confirms, "and yourself."

Chapter Thirty
Interrogation

The mood in the police station couldn't be more different than when Jordan and I came yesterday. Where before there were only a handful of police officers sitting around doing paperwork or relaxing, the place is now crawling with cops. They revolve around the eye of the hurricane in the center of the open ground floor. I assume Holly is there, but I can't see her.

"What's going on?" Toni's mom asks nervously. She seemed to want to stay in the car, but when she found out Toni would come in with me, she decided to follow. Judging by her and Toni's expressions, they both have as much distrust in the police as my family does.

The young woman who welcomed me and Jordan yesterday rushes up. She's wearing a different dress that also shows off a lot of leg and has her golden hair in a bun, which emphasizes her high cheekbones. I find her a lot less distracting today. Maybe because I associate her with yesterday's frustrating experience.

Or maybe because Toni is here.

"Hi," the young woman says breathlessly. I can't remember if we got her name last time. "Sorry, we're in a bit of an uproar right now. Can I help you?"

"The little girl over there." I point to the center of the cluster of cops. "We came to get her. She belongs with us." I don't know where those words came from. I might be channeling Jordan, but badly—she would come up with a much better story.

"Oh!" The young woman turns to Toni and her mother. "Are you her relatives?"

"Us?" Toni's mother asks, meticulously plucked eyebrows lifting high.

Holly looks nothing like Toni and her mother, but I guess the receptionist thought it was more likely that Holly would be related to a Black family than a white one. Pretty silly, really; it's obvious that Holly's family is interracial, but I guess that didn't cross the woman's mind.

"No, we are," I say, though I have no idea what I'm going to do if they ask for proof. Is that something they would do in this situation? I don't imagine they'll hand off a lost child to just anyone who shows up claiming to be her family.

The police officer Jordan and I spoke to yesterday, George, spots me across the room and jogs over. His blue eyes are wide, his face pale and sweaty.

"What are you doing here, sweetheart? Amy, was it?"

I open my mouth to reply but close it again. I didn't think about how suspicious it would look for me to show up to collect a girl who looks exactly like Holly and was found wandering my neighborhood the day after I tried to convince the police that Holly had been murdered.

Maybe if Jordan were here, she would know what to do. I glance at Maddie, who has her hand on my shoulder. She nods, which I take to mean that she will support me but that she's leaving this up to me. Behind her, Toni is chewing her lip. She shoots me a concerned look. It's the second most ruffled I've ever seen her, the first being when she showed up earlier this afternoon to demand an answer about the afterlife. She's having a stressful day, and it's all because of me. I should have encouraged her to wait outside with her mom.

Trust Holly, and yourself, Maddie told me. She probably meant that about dealing with Holly and her grief-stricken family, not with all the people getting in the way. Well, I don't have much of a choice—it's all I can think of to do. I doubt the police are going to let us leave with Holly.

"Can I see her?" I ask George. "The little girl?"

George's eyes widen, then narrow. He crosses his arms. "Are you her parent or legal guardian?"

"No."

"Why don't you go ahead and tell me what you're doing here?"

The knot of cops is still too thick for me to see Holly. Would she want to come with me even if she saw me? She hasn't seemed nearly as attached to me ever since I made her realize she's dead.

"Can I talk to you in private?" I ask.

George nods. "That sounds like a good idea." He frowns slightly. "You're a minor, aren't you? You want your mom or dad or someone to come in with you?"

Mama should be on her way here, but I'm not sure if having her with me will make it any easier. It might even make me doubt myself. If it's just me and George, I can focus on talking to him instead of worrying about anyone else.

"No, it's okay."

"Crystal," George tells the receptionist, "any of the guys ask, I'm taking this young lady to Interrogation Room 3."

"Amy . . . " Toni begins.

"I'm fine," I assure her. It's not even a lie—I'm dissociating just enough to remain calm. I feel only a sliver of the panic I would be drowning in otherwise.

I follow George up the stairs on one side of the former library. My knee throbs in pain with each step, but at least I can walk again. As we near the top, I scan the crowd of cops below and spot Holly in their midst, sitting on a desk in a cubicle as adults in and out of uniform swarm around her. Sandra, the wife of the man who called the police, sits in a chair next to Holly, holding her hand; at least Holly's not alone. As if sensing my gaze, Holly looks up at me. She has that blank expression she's worn without interruption for the last twenty-four hours. I hope that means she's not scared.

George is waiting for me, holding open a door marked with a number 3. I float inside and take the seat he indicates for me. Fluorescent lights buzz overhead, illuminating the prefab walls and cheap metal table. Sadly, there's no two-way mirror or whatever they're called. I don't especially care for crime dramas, but it's still disappointing that the real thing doesn't live up to them.

"Why did you come here today?" George asks, lowering himself onto the chair across the table from me with a grunt.

"To pick up the little girl."

"What's her name?"

I hesitate. I already decided telling the truth is my best option, but it goes against everything I know about necromancy, authority figures, and this whole situation.

"Holly," I say through my teeth. "Holly Myers."

George's eyebrows go up toward his receding hairline. "Holly Myers is dead. There was an autopsy. A funeral. You came in here yesterday asking about the investigation."

"Yes, she is dead."

George stares at me. Maybe he expects me to confess to playing some kind of joke on him. When I don't, he says, "That little girl down there is alive."

"Is she? Have you checked her pulse?"

Again, George hesitates. I have to admit it's pretty satisfying to stump him after the way he dismissed me and Jordan yesterday.

"We haven't," George admits finally. "There's a nurse on her way to do a check-up."

"Well, you'll see I'm right."

"Darling," George says slowly, "are you saying that little girl's Holly Myers come back to life?"

"Not exactly. She's still dead. But her spirit is animating a temporary body that mimics her living body."

"And how . . . how is that possible?"

"Because I'm a necromancer." I'm about to tell him my whole family are necromancers, but there's no reason to out them. Holly is my responsibility.

George sits back in his chair. His mouth isn't quite hanging open, but his jaw is slack and his lips parted. We stare at each other across the table for what feels like an hour. I'm content to wait; judging by how reluctant George is to believe that Holly is Holly, let alone reanimated, I doubt anyone's going to call her family right away. They're probably waiting for the nurse to show up. I'm curious about what she'll find. I don't know much about the differences between a mud-body and a living body except that a mud-body has no heartbeat and doesn't need food or water to survive—though it seems to be able to eat if it wants to.

"You expect me to believe that?" George asks.

"No, not really."

He clearly didn't expect that answer. "Then why are you saying these things? You know it's a crime to lie to an officer."

"I'm not lying." I wonder if I would be nervous if I didn't have this eggshell of numbness over my emotions. There's irrefutable proof downstairs—the nurse will find that Holly doesn't have a heartbeat, and George will have to believe at least some of what I'm saying then.

George rubs his temples. "Okay, girl, let's start from the beginning."

"I raised Holly from the dead last Sunday night. She's been in my house ever since. The way she acted and some of the things she said made me think someone had hurt her before she died or maybe even killed her. That's why I came to talk to you—"

"Wait." George holds up a hand. "No, no. Wait. You say Holly has been at your house since Sunday night?"

"Yes." I can tell this is going to be a long, long talk.

"Holly Myers died two weeks ago."

I sigh. "How do you explain that little girl down there? I'm sure you looked at pictures of her and I guess at her body in the morgue. Don't you recognize her?"

"I met her when she was still alive." Pain flashes across George's face. "Judge Myers . . . he was real proud of her."

Judge Myers. Between Toni's arrival and Holly's disappearance, I forgot that Mama told me Holly's dad is a judge. My calves tense against the metal joining of the chair's legs. It could be nothing—maybe I just distrust authority figures too much—but it could be good to find out more from George.

"Are you friends with him? Judge Myers?" I ask.

"No, not really. But, well, everyone knows him around here." George sniffs in a deep breath and straightens in his chair. "The little girl looks a lot like Holly, that's true. But it's just not possible."

I roll my eyes. Probably not a good idea in an interrogation room when I'm trying to be compliant, but I can't help myself. One step forward, two steps back.

"That's where the necromancy comes in," I say, trying to sound patient.

"Maybe you're not lying to me—maybe you really believe what you're saying—but I need you to think hard about—"

Just then, a scream rattles the flimsy walls of the interrogation room. The cavernous library building, empty of shelves, makes the sound ring out with crystalline shrillness. I recognize the scream; I've heard it plenty this past week.

"JESSIE!"

CHAPTER THIRTY-ONE
Satisfied

I limp out of the interrogation room after George, and we both lean over the bannister to look down at the ground floor. The scene has devolved into even more chaos. I can't figure out what's going on—where's Holly?

"JESSIE!" she screams again, and I spot her. She's running between cubicles with two cops on her heels and a few others trying to herd her in like she's a feral cat.

Either she asked for her sister and the police said she couldn't see her yet, which would probably get the same response for them as it did for me, or she started screaming out of nowhere. Whatever the case, the cops were obviously not ready for her.

"They're scaring her," I snap at George.

He stares back at me, his brow slightly furrowed. He might be about to say something, but I don't have time to wait for him to gather his thoughts. My bruised knee firing darts of pain into me, I gallop down the stairs two at a time and cut across the open ground floor between cubicles to intercept the mad chase.

"Holly!" I call.

"JESSIE?"

Tiny footsteps patter, and Holly pops out from under a desk near me. The cops circle the desk clumsily, trying to catch up with her, but I sprint the last few feet and scoop Holly into my arms.

She squirms in my grasp, frowns up at me, and asks, "Jessie?"

What can I say that won't set her off again? At least she came to me when I called, though I don't know if that's because she thought I was Jessica or because she recognized me.

"I was worried about you," I say softly, trying to keep my words from reaching the two police officers who catch up to Holly and come to stand on each side of us, breathing hard. Are they afraid of a little girl? Afraid I'll hurt her? They're not helping calm either of us down.

"I want Jessie," Holly says, but she puts her arms around my neck. At least she's not running away anymore.

"Are you okay?" I murmur. "Are you scared?"

"Scary." Holly's lower lip trembles, and I brace myself for an outburst. Instead, she looks around at the police officers, scowling, and points a chubby finger at them. "Scary." She buries her face in my neck, and her tears roll down my shoulder.

George appears, eyeing me and Holly, and gestures for the other two officers to give us some space. I glance toward the entrance to the police station; Maddie, Toni, and Toni's mom all stand beside the front desk, which makes my chest feel warm. Toni's mom doesn't even know me, and Toni barely does, but they're still waiting for me. Maddie gives me an encouraging smile. Toni seems like she's trying to decide whether to come over, her body angled forward as though poised for flight. I shake my head at her; more people will only complicate things.

"She obviously knows you," George tells me.

"Look, if you talk to both of us in private, it'll be a lot easier." I don't look forward to going back in that cramped interrogation room or taking Holly in there with me, but Holly isn't going to talk to George out here with all these people. She hasn't looked up from my shoulder since she put her head down.

George shakes his head slowly. "I don't . . . this isn't really how we . . . "

I might feel bad for him if I had room inside me, but I'm about to spill over.

"I see Jessie?" Holly whimpers into my shoulder.

Trust Holly, and yourself. Maddie's words echo in my head yet again, like a mantra. Ever since Holly remembered her identity, she's been fixated on seeing Jessica. I've spent all this time weighing the risks and consequences of allowing Jessica, let alone the rest of her family, to see Holly. I've assumed Holly wants to see her sister because she misses her, but what if it's more than that? What if it's the whole reason she came back from the dead?

Earlier today, I was afraid Holly would never speak again. But Mama said if she had nothing left to say, she wouldn't still be clinging to the world of the living. I've always assumed that I bring creatures back from the dead so they can accept their death and understand that they don't belong here anymore. Often, the animals will be excited about life at first—the dogs will want to play fetch, the cats will pounce on any small thing that moves, the birds will swoop around the garden. After a few days, they grow more and more mellow until nothing catches their interest anymore. Finally, they'll go out into the garden, lie down in the soil, and dissolve back into the mud I made them from.

In Holly's case, ever since I realized something terrible might have happened to her, I've assumed she needs some sort of justice in order to move on. Isn't that what ghosts usually want, in stories? But—I close my eyes and pat Holly on the back, trying to soothe her—haven't I reaffirmed to myself that the dead I bring back aren't ghosts?

Few of the animals have ever been fixated on the manner of their deaths; mostly, they have seemed to want to recreate their lives, and when they find out those lives don't fit them anymore, they're able to shuck them. Maybe Holly just needs to see Jessica, and that will convince her to move on. Maybe the reason she hasn't answered any of my questions about what happened to her is that it's not important to her anymore.

I open my eyes and bite my lip. George is watching me, frowning slightly. His lips move, but if he's talking, I'm too preoccupied to even register the sounds coming from his mouth.

There's a complication: if I want to help Holly see Jessica, how will I deal with their parents? Holly hasn't asked for her mom or dad once, only her sister. It's still a fact Holly was scared of my daddy, and she seemed scared of her daddy, too. *Jessie said no telling. Daddy's going to get mad.* I shiver. Could I let Holly see Jessica, but not her parents? Would that be enough to satisfy Holly and help her leave this world?

Would that be enough to satisfy me?

CHAPTER THIRTY-TWO

Pulse

I'm so preoccupied trying to figure out how to reunite Holly and Jessica that I don't notice George approaching me. Now, he's looming over me, reaching for Holly. I take a step back, but all he has to do is reach a little further to grab Holly's wrist. He frowns, gazing at his watch—he's taking Holly's pulse. About a minute passes as he shifts his fingers around on Holly's wrist, evidently looking for her heartbeat. He tries the side of her neck, her other wrist. Finally, Holly sits up in my arms and turns to scowl at him.

"I see Jessie," she informs him.

George takes a step back, his eyes wide, and looks between Holly and me. "She . . . she really doesn't . . . " He trails off, then grabs a phone from the desk closest to him and dials. "Hello, this is Sergeant James. I need an ambulance at the police station. We have a three-year-old child without a pulse. Yes, thank you." He hangs up.

"That's not going to help." I hesitate, but I can't contain myself. "Your name is really George James?"

George ignores me, running a hand through his thinning hair, and turns in a quarter circle one way, then the other. He mutters something to himself. Then he walks back over to me and grabs Holly's wrist again.

"It's not going to be different," I tell him. I take another step back, forcing him to let go of Holly, who grips me tight again. "Does she look like she needs an ambulance?"

"It doesn't matter what she looks like," George mumbles, casting his gaze all around as though searching for a report or instruction manual that will tell him what to do next. "She doesn't have a pulse. She needs to go to the hospital. We need to confirm . . . We need a doctor to verify."

I start to argue but think better of it. Maybe it will be easier to control the situation in the hospital. If I can get Jessica there, maybe she can talk to Holly without police hovering all around, asking questions and making demands. Now the question is how I can get Jessica to come meet us without her parents when she probably won't trust anything I say. Maybe I could ask Jordan for help? Or someone else, a neutral party? Maddie might be able to convince her . . . or she might convince Jessica that our family is off our collective rocker.

George is conferring in a low voice with the other police officers. He keeps shaking his head, which I assume means he's either unable to answer their questions or expressing disbelief. The others shoot us looks every now and then.

"Amy." Toni has appeared at my elbow. Her mom and Maddie still wait by the front desk, watching us. "What's going on?"

"They called an ambulance because Holly doesn't have a pulse."

"Really? What will the doctors even do?"

I shrug. "I guess it's the best thing they can think of. Make her someone else's problem. Though they probably still won't leave us alone until they have something to write in a report, like 'girl was found to be a look-alike for recently deceased Holly Myers.'"

"What did you tell them?" Toni asks, eyeing George and the others.

"I tried to tell him the truth, but I don't think I got through to him. Well, I guess I convinced him to take her pulse."

The front doors of the police station burst open and

several paramedics march in. I didn't expect them to get here so soon; I guess it's one of the perks of being the police. George comes back to stand beside me, beckoning to the paramedics. They take Holly's pulse again and try a stethoscope. One of them is tall and pale—seriously pale and puffy, like he only goes out at night. The other has warm brown skin and a crew cut.

"We can't get a heartbeat," the crew-cut guy says. "She seems okay, but if you want us to, we'll take her to get checked out."

George nods. "I'll be right behind you."

"I'm coming with her," I say before anyone can ask or suggest otherwise. No one objects; they'd have to pry Holly's arms from around my neck if they wanted to separate us. I turn to Toni. "Could you get in contact with Jordan or Adela?"

Instead of answering, Toni presses her phone into my hand. Her expression has reverted to the calm mask she wears at school. I wonder what has more to do with her ability to disguise her emotions—is it her mom, who seems good at doing the same thing, or the fact she was on the edge of death for years? I've seen her in distress today, but rather than convince me that her emotionless mask is a disguise, I think it reflects some sort of internal balance inside of her. I want to spend hours talking to her, not about this whole mess but about anything and everything else. I want to know if I'm right about the way she processes the world around her.

But the paramedics are whisking me away with them, leaving Toni and Maddie and the police station behind. They usher me into the back of the ambulance, where they have me sit on a stretcher with Holly in my lap. As the ambulance rattles away from the police station, they connect Holly to a cardiac monitor; the line stays flat. The two paramedics wear expressions of utter incomprehension.

"Malfunction?" the pale guy suggests and goes to check that everything's okay with the cardiac monitor machine.

"I see Jessie," Holly informs the paramedics.

"She's dead," I add.

"What do you mean?" the crew-cut guy asks.

"She's been dead for two weeks," I say. "That's why she doesn't have a heartbeat."

The paramedics check Holly's other vitals—blood pressure, breathing, pupil reaction. Then they sit back and stare at us, eyes showing white all the way around. The tall, puffy guy goes slack, while the guy with the crew cut tightens his jaw and shakes his head back and forth in short jerks. I'll probably be seeing a lot of this sort of thing in the next few hours. I'm torn between a weird sort of embarrassment, like strangers are seeing me naked, and an amusement I know isn't fair to these poor paramedics who are only trying to help.

"What's going to happen once we get to the hospital?" I ask since that's probably a question they'll know how to answer, and I really would like to know.

"Since . . . since . . . " The crew-cut guy gestures at the cardiac monitor screen, which still displays a flat line. "A doctor will see her straight away."

"What do you think the doctor will do?" I ask.

"Run more tests," the pale guy says. "Probably do a full checkup."

"She talks," the crew-cut guy mutters, almost to himself. "So, she must be breathing."

"I've thought about that, too," I say. "I think she just breathes in when she needs the air to talk. I haven't paid that close attention to it, though."

The crew-cut guy puts his stethoscope to Holly's torso again, then puts his ear in front of her mouth. Holly draws back, tightening her grip on my neck even more. Pretty soon, *I'm* going to have an obstructed airway.

"I see Jessie!" she shouts, which makes the crew-cut guy jump back.

"Who's Jessie?" he asks.

"Her sister," I reply. "We'll see her soon, Holly."

She looks up at me, her eyes wide, her face slightly out of focus since it's so close to mine. "Now?"

"She's on her way."

Immediately, I wish I had said something less definite.

What if I can't deliver on my promise? But no—no matter what I tell Holly, there's no going back. I have to get Holly and Jessica together one way or another.

I pull Toni's cell phone from my pocket. "Is it okay if I make a call?" I ask the paramedics.

"Go ahead," crew-cut guy says. He and the pale guy have both gone back to staring at us in disbelief.

Jordan's number is the only one I know by heart. She doesn't pick up the first time I call—she never picks up calls from numbers she doesn't recognize—but when I call a second time, she answers after a few rings.

"Hello?"

"Jordan, it's me. Amy."

"Amy! Are you okay? You weren't in school—"

"I'm fine. Well . . . I'm in an ambulance. Holly is being taken to the hospital."

"What? Why?"

"It's a long story. But I think . . . " I inhale deeply, feeling Holly's small shape against my side and her too-tight grip on my neck. She's so present, and at the same time, as everything has proved over the past few minutes, so dead. No body heat emanates from her, no breaths inflate and deflate her chest. "I think she needs to see Jessica. Just Jessica, though—not her parents. Do you think you could convince Jessica to come to the hospital?"

There's silence on the other end. "That's a lot to ask," Jordan says finally, her voice quiet. "Jessica didn't listen to me or you last time."

"I know." I run through my options. It's a very short list. "Could you find out Jessica's number? Maybe ask Adela? This is Toni Davis's phone, so just send it here."

"You have Toni Davis's phone?" Jordan asks, her tone changing from meek and skeptical to intrigued in a second. I guess she doesn't resent Toni anymore now that I've told our friends the truth about myself. Or maybe it was just me she resented. "How did that happen?"

My cheeks burn. Will they ever stop doing that? "We were, um, taking a walk when Holly . . . anyway, we were hanging out when this whole thing happened, and she let me borrow her phone."

"Okay," Jordan says, drawing out the vowels.

"You'll get me Jessica's phone number?" I press.

Fortunately, she drops the Toni thing. "Yes. I will."

We ride in silence all the way to the hospital. The paramedics are opening the back doors and stepping out when Toni's phone dings with a message from Jordan containing Jessica's number. Adela is fast; I bet even the police couldn't have come up with Jessica's contact information as quick as Adela did. I stuff the phone in my pocket and accept the crew-cut guy's hand to help descend from the ambulance, Holly keeping me in a stranglehold. I let the paramedics lead the way and don't pay much attention to where we're walking—double doors, through the waiting room—and pull Toni's phone back out.

With each ring, ice builds in my stomach. I fight the urge to hang up. The paramedics check in briefly with a triage nurse before taking us out of the waiting room and down a hallway. The phone rings some more. It must be about to go to voicemail.

But before it does, the line connects and a voice says, "Hello, who is this?"

That voice brings me back to the white and beige interior of that old house. The inspirational posters on the walls. The smell of coconut and lavender. The hammer of my heart against the back of my throat.

In my arms, Holly stiffens. She must have heard Jessica's voice, too.

"Hear me out, Jessica," I say, deciding that identifying myself too soon won't do me any favors. The paramedics lead us to an examination room and head off, shooting Holly looks of confusion and curiosity. The room is empty, so I sit on the chair by the examination table. "You need to come to the hospital." There's only one hospital in town, so there's no need to tell her which one.

"Who is this?" Jessica snaps.

"Holly's here. Holly? It's Jessie."

I hold the phone so Holly can speak into it. I know I don't have any better way to prove my point, though it's a pretty blunt approach.

"Jessie?!" Holly wails. "Jessie!"

"Oh, my God." I hear Jessie faintly through the phone speakers. "Oh, my God. Holly?"

"Jessie, I want to go home! Come now! Come, Jessie!"

"Oh my god."

I put the phone back to my ear. "She just wants to talk to you, okay? Don't come with your parents. Please. We're at the hospital."

"Oh, God," is all Jessica seems able to reply. Her voice is flat, small.

"It'll be okay," I tell her. I have to trust myself. Trust Holly. "It won't be easy, but it'll be okay. Please come as soon as you can. She just got admitted to the ER."

There's silence for a moment. Then Jessica says, "Okay. Yes. Okay. I'm coming."

CHAPTER THIRTY-THREE

Sense

The doctor seems just as baffled as the paramedics by Holly's lack of a heartbeat, though she's better at disguising it. She runs an EKG, and when the monitor shows nothing but the same flat line and she's fiddled with the machine for several minutes, she calls in a technician. The technician fiddles with the electrodes on Holly, with the connections to the machine, with the settings. He even restarts the machine, just like you would do with a computer that's acting up. I almost laugh at that, but it's clear no one else would appreciate the humor in this situation.

While the technician goes off to get a different EKG machine, the doctor starts interrogating me. I try to tell her Holly's dead, but the doctor seems even less willing to entertain that idea than George or the paramedics. She ignores me as if she thinks that will make me change my answer. Her questions blur into each other, full of demands I can't fulfill. The whole time, Holly is wailing, not seeming to notice my half-hearted attempts to comfort her. My mind is on Jessica, who's on her way to see Holly. How will she take it? How will she react? Will she refuse to accept that Holly's dead and try to take her home?

The technician comes back with a new EKG machine. The doctor waits a few minutes while he tries to get it to register a heartbeat. When it doesn't, the doctor shakes her head.

"Okay. She doesn't seem to be in any immediate danger, so I'll send in a nurse to check the rest of her vitals and draw her blood. We'll run some tests and see what we can find." She writes a few notes on a clipboard and leaves the examination room without a goodbye.

"This has never happened before," the technician admits as he plucks the electrodes from Holly's skin. "When was her last check-up?"

"Four months ago," I lie. I've already gone through the whole routine with the doctor, and I don't have the patience to keep trying to tell the truth. For all I know, Holly's last check-up really could have been four months ago.

"And everything was normal then?"

"Yeah."

The technician shakes his head, dumbfounded, and leaves the room. I take Holly from the examination table and back into my lap, where she keeps crying, the sound almost monotonous by now. It's not the same as those screams back at my house all the times I told her she couldn't see Jessica—not nearly as loud or shrill. Weirdly, it's hard to read an emotion from her cries. She doesn't seem angry, or grieving, or even particularly upset. It's like these cries are just echoes of the real thing.

A nurse comes to take Holly's vitals and blood, trailed by two others. I assume they're nursing students or something. But instead of watching what the main nurse is doing, they stare at Holly and whisper to each other for a few minutes before leaving.

"We're going to be famous," I say. I didn't mean to speak the words out loud, but the nurse smiles slightly without taking her attention from the syringe she's using to draw Holly's blood. She's short and curly-haired, and she has even more freckles than me. Her name tag tells me her name is Serenity.

Serenity withdraws the needle and distributes Holly's blood among a few vials, labeling them in marker. Then she looks back at us.

"Hey, sweetie," she says to Holly, crouching down to Holly's height and resting a hand on her upper back. "Does something hurt?"

Holly keeps crying in that same hollow way and doesn't look at the nurse. She might not even realize she's there or talking to her.

"Her sister is on her way," I say. "I'm sure Holly will feel better when she gets here."

Serenity nods, patting Holly's back. Then she gets a thermometer. "Open up," she says, and when Holly opens her mouth for another wail, she pops the thermometer in. Holly jerks back into my side, and her cries abruptly cut off as she stares at the nurse. "Good girl," the nurse says. "Keep it closed for a minute, okay, sweetie? What's her name?" she asks me.

"Holly."

"Holly. That's a pretty name."

The thermometer beeps, and Serenity takes it out. She frowns at the display, then feels Holly's forehead with the back of her hand.

"Let's try that again," she tells Holly, and pops the thermometer back into Holly's mouth. The little girl seems too shocked to object. Again, the thermometer beeps after only a few seconds. Serenity checks the display.

"What does it say?" I ask curiously.

"Eighty-two point six, both times," Serenity murmurs, clearly more focused on the thermometer than me. She gets a new thermometer from a drawer and goes in for another try, but Holly whips her head around, facing away from her.

"I don't think it's going to be different," I tell the nurse. "You probably won't believe me, but she's dead. Her body's made of mud."

I glance at the vials of Holly's blood, which now that I think about it, I'm surprised she even has. I guess her spirit remembers her body well enough to replicate that much, but I'd be a lot more surprised if the blood looks normal under a microscope.

Serenity stands there staring at me for a moment. She doesn't dismiss me or try to argue with me. Is it possible she might believe me?

"I just don't want you to waste your time," I explain. "You probably have other patients who need your help. Holly just needs to see her sister."

Serenity seems about to answer, but she looks up. There are voices outside one of the doors. The room has two entrances; the one we came in through is connected to the hallway that leads to the waiting room, while the other door—the one the doctor, EKG technician, and nurses all used—seems to lead to a staff hallway. The voices are on the patient side. Could Jessica be here? I can't remember what time I called her, but it must have been a good while ago.

Holly jerks in my grasp, startling me, and escapes my grip before I can react. Her sandals thunk to the floor, and she patters over to the patients' side door. She reaches up on tiptoe to turn the doorknob.

Serenity makes a sound of protest and starts toward Holly, but before she can reach her, Holly pulls the door open, revealing Jessica and Officer George James, who has his back to us. He turns around and looks down at Holly.

Jessica stands in the hallway beyond George, limbs stiff and jaw locked. She doesn't seem to be breathing as she stares at Holly with wide eyes. Her hair is tied back in a messy ponytail, frizzy locks escaping to frame her face.

"Jessie!" Holly cries and launches herself toward her sister. George intercepts her, scooping her off her feet.

"Easy, now," he says.

Jessica shudders once from head to toe. She's gone sickly pale. Then she turns and sprints away, back toward the waiting room.

"Wait!" I say. I lurch out of my chair.

"Jessie!" Holly wails, squirming and kicking in George's arms.

"Did you tell that girl to come here?" George demands, rounding on me. In contrast to Jessica, he's gone flaming red, but it's hard for me to imagine how I could care less about his feelings at the moment.

I brush past him and run after Jessica. She's much more athletic than me, so there's no way I can catch up with her; this is what I get for spending every gym class chatting with my friends. She's almost at the doors to the waiting room.

"Wait, Jessica!" I call. "Holly's been asking for you for days. You can't just leave her here!"

A nurse and a man in a wheelchair emerge from an examination room and pass me, going in the opposite direction. The nurse shoots me a stern look. I'm probably not supposed to run or shout in the emergency room. Again, it would be hard for me to care less.

Jessica halts just outside the waiting room, bends over, and vomits into the corner. I draw up short in spite of myself, my stomach heaving with the sound and the smell. I take several deep breaths through my mouth and avert my eyes. I manage not to follow Jessica's example. Jessica stays bent over, one hand on the wall, panting. Tears fall down her face; she looks too shocked to be crying, but maybe the tears are from throwing up.

Serenity rushes over. She puts a hand on Jessica's back, just like she did with Holly a minute ago. "I'll get someone to come clean this up. Come on, honey. We can go into the exam room to get a bit more peace and quiet, all right?"

The doors to the waiting room swing open, admitting a mother and son. The kid seems to have a broken arm. They both stare at Jessica as they pass, even though the kid is ashen-faced and tear stained.

After they're gone, Jessica slowly straightens. Serenity keeps her hand on Jessica's back and uses it to gently steer her back the way we came.

"I still have to finish doing a few checks," Serenity says, her voice soothing and conversational, as I follow her and Jessica to meet up with George and Holly. The nurse kind of reminds me of Mama and how easy it is for her to remain calm when everyone else is falling apart. "We might have to admit Holly to the hospital for observation, but it all depends on what the doctor thinks."

George scowls at me as we reach him. Holly still squirms in his arms, straining to reach for Jessica, who keeps her eyes on the ground.

"I'm sorry, ladies. I'm afraid there's been a misunderstanding." George turns to Jessica. "This young lady—" he nods toward me— "called you without my knowledge. We haven't confirmed this little girl's identity yet. She shouldn't have—"

Jessica looks up and locks eyes with Holly, who finally stops struggling. Jessica's voice is hoarse and choked as she asks, "What do you mean? Are you saying that's not Holly?"

"Well, I . . . we don't know. The circumstances are not very . . . not usual. We're working on getting a warrant to collect a DNA sample."

"I Howee," Holly snaps. "I Howee. I want Jessie." Again, she reaches out her chubby arms for Jessica.

Jessica starts shivering violently, and Serenity ushers her inside the exam room and sits her down in my vacated seat. George and I follow, and I close the door behind us.

"Are your parents here, Jessie?" George asks.

Jessica shakes her head. "I came by myself." She looks at me. "You told me to. You're the one who called me?"

I forgot I didn't tell Jessica who I was on the phone. I nod sheepishly.

George lets out a long-suffering sigh. He doesn't face me; I guess he's that angry at me. "Well, that was a mistake," he says firmly.

"Is this why you came to my house?" Jessica asks me, still shaking, her face growing even paler. I hope she doesn't pass out or something, but if she does, at least there's a nurse right here.

"Yeah," I say. "Holly . . . Holly came to me and told me she wanted to see you, but I wasn't sure how you'd take it, so I went to talk to you instead."

Jessica lets out a humorless gasp of laughter. Her eyes are so wide, I'm worried she's straining her optic nerves. "That's . . . that's . . . that doesn't make any sense." She turns to George and Serenity. "That doesn't make sense, does it?"

"No." George eyes me. "None of this makes sense."

"Well, that's not my fault," I reply, annoyed. "I'm just trying to help." I bite back further retorts. I could go on about how no one believes me when I tell the truth, or about how much pain this has caused me even though it has nothing to do with me. But Jessica is on the verge of some sort of breakdown, and everything I've gone through can't compare to what she has.

"Jessie," Holly whimpers, reaching out yet again. I want to scream at Jessica to just hold her sister. I take a deep breath, willing myself to stay calm.

Jessica squeezes her eyes shut and turns away.

"What have you found?" George asks Serenity.

"Oh," she says, as though remembering she's supposed to be in charge here. "Well . . . we had some trouble picking up a heartbeat, and her temperature keeps showing up as unusually low. I've drawn some blood samples—"

She continues, but I don't listen. I'm remembering something Mama said years ago, when I was a little kid. Something about how all living creatures know, deep down, how to die. Is that the sort of instinct Maddie was talking about? Is that why she told me to trust Holly and myself?

I look at the little girl, who sits deflated in George's arms, staring with blank eyes at Jessica. Her sister, who won't talk to her or hold her, who won't even look at her. I don't know exactly what Holly needs from Jessica, but I know it's not this. This won't help her rest in peace.

While George is distracted talking to Serenity, I step over and pluck Holly out of his grasp. The two adults turn to me, but I ignore them. Instead, I walk over to Jessica. I wait for her to look up at me, her eyes wide and terrified. Holly doesn't reach out for her this time—maybe she's gotten tired of being rejected—but I feel her tremble. I hold her out and lower her into Jessica's lap.

Chapter Thirty-Four

Authority

Jessica stares at Holly. Her face goes slack, and she lets out a small, almost inaudible whimper. Holly throws her arms around Jessica's neck and holds her tight. After this past week, I know exactly what that feels like: the discomfort and slight difficulty breathing but also the softness of her skin and hair, and the knowledge of being needed so desperately. Jessica doesn't respond to Holly's hug, though. Her arms stay at her sides, her hands limp.

"No telling, Howee," Holly murmurs. "I don't tell anyone. I keep secrets."

George and Serenity stare at the pair of them. Neither questions us or tries to get in the way anymore.

"H-Holly," Jessica chokes out. "You can't . . . " Her eyes meet mine, the dark circles under hers in stark contrast to how pale the rest of her face has gotten. "What did you do?"

I let out a measured exhale, hoping it doesn't sound like a sigh of exasperation. I've explained myself so many times today, it's like I'm in a time loop.

"I'm a necromancer," I say. "I brought Holly back from the dead, but she's not alive. She's just animate. I think she came back because she wanted to see you again."

"She's still . . . dead?" Jessica asks.

"Yes," I reply. "I'm sorry." I wish I hadn't apologized. I made the choice to trust Holly, and that means I have to believe she made the right choice in coming back and I made the right choice in bringing her. "I'm sorry that it's so hard," I amend. "I'm sorry for what happened to her, and to you."

The stark light of the examination room accents the bruise on Jessica's temple like it does the shadows under her eyes. Her hair sticks up in clumps where it isn't confined by her ponytail. Combined with how pale she looks, you'd almost think she's the one who pulled herself out of the grave, not Holly.

"Jessica, honey," George begins. "Is this . . . is this true? Is that your sister?"

Jessica squeezes her eyes shut, opens them again. Tears trickle down her face. "I can't do this. I can't."

She grabs Holly under the armpits and pries the little girl off her neck, holding her out to me. Holly goes rigid in shock but doesn't take her eyes off her sister. I hesitate before grabbing Holly and holding her close. She doesn't relax against me—which isn't surprising, of course.

Jessica lurches to her feet and starts toward the door. George intercepts her, laying a hand on her shoulder.

"I'm sorry, sweetheart, but I need you to stay," he says.

"No," Jessica whimpers. "No, I can't, I have to—I have to go home."

"Is that little girl your sister?" George asks again firmly.

Jessica shudders and doesn't reply. George beckons me, and I step into Jessica's line of sight with Holly in my arms. Jessica shudders again, averting her gaze.

"Sweetheart, look at her. Is that your sister?" George asks gently.

I remember Jordan's outrage at all George's pet names. She would be disappointed in me for not putting down my foot sooner. This moment is hard enough for Jessica without having to deal with being looked down on.

"Her name is Jessica," I say.

George shoots me an annoyed look. Jessica looks at me too, then down at Holly. Holly stares back at her, still as a porcelain doll. It's more evident than ever that she's not breathing. Jessica's eyes overflow, and she turns into George's chest, crying against his uniform. George stands there in surprise for a moment before patting her back.

"There, there, sw—Jessica. Just tell me."

"Yes, it's her," Jessica sobs. "It's Holly."

George lets Jessica cry for a bit, then says over her shoulder to Serenity, "Have you done the full examination? Can you pronounce her dead?"

"I can, but . . . " Serenity glances at me and Holly. "I have the legal ability to pronounce death, but I can't ethically do that when she's moving around and talking, no matter what her vital signs are. The equipment might be malfunctioning."

"All of it at the same time?" I ask.

"It's possible."

I understand what she really means: it's more likely that all the equipment is malfunctioning than that Holly is back from the dead. At least as far as the hospital is concerned.

"She has a death certificate," I say. "Isn't that enough?"

"This . . . " Serenity gestures at Holly. "This suggests the death certificate is wrong."

I take a deep breath in and out. This is why my family avoids dealing with the police and the medical establishment. Serenity is reasonable—I think she might even believe me—but she's confined by bureaucracy. George and Serenity aren't going to resolve this situation. This should be between Holly and Jessica, with me there to guide them. But how can I get them away from here now?

George gently pushes Jessica away from him and puts both hands on her shoulders, hunching down so their eyes are level. "We're going back to the station, and we're calling your parents, all right?"

"No," I say. Where did that tone of authority come from? Everyone looks at me in surprise.

"This isn't your decision, young lady," George says.

"As the reason why Holly is here, I think it is. I know you both mean well, but you don't know what you're doing. I do." A pressure lifts from my chest, a weight I didn't know I carried. It's like finally telling all my friends the truth about me only on a wider scale. I'm talking to adults, professionals, authority figures. I'm tired of them calling the shots, and I finally feel like I'm doing the right thing.

"Um . . . I don't know your name," Serenity says.

"Amy."

"Amy, I understand what you're saying. You're the only one who really knows what's going on here, I see that. But we have to follow the law."

"The law about people coming back from the dead?" I ask. "The law that covers this exact situation?"

Serenity sighs, regret making her look older. "As far as the law is concerned, Holly isn't dead. She's alive."

"What do you think we should do?" Jessica asks.

We all turn to her. She's pulled away from George's grasp and stands beside him, her arms wrapped around her torso, shivering. Waiting for my answer.

"I think you should talk to Holly somewhere private," I say.

"I can't." Tears spill down Jessica's pale face again. "You don't understand."

"Would you rather go back to the police station?" I ask.

"That's not up to you, young lady," George snaps at me.

Jessica shakes her head, avoiding looking at me or Holly, though we're both fixated on her. "I don't know. I don't know what to do."

"You don't have to worry about that," George assures her. "We'll all go back to the station—"

Holly screams, the shrill sound bouncing off the walls of the examination room. My skull vibrates, and my eardrums shrivel up. This scream is unlike anything I've heard from her; no living child could make this noise. It's metallic, unwavering, devoid of emotion or strain. I flinch away from her—so does everyone else, but at least they can escape. The scream goes on, and the vibration in my skull grows almost unbearable.

The test tubes holding Holly's blood burst open. Instead of red liquid, what spills is thick black mud. The fluorescent lights shatter next, leaving us in the otherworldly blue glow from the digital clock.

I don't know how much longer I can hold onto Holly. Maybe I should let her go and get away from her. But as soon as I think that, something changes about Holly's body. It gets less solid, like I'm holding onto a soft pillow—no. Like I have an armful of mud.

And then Holly's body dissolves and mud splatters to the floor at my feet.

CHAPTER THIRTY-FIVE

Opposites

I don't know how long I stay in Interrogation Room 3, answering questions from George and another policeman whose name I didn't retain, but when they finally let me go, it's dark outside. Maddie, Mama, and Grandma are waiting for me by the front desk, sitting in folding chairs and looking exhausted. They spring to their feet when I approach.

Mama wraps me in a hug. "How are you doing, sweetie?" she asks.

"Tired," I mumble.

"Let's go home."

I glance up as footsteps sound behind us. Jessica and her mom have been released from their interrogation room, too; Jessica's mom has a hand on Jessica's shoulder, though I'm not sure if she's guiding her daughter or leaning on her for support. They both look even more exhausted than I feel. As they pass us on their way out of the station, Jessica flicks her eyes toward me, then away. Her mom stares at me for longer, her eyebrows pulled down. I wish I knew what she's thinking.

Mama leads me out after them, Grandma and Maddie following close behind us. Out on the sidewalk, a man gets out of a car and exchanges a few words with Jessica's mom, then with Jessica. He's a tall, dark-haired white man, neat in a button-down and slacks.

As we head toward our truck, he must sense me watching him, because he meets my eyes. His are deep-set and green or gray—it's impossible to tell with only the lights from the police station to illuminate his face. His hands, which he rests on the edge of the car door, are huge. He looks away from me and rests one of those huge hands on the small of Jessica's mom's back, guiding her into the passenger side of the car. Jessica gets in the back, and her stepdad closes both doors before going around to the driver's side.

I've gotten my first glimpse of Judge Myers.

Our family climbs into Daddy's truck, and Mama drives us, finally, away from the police station. I'm in the back with Maddie, who pats my knee but doesn't say anything. No one speaks as we drive out of downtown and up the winding main road of Whaleback Hill. I'm relieved, because I feel like I've talked as much today as I did the whole previous week.

We're about a block from our house when I finally force myself to ask, "Do you know if Toni and her mom are okay? I didn't get to thank them for helping out."

"They were pretty tired, but Toni seemed more worried about you than anything else," Mama says from the front. "They left a few minutes after Grandma and I got to the station."

"Good." I shouldn't be disappointed that they didn't wait for me. They have their own lives to get back to. But if there's one person I wouldn't mind sitting quietly with after this long day, it's Toni. "Oh." I reach into my pocket and draw out Toni's phone. "I have to get this back to her."

"She said not to worry about it," Maddie tells me. "She'll stop by after school tomorrow to pick it up."

My lips pull up at the corners of their own accord. Toni's coming by again tomorrow.

Mama parks the truck, and we troop through the side door into the kitchen. Daddy and Sarah sit at the island counter with mugs of tea. Daddy jumps up and throws his arms around me and Mama. I'm not used to this sort of effusiveness from him, but I cling to his shirt gratefully.

He smells like his favorite shampoo, which Maddie makes for him with peppermint and rosemary from the garden. I hold onto him until Mama pulls away from the hug to accept a mug of tea from Sarah. Reluctantly, I let go of Daddy and take my own tea.

There's not room enough for the whole family in the kitchen, so we move into the living room, and a few people pull up chairs from the dining area. I sink into the couch, tucked between Mama and Daddy. We all sip our tea in silence.

"Well, today was something," Sarah finally declares, breaking the silence.

Maddie lets out a breathy laugh. "Yeah."

"What happened to little Holly?" Daddy asks.

"She's gone," I mumble.

"She turned back into mud while Amy was in the hospital with her," Maddie supplies. She, Mama, and Grandma heard the abbreviated story from me earlier, before George pulled me into Interrogation Room 3.

"You think she's gone for good?" Sarah asks me.

I shrug. I've turned it over in my mind for hours. When the creatures I've brought back have left behind their mud bodies, they've always done it peacefully. Did Holly's scream and sudden change mean that she wasn't able to find peace and gave up on trying? Was she just so frustrated with Jessica's refusal to acknowledge her and the world's general lack of helpfulness that she lashed out in the most violent way she knew how? Could she come back and try again, or will she move on and leave behind an angry spirit that Aunt Betty will have to tame?

I'm starting to see myself from the outside, my thoughts dissolving into white noise. I close my eyes and struggle to feel the warmth of the mug in my hands, the gentle pressure of Mama and Daddy's sides against my body. I inhale the scent of Maddie's herbal tea.

"How did the police react to her when she turned into mud?" Sarah asks. "They were probably pissed, weren't they?" She sounds a little too satisfied.

In a strange way, I understand how she feels. Every interaction I've had with the police has been so frustrating and unhelpful that it feels like a bit of comeuppance for them to fail so spectacularly. But if it comes at the cost of Holly and Jessica getting the resolution they need, it's not worth it.

"They tried to get me to admit I had played some kind of trick on them," I reply, opening my eyes. I feel a little more connected with my body. Mama is combing my hair with her fingers, which helps. "I guess that's the best thing they could think of."

"A trick? How were you supposed to have done that?" Sarah demands. It's nice that she's so outraged on my behalf; I don't have the energy to do it for myself.

"I think George believed me, but he needed something more realistic to put in his report," I say.

"Are they going to charge you with anything?" Daddy asks.

I shake my head. "I don't think so. I don't think they have enough evidence to say I interfered with an investigation or anything. I mean, Holly's case is already closed, anyway."

"Poor Holly," Maddie says, shaking her head.

"Poor Jessica and her mother," Mama says, still stroking my hair. "They looked like they'd been put through the wringer."

I cringe, waiting for someone to criticize me for calling Jessica and failing to solve the situation between her and Holly, but no one does. I'm not convinced they're not thinking it, though. I felt so sure of my actions in the moment—I was trusting myself and Holly, like Maddie told me to—but it ended up making even more of a mess for everyone else.

What does Jessica think of me? And her mom? They must both hate me. And Jessica's stepdad, Holly's dad? I shiver, thinking of his cold stare and huge hands. Could he be capable of murdering his daughter and leaving that bruise on Jessica's face? Of putting pressure on the police department to stop investigating Holly's death? I don't know what to think anymore. Worse, now that Holly's gone, I don't know if there's anything I can do.

My tea drunk, I set the empty mug on the coffee tables and push myself to my feet. "I need to go to bed."

Everyone else murmurs in agreement and chairs scrape as the rest of my family gets up. I start toward my room, but a hand lands on my shoulder, startling me. I turn around to see Grandma frowning at me.

"Amy," she says. "Madeline told me you were worried about whether your powers do any good."

It's so rare for anyone to call Maddie by her full name, but of course it would be Grandma who did it. And of course, Grandma would be the one to confront me rather than let me be. I take a step back, getting out from under her grip, and cross my arms over my chest.

Grandma is not impressed by my defiance, simply raising an eyebrow. "Do you still think that?" she asks.

I open my mouth to snap at her to leave me alone, but it's Grandma. Her blue eyes are unflinching.

"I don't know," I mutter, breaking eye contact. "I don't think I did a good job today."

"Things always get trickier when there are inflexible people involved," Grandma tells me—that's what she calls people who have to follow strict rules, like the police. Everyone else is watching me over her shoulders. I wish they all had urgent tasks to get on with. "I think you did your best in a bad situation. That's all any of us can do. We have power over death—not the living."

I nod numbly.

"Don't let this shake your confidence, girl. I don't think it's over."

"You don't?"

She shakes her head. "The dead are tenacious. Just ask your aunt."

I glance toward the room shared by Grandma and Aunt Betty. Aunt Betty is the only member of my family who didn't welcome me home. Come to think of it, I haven't even seen her for a couple of days. Not since the day Jordan found out about Amy. When was that? Two days ago? Time has gotten so confusing; it seems like this week has gone on for a lifetime.

"Good night," I say firmly. Before Grandma can say anything else, I turn on my heel and stalk into my bedroom.

I'm lying in my bed, staring at the ceiling, when Sarah

comes in. Without turning on the light, she changes into her nightgown and slips into her bed below me. Neither of us makes a sound for a few minutes, and I assume Sarah has gone to sleep. For my part, I can't stop replaying the events of the day over and over again.

If only I hadn't let Holly out of my sight, allowing her to wander off. If only I had better answers for the police and they let us go before things got out of hand. If only I'd known what to say to Jessica to get her to talk to Holly and resolve things before George interfered and made Holly freak out. Should I have tried to speak to Jessica one last time as we were both leaving the police station? What did the police ask her? They kept her as long as they did me, even though she couldn't have had that much to say. Did she bad-mouth me? She had plenty of reasons to.

"Amy, you awake?" Sarah asks quietly from the lower bunk.

I consider pretending to be asleep, but it's so rare for Sarah to want to speak to me one-on-one, I can't help but feel curious. "Yes."

She doesn't say anything for a moment. Then, "I think that girl likes you."

My face heats, and I pull my sheets up to my chin. "Who?" I ask.

"The one who helped us look for Holly."

"Toni?" I ask, though it's obvious.

"Yeah. I only saw you two together for a few minutes, but I saw the way she looked at you. I think she's interested."

Sarah has never, ever spoken to me like this before. When I told her I like girls last year, she only responded with a shrug. A few times, she's told me about boys she likes, but it's never been a full conversation. Is she just trying to get my mind off the whole Holly fiasco? Even that seems like a stretch for Sarah; she's never tried hard to spare people's feelings.

"Do you like her?" Sarah asks.

"Um," I say. My face grows even hotter. I'm going to burn a hole through the ceiling if I'm not careful. "Yeah." I hesitate before asking, "What could she see in me, though?"

Sarah gives a disgusted sigh. "I'm not even going to answer that. This isn't going to turn into an Amy pity party."

"That's not what I meant," I amend. "I mean, do we seem compatible? She's so . . . so put-together and graceful and elegant, and I'm . . . "

"A slob?" Sarah snickers. "Well, they say opposites attract."

If I had a clear shot, I would throw a pillow at her face. "Forget I asked."

I lie awake long after Sarah has started snoring softly, replaying every interaction Toni and I had today. Could Sarah be right? Does Toni really like me? And even more important—does she still like me even after everything she saw today?

CHAPTER THIRTY-SIX

Aunt Betty

I wake gasping and lurch into a sitting position. Where am I? My hands feel cool dirt underneath, and I smell flowers and a slight scent of decay. I curl my toes and clench my hands, shake my head, and blink several times. Am I really outside in the garden? No—there are sheets tangled around my ankles, and my bedroom comes into focus around me. I'm in my bed. I must have just had a vivid dream.

I sit there and work to steady my breath for several minutes. Moonlight brushes the slits between the blinds, so it's early. I should go back to sleep. But my body pilots me to the edge of the bed, and before I have the chance to reconsider, I'm climbing down the ladder. Sarah sprawls fast asleep in her bed, so I tiptoe out of the room.

As I pad through the living room, I lift my hands to see why they're itching and stop short. Why are my palms covered in dirt? I turn my hands over; there's black soil under my fingernails and caked into the folds between my fingers. Did I sleepwalk? I've never done that before. In a house this crowded, I would know if I had.

I double back to the bathroom and switch on the light. In the brightly lit bathroom, my hands are as clean as they were last night. My vision tunnels, and the walls feel like they're closing in on me. I put a hand on the wall to make sure it's not moving and steady myself. What's happening to me? Am I still dreaming? I splash water on my face and leave the bathroom, heading into the kitchen.

All the bedroom doors are closed. I pause in front of Grandma and Aunt Betty's door, my knuckles hovering a couple of inches from the plywood. What am I doing, waking them up in the middle of the night? I probably just had a bad dream. Yesterday was stressful, after all.

But I knock anyway. Something's bothering me, something I can't name, and I have the feeling that Aunt Betty is the person to talk to. I knock again, trying to make it loud enough for the room's occupants to hear me, but not loud enough to wake up Mama and Daddy next door.

The door opens, and Grandma peers at me blearily from the other side. "What's this, Amy?" she asks, her tone as sharp as ever despite her sleepy expression.

"I, um, need to talk to Aunt Betty."

Grandma frowns, but steps aside to let me in. I haven't been inside their room in a long time, since Aunt Betty usually locks herself in it during the day. There are two twin beds separated by a nightstand, like in a hotel. An ancient vanity table looms on the other end of the room, its bulk made up of a dozen drawers on either side of the table itself, which is covered with knickknacks and heirlooms. A lace-trimmed cloth, maybe a fancy tablecloth, is draped over the mirror, obscuring its reflection of the room. When we were little, Sarah and I were freaked out by Grandma and Aunt Betty's room and all its mysteries. Now, I think Aunt Betty might be a hoarder kept narrowly in check by Grandma's no-nonsense attitude; there are even more knickknacks on shelves nailed to the walls, and several plastic drawers under Aunt Betty's bed. It's all neat, which is the only way Grandma would tolerate it, but it's verging on cluttered.

Aunt Betty sits in bed, arms wrapped around her knees. She's wearing her usual flowing white nightgown, her hair in need of a good comb. She doesn't look at me as I enter but stares out the window. The blinds are up, revealing a moonlit view of the garden.

"Sorry to bother you," I say as Grandma closes the door softly behind me. "I . . . I had a weird dream."

"Yesterday was hard on you," Grandma says.

"I know, but I think this is something else." I tell them about how I woke up and how I thought my hands were covered in dirt. Aunt Betty still doesn't look my way or give any indication that she's listening.

"It was dark," Grandma reassures me. "There were probably shadows on your hands that made you think they were dirty."

"Maybe. But . . . something feels weird. I thought I needed to talk to Aunt Betty. Aunt Betty, did you hear about what happened yesterday?"

My aunt finally turns from the window to stare at me. In that moment, she looks unnervingly like Mama, minus a few pounds and a lot of care in her appearance. "I heard. Did you dream about Holly while she was here?"

"Yeah, pretty much every night since I raised her," I reply.

Aunt Betty nods to herself. "And you've had some of Holly's feelings and memories, too?"

"Yes."

"You do tend to get the Itch at night," Grandma muses, folding her arms across her front. "Your mama and I have thought it's because your conscious mind doesn't get in the way of your instincts when you're asleep."

"You have a psychic connection to Holly," Aunt Betty tells me, with the tone of someone commenting on the weather. "Maybe it wasn't broken when Holly disappeared at the hospital."

"But my dream didn't have anything to do with Holly," I counter. "I just dreamed that I was out in the garden . . . "

I trail off as more of the dream comes back to me. Jessica was there, and someone else . . . a boy? Jessica's boyfriend, Peter. What were they doing? I remember the flower decals on the bedroom door—Holly's bedroom door. Or am I mixing dreams with memories? The more I try to remember details, the more muddled everything becomes. When I think about it, it's the kind of dream I might have had without supernatural intervention. I saw a lot of Jessica yesterday, and of course I would associate her with her house, which I visited the day before, and with her ex-boyfriend, who Adela kept talking about.

Without warning, the walls of the bedroom balloon toward me and my vision narrows. I gasp for air— something's stuck in my throat, clogging it, and I fall to my knees, coughing and retching so hard my chest aches and my stomach cramps. Someone calls my name, but I can't tell who.

Something cold and gritty dislodges from my throat, and I spit it out onto the carpet. Sweat saran-wraps my nightgown to my skin as if I had a fever that broke. Through watering eyes, I squint at what I coughed up.

Mud.

Aunt Betty crouches in front of me, nightgown draped over her knees like a tent. I brush tears from my eyes and spit out the remainder of the mud. Grandma touches my shoulder, and I look up to find her holding out a glass of water. I take it gratefully and rinse the gritty taste from my mouth. It still feels like it's coating my teeth. I gag but keep myself from retching again.

"Did you see something?" Aunt Betty asks.

"No, I just . . . "

I stop myself. The walls are gliding toward me on all four sides, crowding me and sapping the oxygen from my lungs. I squeeze my eyes shut and press my hands and feet into the carpet with all my strength. My therapist has me do this sometimes, and it usually helps. I focus on the support the floor gives my body, on the reminder that I'm here in the world: flesh and bone, muscle and skeleton.

But when I open my eyes, the walls are even closer. Aunt Betty and Grandma are gone, and something soft and heavy weighs on my back and shoulders; it smells like fabric softener and vomit. The only source of light is a series of horizontal lines straight in front of me, like blinds. I reach for the light, hoping to find a way out. But my hands never reach anything solid, just folds of cloth that get in my face, cling to my throat, wrap around my arms.

"Come back, Amy," a voice says.

Amy. I'm Amy. A hand strokes my cheek, recalling me

to Aunt Betty and Grandma's moonlit bedroom, to the walls that leave room to breathe. I'm lying on the carpet with my head in someone's lap. Aunt Betty? I'm not sure if I'm more surprised that she's touching me, or that I can touch her—part of me has been convinced for a while that she's a ghost herself.

"Where did you go?" Aunt Betty asks in a calm, commanding voice that's most unlike her. She only ever talks to the dead this way.

"I was in a little room," I mumble. "It was dark. I think there were clothes or something all around me. I couldn't get out. A closet, maybe?"

"What else?" Aunt Betty asks, stroking my cheek again.

"There were voices in the distance." I frown, struggling to remember. Did I really hear voices? I was mostly focused on getting out of there. "Maybe they were arguing. I'm not sure." I'm doubting my memories now, like what happens a few minutes after you wake up and your dream starts unraveling. I concentrate on the details I remember, trying to draw something useful out of them.

"Shh, that's enough," Aunt Betty tells me, tapping my chin. "You're back here now."

I nod and sit up. She's right—I could start making up things if I force myself to remember anything else. Grandma is nearby, using paper towels to clean a spot on the carpet.

"Did I really vomit up mud?" I ask.

"That's what it looked like," Grandma replies. There's a troubled line between her eyebrows that I've rarely seen before.

"Am I . . . going to die?" I ask in a small voice.

"What?" Grandma snaps. She tosses the dirty paper towels in the trash and scowls down at me. "Of course not. Why would you say such a thing?"

"Am I being punished because I didn't help Holly and Jessica find peace?" I don't know what's making me say these things. It's like my brain has shut off the part that decides when to speak and is just translating thoughts into words before I even know I've had them. "I threw up mud. Like the mud I used to bring Holly back."

Grandma shakes her head. "Don't be silly. I told you, this isn't over. Holly still has a chance to get what she needs before she moves on."

"Why is she doing this to me, then?" I ask. I sound pitiful to my own ears. Some necromancer I am.

"She's not doing this to you," Grandma tells me. "You're the one with the power."

"You mean I'm doing this to myself?" I ask.

"You're letting her in," Aunt Betty murmurs. "You're listening to her."

Grandma and I both turn to look at Aunt Betty. She's wrapped her arms around her knees and is looking out the window again.

I grab Aunt Betty's shoulder. Why isn't she looking at me? "Do you think Holly is trying to tell me something?"

"Hmm. Tell, no. That suggests intention."

Yes, "tell" does suggest intention, and Holly refused over and over to tell me what happened to her. *Jessie said no telling.* But now that Holly's body is gone and I'm only hearing her through our psychic connection, could I get more of the story? Could I use these clues to figure out how she died? Will that help Holly and Jessica?

"Back to bed," Grandma orders me.

"But—"

"You need your rest. We all do."

"But shouldn't I—"

"If you're going to get anything else out of that girl's memories, you'll get it. If not, you still need to sleep."

I sigh. Exhaustion steamrolls me, as if it were waiting for Grandma to bring it up before making itself known. She's right.

Trust Holly, and yourself.

CHAPTER THIRTY-SEVEN
Normal

I stare at myself in the bathroom mirror for several minutes the next morning. My sunken eyes have bags under them now. Did last night really happen? Did I really vomit mud and have a vision of Holly's past? Maybe it was all a dream. I try to convince myself for a few minutes, but it doesn't work. My gut knows it was all real.

But that doesn't mean I have to dwell on it all day. Since I slept through the rest of the night after the whole incident, it must mean either Holly thinks I've gotten the message, or my brain decided not to listen anymore. Either way, I need this sliver of normalcy, even if it only lasts from now until school lets out. A short vacation from being a necromancer. No visions, no vomiting mud, no Itches or memories. Just Amy—Amy who is not going to fail her classes.

Mama and Maddie raise their eyebrows at me when I shuffle into the kitchen. It's hard to remember they're mother and daughter sometimes; Maddie is several inches taller, blond where Mama is dark-haired, tanned where Mama is pale, curvy where Mama is plump. But then they'll wear the exact same expression, like now, and make it impossible to forget.

"You're going to school?" Mama asks.

"I'm not going to sit around here all day." I serve myself coffee and plop into a chair at the island counter. "I've already missed a lot this week. I don't want to fall behind."

"Well, it's your decision," Mama says.

"You look tired," Maddie observes.

I shrug and take a swig of coffee. Grandma must not have told them I woke her up in the middle of the night, or Maddie would mention it. I guess privacy isn't completely dead in this house. Thank God because Mama and Maddie are already hovering enough as it is. When I came home from the police station last night, I enjoyed getting coddled. Now, I'm ready to put yesterday behind me.

The dark coffee stares up at me, and I remember the mud I spat out last night. My stomach roils. I pour in creamer until the coffee is much lighter than I usually drink it—and impossible to compare to mud.

Sarah strides into the kitchen and smirks at the sight of me. "Are you wearing jeans? And an actually decent shirt? What happened to sweatpants and baggy T-shirts?"

I blush and scowl at her. "I can wear whatever I want."

Sarah shrugs, still smirking. "Sure."

At least Mama and Maddie aren't looking so worried anymore—now they're trying to hide their amusement. I blush some more and ignore everyone as I drink the rest of my coffee.

Sarah's getting a ride from a friend, so I leave for the bus stop a few minutes later. On the way out, Mama calls, "I can pick you up if you don't feel well, okay? Just call me."

"I will, Mama. Thanks." I slam the door behind me and jog a few steps before settling into a walk, eager to avoid any other last-minute comments from concerned family members.

The morning is bright and warm but not too humid; a breeze lightens the air even more. Maybe we'll finally have a day without rain.

"Jordan!" I call when I spot her ahead of me, walking down the winding road.

She turns, eyes wide, and waits for me to catch up. "Amy, are you okay? Yesterday—"

"Yeah. It's a long story. Do you mind if I tell you later?"

"Sure."

Jordan's eyes are dark with worry, but she falls in step beside me and doesn't insist. We walk in silence for a few minutes.

"So . . . " Jordan hedges. "Did you get a chance to study for the chemistry quiz today?"

My stomach sinks. "There's a chemistry quiz?"

"Yeah, remember? He told us on Tuesday."

"Was Tuesday this year?" I mutter. I don't think I've done any homework this week. I barely remember which classes I'm in. On the positive side, I guess I won't have trouble getting distracted from Holly today.

"We can do a quick review in the bus," Jordan assures me.

"Thanks."

"You look nice, by the way. I like your shirt."

I grin from ear to ear. It's the first time I can remember that Jordan has complimented my clothing.

We chat lightly about some reality show Jordan has been watching. The conversation is a little stiffer than usual, but it's something. I'm sure Adela will have a lot more trouble pretending everything is normal, so I need to enjoy this while I can.

I spot Toni's house up ahead, and my heartbeat makes great conversation with my ribcage. I'd almost forgotten she lives along our route. I grab Jordan's arm, pulling us both to a stop.

"Sarah thinks Toni likes me," I stammer, my words falling over each other to get out of my mouth. "Do you think she likes me?"

Jordan stares at me for a moment as if I've started speaking another language. Then she eyes Toni's house. "Um, I don't really . . . "

The front door opens, and Toni steps out, book bag over one slender shoulder, hoop earrings accenting the length of her neck and graceful shape of her jaw. I open my mouth to call out to her, but my voice sticks in my throat.

Toni looks our way anyway; her lips part in surprise, and she waits for us to reach her. I have to focus on my feet to keep from tripping over them. Or maybe it's because I'm focusing on them that walking suddenly feels like such an unfamiliar task. Am I imagining the warmth in Toni's expression as I get to her side? She's not smiling, but something about her eyes, which seemed so distant and inscrutable before, welcomes me.

I take her phone from my pocket. Our fingers brush as she takes it from my hand, sending a shiver up my arm.

"Thank you," I say.

"You're welcome. Are you—" Toni begins.

"Nice day, isn't it?" I burst out. "No rain this time."

Jordan and Toni both look up at the sky as if what I said is so outlandish that they have to see for themselves. My cheeks warm, and I scuff my shoe along the curb.

"Yeah, that's nice," Toni says.

"Um, shall we?" Jordan asks, gesturing stiffly downhill.

Toni and I nod, and we all start walking. Is Toni about to try to ask me how I am again? I should offer her some explanation, like I sort of did with Jordan. But something better. Toni doesn't know me as well as Jordan, after all. I open my mouth to say something, hoping the right words will come if I start making sounds.

"That concert is tonight, right?" Toni asks, interrupting me.

"What? Oh!" Jordan shakes her head as if emerging from her thoughts. "Yeah, it is. Do you think you might come?"

"Oh, that concert," I say. I didn't mean to speak my revelation out loud, but it took me a few seconds to figure out what Toni was asking about. Discarded Infernal, the band Jordan has been looking forward to seeing all summer.

Toni and Jordan both eye me. Sometimes I wonder if people are searching for signs of a concussion when they do that.

"Maybe," Toni says, replying to Jordan's question. "Are you going, Amy?"

My heart trips over itself. She wants to know if I'm going. Does that mean she'll go if I go? Could this be a date? No, of course not—Jordan is going, too. It would be rude for it to be a date. But it could be a chance to hang out and get closer, and who knows? Maybe it could turn into a date afterwards.

Cool it, Amy, I tell myself. I'm getting ahead of myself. Toni might not even be going. Sarah might be wrong, and she just wants to be friends.

"Probably," I find myself saying. I did say I was going the other day without thinking it through.

"Do you have a ticket?" Jordan asks.

Ticket. Right. Deciding I'm going isn't enough. I should have thought this through earlier. But to be fair, I've had a lot on my mind.

"I, um, forgot," I say. "Do you think there's still tickets?"

I'm not sure what answer I'm hoping for. I've never been to a concert before, but it sounds stressful. I'm not exactly my own person these days; what if Holly decides to send me another vision? On the other hand, Jordan has been asking me to go to a concert with her for years. And of course, Toni might come, too.

"You can pay at the door, but it'll be more expensive. I can check if they're still selling tickets." Jordan pulls out her phone. I don't know how she looks at that thing while she's walking and doesn't fall flat on her face. "It looks like you can buy them until twelve hours before the show. Eight AM."

That's in less than an hour. "How much is it?" I ask.

"Thirty dollars."

I have about a hundred dollars saved up from birthday cards and that babysitting gig last month. I don't have enough ambition to be saving up for anything in particular, so it might be worth it.

"Oh." Toni's expression closes off, and a lot more space suddenly seems to separate us.

I remember what she told me—that she and her parents have spent the last couple of years traveling all over the world, trying to find a treatment to cure whatever was wrong with her. They could be thousands of dollars in debt for all I know.

"My mom probably won't want me to go," Toni says. "She's kind of overprotective."

"I can get you a ticket," my voice says.

Toni shakes her head. "I can't let you do that."

"If you want to go, you can pay me back later," I say. This time, it feels like me saying it.

Toni bites her lip. It really, really suits her. The day grows a little warmer.

Jordan looks from me to Toni and back. Her face goes carefully neutral. "Well, you have a little while to decide."

"Okay," Toni says quickly, as if she had to get the word out before someone snatched it away from her. "I guess if you don't mind, Amy . . . " She glances back toward her house. "I probably shouldn't tell my mom."

My chest swells. It's really happening. We're all going to the concert together. Maybe it's a terrible mistake—maybe I'll have a panic attack or start vomiting mud again. But I don't want to think about that. The day's too bright and Toni's too pretty and Jordan's too excited, in her own low-key way, for me to worry.

"You can tell her you're over at my house," I tell Toni.

CHAPTER THIRTY-EIGHT
Conviction

Adela takes even less time to confront me about last night than I thought she would. As soon as she spots me in the school hallway, she marches over to me and demands, "What happened last night? Did you call Jessica? Did she meet Holly?"

I nearly dislocate my head whipping it around to see if anyone is listening to us—and most of all, if Jessica is nearby. But no one seems concerned with our conversation. I guess Adela didn't yell her questions, though it felt like she did.

"Can we talk about this later?" I ask.

Adela looks up from me, seeming to notice Toni for the first time. Toni, Jordan, and I walked into the school building together, which wraps me in a warm blanket of comfort.

Not comforting enough to withstand Adela, though.

"Ha," she says. "Not a chance. I know you're going to keep avoiding me if I let you get away with it."

I sigh. I guess Adela both knows me too well and has too little patience.

"I'm just trying to have a normal day," I mutter. "Can't I have a break?"

"Sure. After you tell us what's going on."

Harper approaches us. Their raised eyebrows, their aura of cool not quite concealing their earnest interest, tell me Adela must have shared with them what she knows about last night.

This is the opposite of what I wanted to accomplish by coming to school. But at the same time, it's reassuring to have all my friends be concerned and ready to support me. Adela really did help me a lot by getting me Jessica's phone number within a few minutes. If I give everyone the run-down now, I'll only have to explain it once, and then maybe I can forget about it for the rest of the day.

"Okay, let's find somewhere private," I relent.

Adela grabs my hand and drags me to a niche near a cleaning closet. Everyone else crowds around me with intent looks on their faces, even Jordan and Toni, who seemed to accept my evasion earlier. It's proof of how focused everyone is on the Holly situation that no one questions or even seems that surprised by Toni's presence in our group.

"So, Holly got taken to the police by my neighbor," I begin.

"What?" Harper demands. "Why?"

"They found her wandering around by herself. She was trying to get to Jessica on her own."

"Poor baby," Jordan says.

Poor baby who nearly gave me several heart attacks. "Yeah, well, the police questioned me for a while, and I tried to tell them the truth, but they—"

"You told them the truth?" Adela asks. "That you're a . . . a necromancer?" She says the word with uncertainty, like she's still figuring out the sound of it.

"What else was I supposed to do? Can you think of a believable lie?"

"What then, Amy?" Jordan asks, cutting off Adela from making any further interjections. "When you called me, you said you and Holly were in an ambulance, and she needed to see Jessie."

"A police officer checked Holly's pulse and realized she didn't have one, so he called the paramedics. I think he wanted confirmation that she was dead, or I guess he wanted to cover his bases in case she wasn't and needed medical attention. I rode in the ambulance with her. She kept insisting she wanted to see Jessica, and I decided it was time."

"Why?" Adela asks. "The other day, you said Holly couldn't see her family or they would assume she was alive and want to take her home. Right?"

"Yeah, but look how far it got me to keep ignoring what she wanted," I point out. "I realized I needed to trust her, or she would never get to rest in peace."

"Wow," Adela breathes.

Could it be that I'm actually impressive? Maybe even kind of cool? Jordan and Toni both keep their eyes narrowed and focused, though, waiting for what I say next.

"Um, well," I continue, "Adela got me Jessica's number, and I called her and convinced her to come to the emergency room without her parents, since Holly seemed to only want to see her."

"How did you convince her?" Jordan asks, probably remembering our disastrous conversation with Jessica the day before yesterday. It occurs to me that that conversation finally convinced Jordan I was right in not wanting to tell Jessica the truth—and then the next day, I turned around and told Jessica anyway. Maybe that's why Jordan doesn't seem that impressed with me.

"I put Holly on the line," I admit.

Adela gasps. Harper shakes their head slightly. Jordan winces. I guess I made it sound kind of tactless.

"Look, I talked to Maddie about my powers yesterday, and she convinced me that the only way I can use them responsibly is to trust and follow my instincts. It was . . . arrogant, I guess, to think that I knew better than Holly how to deal with her own family. You never really know what people need or how they'll react when it comes to death."

Saying it all out loud eases a tightness in me that I didn't know was there. I'm still not sure I made the right choice—I know I messed up a few times—but at least the argument sounds convincing to my own ears. That counts for something, right?

"So how did Jessica react when she saw Holly?" Jordan asks.

I hesitate. After that speech I just gave, it's about to seem like I'm contradicting myself. And maybe what happened in the ER really does prove me and Maddie wrong; maybe I really should have left Jessica out of it. I consider spinning it in a more positive light to make myself sound like I know what I'm doing, but even if I thought I could pull off a half-lie, I owe my friends better. Besides, my conviction wouldn't be very strong if it couldn't take a few challenges.

"Uh . . . not great."

Jordan nods, a taste of I-told-you-so in her expression.

"But I knew it wouldn't be easy," I continue. "It's never going to be easy to deal with death."

"What did Jessica do?" Adela asks.

"What did *Holly* do?" Harper asks.

"Jessica sort of . . . freaked out and tried to run away. I got her to hold Holly for a bit, and it seemed like we were making some progress. At least, she accepted it really was Holly and that I knew what I was talking about. But then the police officer who was there got in the way, and Holly got frustrated and started screaming."

"Like she did the other day at your house?" Harper asks.

"Not . . . not quite. More like a drill or something. She didn't sound human. She made some glass explode, and then she . . . collapsed into mud."

"She fell into the mud?" Adela asks. "There was mud in the ER?"

"No, she kind of melted. Her body burst and turned back into mud. She's gone—for now, anyway. My grandma thinks she'll be back, and I . . . I agree with her."

Everyone stares at me with various shades of disbelief, shock, confusion, and worry painted across their faces. The bell rings for homeroom, but no one moves.

"Are you okay?" Toni asks quietly. It's the first thing she's said since we got to school. Everyone glances at her; I can tell Adela is boiling over with questions about Toni's presence, but she must be too preoccupied to ask them.

"Yeah, I'm fine." I consider telling them about last night's dreams and visions, but I don't feel like reliving them after everything I just had to explain. Besides, my friends are freaked out enough already. "I want to take a break while Holly's gone and just be a regular person. I'm sure she'll need me again soon."

Students are streaming past us on their way to their homerooms. If we don't hurry, I'll be late for the second time this week—and that's not even counting yesterday, which I missed completely.

"Oh, yeah," Jordan says, straightening. I didn't realize until now that she was hunched forward, leaning toward me. "Amy and Toni are coming with me to the Discarded Infernal concert tonight."

"What?" Adela asks, her eyebrows shooting up.

"You like alternative grunge?" Harper asks Toni. There's an amused note in their voice that makes me want to rush to Toni's defense. Harper can be so callous sometimes.

Toni's gaze drops to her cute sandals. "I thought I'd try it out."

"Maybe we should all go," Adela declares.

"You would definitely hate it," Jordan tells her.

"Well, we can at least all hang out together in Glendock Park before the concert," Adela says, wiggling her eyebrows.

"What's in Glendock Park?" Toni asks.

"Great place for smoking pot," Adela stage-whispers.

"Oh," Toni says, her expression relaxing. "I probably have enough to share with everyone, if you don't mind the strong stuff."

Everyone goes some degree of slack-jawed and wide-eyed at Toni's casual comment. I remember that, earlier this week, Adela and Harper were speculating whether Toni was too uptight to have ever smoked weed. I giggle at their expressions. Toni shoots me a smile that warms me from toes to fingertips.

"Yeah, you're definitely invited," Harper says.

"Oh my God," Adela says, looking over Harper's shoulder, all levity gone from her face. "She came to school?"

Everyone who's facing away from the stream of students turns to look, which gives me a window into the rest of the corridor. None of us has to wonder who Adela was talking about.

Walking by on her own, a few books wrapped in her arms, hair messy and looking almost as pale and exhausted as last night, is Jessica. She notices us staring at her and glances our way. Her eyes, circled by dark shadows, meet mine. It hurls me back into that same vision I had last night or a vivid memory of it. I hear Jessica and her boyfriend, Peter, arguing nearby. It's getting harder and harder to breathe, or maybe it's the fear.

Then I'm back in the school hallway, surrounded by my friends. Jessica breaks eye contact with me and hurries away without a word.

CHAPTER THIRTY-NINE

Misfits

I want to ignore Jessica and have my well-deserved normal day, but I keep running into her. It's like we're tied together with bungee cords that keep snapping taut and yanking us into meeting in the bathroom, on our way to our desks, on our way in or out of a classroom door, in the hallway. She's not accompanied by her usual posse, though I catch a few of them trying to talk to her.

We end up next to each other in the lunch line, and our eyes meet for the millionth time today before we both look away. I swear I taste mud in my mouth and my breath wheezes as if there's some obstruction in my throat, but I tell myself it's my imagination. The sensation fades.

"Why are you following me?" Jessica hisses.

I look at her, surprised. I thought it would be obvious that I don't want to run into her anymore than she wants to run into me. I haven't tried to talk to her, and I always scurry away as soon as I can.

"I'm not," I tell her.

"What more do you want from me?" she asks. "Wasn't last night enough for you?"

Now *that* pisses me off. "I didn't ask for any of this. I'm just trying to do the right thing."

"Well, good job. Really excellent work."

I stare at her for a moment. I've never punched anyone, but I'm tempted to make my debut. I force myself to look away instead. She's grieving, she's hurt, and she's trying to take it out on someone. I guess I'm an easy target.

I leave the lunch line without another word, even though I haven't gotten my pizza, just the weird vegetable sides they give us to disguise the fact they're feeding us greasy heart failure. I drop into a seat at my friends' table and eye their pizzas enviously.

"You okay?" Jordan asks. "I saw you finally talking to Jessica."

"She's being an asshole," I say. "There's no point in talking to her."

"May I sit here?"

Toni is standing beside me with her tray and her lilac blouse and her hoop earrings that look so good on her. Her cheek is pulled in slightly, which must mean she's biting the inside of it—a nervous habit, I guess.

Across the table, Adela laughs. "You don't have to be so serious about it. Sure, sit. Join us."

"Welcome to our circle of misfits," Jordan says as Toni takes the seat next to me.

The side of my body closest to her seems to grow several degrees warmer than my other side. I stare at her tray—she has two slices of pizza. No one ever gets two slices.

"Did you bribe the lunch lady?" I ask.

"She knows I spent the last two years on death's door," Toni replies. "I get extra pudding, too."

The table falls silent as Adela and Harper break off their conversation to stare at Toni.

"What do you mean?" Adela asks.

"I was sick," Toni explains calmly.

Her hands shake as she arranges her silverware, though. Is she scared to tell my friends what she told me? Why? Does she think they'll judge her for it, or is she just not used to opening up to this many people? It must be a change, going from eating lunch alone to having four pairs of eyes glued to you.

"Sick how?" Harper asks.

"A rare autoimmune disorder. Doctors here didn't even know how to diagnose it, so we had to go around the country until we found someone who could tell us what was wrong. Then we basically had to travel the world looking for a treatment." Toni tells all this to her vegetables. She's making an obvious effort to keep her voice light.

"So you're better now?" Adela asks.

It's an obvious question, one I didn't think to ask yesterday. My chest tightens. Is Toni still in danger?

"It's possible I'll never have another episode again. Apparently, I survived the deadliest part, which is the initial onset."

"But you could still die?" Adela asks.

Harper elbows her. "Jeez, girl. You have no filter."

I watch Toni anxiously. She smiles slightly, her eyes sliding away from everyone's faces and toward the crowd beyond our table. Is she really unaffected, or is she just trying not to face anyone?

"Maybe. But I could also get hit by a car, just like anyone else."

Harper snorts, and Adela laughs nervously. I breathe a little easier—the tension at the table has lessened.

"You didn't get pizza?" Toni asks me.

"I left the line. Jessica was being a jerk."

Toni scoots her tray toward me, offering me my pick of her two slices. "Here."

"You don't have to." My face is the color of a fire truck, I'm sure of it.

Toni shakes her head. "You'll be doing me a favor."

Resolutely not looking at anyone else at the table, who I'm sure are all staring at me, I take the slightly smaller of Toni's pizza slices.

Just then, a voice makes me look up. Peter and his new girlfriend, Angela, are walking by our table. Angela is hanging on his every word, walking closer to him than must be practical. He's tall, attractive, with an athletic build and cheekbones that could slice cheese. The sound of his voice drills into my skull, and the memory of being in that dark, enclosed space with him talking outside imprints itself onto the insides of my eyelids.

"Amy?" Jordan asks.

I realize I've stood up, my fists planted on the table, my whole body shaking and tense. I ignore Jordan.

The voice that comes out of me isn't my own, but Holly's—young, high-pitched, unsure of the precise shape of words. And loud enough to carry to everyone on our side of the cafeteria.

"Did you hurt Jessie?"

Chapter Forty

Theory

My friends sit on our usual log in Glendock Park, passing around a joint. Adela and Harper quiz Toni about her weed stash, which is apparently left over from her medical marijuana supply. I sit on a rock a little bit apart from everyone, relishing not being confined by the walls of the school building or the stares of my classmates.

Jordan comes over to me. "Want to scoot?"

I make room for her on the rock and she sits beside me. Neither of us speaks for a few minutes.

"I can't believe I yelled at Peter in the middle of the cafeteria," I mutter.

"Yeah, it was pretty unbelievable," Jordan agrees.

"Thanks."

The look on Peter's face was about as shocked as I felt. *Did you hurt Jessie?* I don't know what came over me. No, that's a lie—I know it was Holly. But I never expected to do what she wanted so immediately, without even thinking about it. With other things Holly has wanted me to do, like fling my arms around Jessica, I've been able to separate urge from action and stop myself.

"Did he say anything?" I ask. After my outburst, I stared at Peter for about two seconds before fleeing the cafeteria.

"No," Jordan says. "Angela asked him what was going

on as they were leaving, but I didn't hear whether he answered."

One sight I managed to take in as I was running away was Jessica, who froze on her way to an empty table, tray in hand. She stared at me with an expression pretty similar to Peter's.

"You said Jessica left the cafeteria right after that?" I ask Jordan. That's about all Jordan had the chance to tell me when we spoke before gym class, which I skipped to go hide in the bathroom.

"Yeah, she just dumped her tray and disappeared. I can't blame her—everyone was staring at her."

My cheeks heat in shame. "Of course they were."

Jordan bumps my arm with her elbow. "It's okay, Amy. It's not your fault."

"Aunt Betty told me I was letting Holly in. Listening to her. She wouldn't be able to make me say things or remember things if I wasn't letting her."

Jordan purses her lips in thought. "Do you think listening to her is the right thing to do?"

"Yes," I say without hesitation. Then I pause. "I don't know. If it makes me act like this, maybe not. Shouting at Peter in the cafeteria didn't help anything, it just made Jessica have a terrible day."

"Are we talking about it now?" Adela calls from the log. "Have you finished being embarrassed, Amy?"

"No," I snap, blushing.

"What did you tell the counselor?" Harper asks. "He's an asshole."

The counselor pulled me out of class after lunch to ask me about my outburst. Apparently, he talked to Jessica and Peter, too. People saw them each going in separately and wouldn't stop gossiping about it.

"I didn't tell him anything," I say. "I just said I had a headache and had no idea why I'd said it."

"Did he believe you?" Adela asks, eyes widening.

I shrug. "I don't really care."

I've reached my limit for dealing with people who I know will never listen to me, no matter how much they say they want to help. I spent hours being interrogated by the police last night, so a few minutes in the counselor's office wasn't that big of a deal.

"You're turning into such a badass, Amy," Harper observes. I can't tell if they're impressed or amused. "Everyone's probably so surprised."

"I'm surprised," Adela declares. "Amy's always been so mousy."

"Thanks, everyone. I feel really supported." I kind of do, though, weirdly. Maybe because I know that, unlike everyone else apart from my family, they're actually on my side.

"Do we think Peter killed Holly, then?" Adela asks.

"That's a leap," Jordan says. "Even if he's the one who hit Jessica, that doesn't mean he's capable of killing someone. Besides, why would he do it?"

"Maybe Holly saw him hitting Jessica, and he panicked because he thought she would tell someone," Harper suggests.

Adela shakes her head. "I don't think a man who hits a woman is that scared of getting caught."

We all fall silent and look away, except for Toni, who's obviously out of the loop. A couple of years ago, Adela told us her mom's old boyfriend hit her mom. Her mom was able to dump him right afterwards, luckily. I can't imagine seeing Daddy hurt Mama; it would probably break me in half.

"I think her daddy—I mean, her dad, is more likely," I say, looking back up. "Holly was scared of my dad. And she said hers would get angry if he found out about some secret Jessica didn't want her to tell. Also . . . "

I lick my lips, wondering if I should even voice this suspicion. I haven't told anyone. It might sound far-fetched. But then I remember that my friends just found out I can bring people back from the dead and believed me.

"Her dad's a judge, and everyone at the police station knows him," I explain. "They would probably do him a favor and get through the investigation quickly, without looking into things too much."

Adela gasps, and Harper raises an eyebrow. Toni frowns as though considering it. Jordan shakes her head slowly, but I think she's taking it in rather than denying it.

"A cover-up?" Adela asks in a hushed voice, leaning forward.

I remember everyone else has been smoking weed—I don't know how much, since I was in my own little world until Jordan came to sit beside me. I should be careful about how hard I push the conspiracy angle, or Adela could start speculating about aliens.

"It's just a theory," I say. "I don't have any proof, just the things I told you."

"What are you going to do about it?" Harper asks.

I prop my elbows on my knees and dig my fingertips into my temples, massaging in circles. "I'm not sure. At first, when Holly seemed so traumatized, I thought she might have come back so I could solve her murder. But then, I started to think she just needed to speak with Jessica and make peace before moving on. Maybe she doesn't care who killed her. Maybe she's beyond that. Maybe . . . maybe it isn't my purpose to meddle."

"So you're just going to give up?" Adela demands.

"It's not her job to solve murders," Jordan says. "That's what the police are supposed to do."

"But they're not doing it," Harper points out.

"That doesn't mean it's Amy's responsibility," Jordan counters. "She can't force people to answer questions. She can't collect evidence. What is she supposed to do?"

I lean into Jordan gratefully. She puts her arm around my shoulders, and I put mine around her waist.

"I spent all day yesterday trying to deal with this," I say. I hope I sound reasonable and not whiny. "I wanted today to just be normal."

Harper and Adela exchange looks. I can tell they want to keep asking questions. But then Adela leaps to her feet.

"Let's be normal, then," she pronounces. "Let's go to the furniture store and pretend to be sister-wives shopping for our new house."

"Is that something you normally do?" Toni asks, bemused.

"Adela always comes up with something," Harper says.

"Come on, everyone." Adela starts off down the path we usually take in and out of the forest. Then she pauses and turns back to us with a look of concern. "Hey, guys. Do I smell like weed?"

CHAPTER FORTY-ONE

Grass-by-the-River

Jordan, Toni, and I say goodbye to Jordan's mom and get in line outside the Grass-by-the-River, the club where Discarded Infernal is playing. Well, "club" is a generous term; it's an area enclosed by a tall wooden fence, and from what I can see through the cracks between the planks, there's little more than a stage and an outhouse. I didn't realize the concert would be outside. What if it rains? What if it gets cold? I didn't bring a jacket.

"Are you okay, Amy?" Jordan asks. She looks natural and at ease in this line full of people mostly in their twenties and thirties.

"Mm-hmm," I respond.

On my other side, Toni stands with her hands in her pockets, her wide eyes taking in everything—the clouds of cigarette smoke, the people with buzz cuts or with hair dyed bright colors, the cluster of cars parked in the mud that formed after a rain shower earlier today. I'm glad I'm not the only one out of their depth.

"After we get in, we can go to the back," Jordan assures us. "There's some old bleachers we can sit on and see the show but not be in the middle of everything."

"Don't you want to be closer to the stage?" I ask. Jordan has been looking forward to this concert all summer.

She shrugs. "It's not big. I'll still be able to see and hear everything."

We stand there another few minutes before the line finally starts moving as they open the door to let people in. I know Adela probably wouldn't have enjoyed herself, and Harper already had plans to hang out with their not-boyfriend Josh tonight, but I wish everyone had come. Strength in numbers and all that. Jordan, Toni, and I could easily get swallowed up by this crowd.

A girl not much older than us checks our tickets on Jordan's phone and stamps the back of our hands to show we're not allowed to drink alcohol. The three of us move through a turnstile and into the "club" area. There are a few tables and chairs, as well as a food truck and a beer truck. Most of the people are gathering in the clear area in front of the stage, where a couple of guys are testing the sound system. I assume the band is lurking in the small building behind the stage.

"Come on," Jordan says, and pulls Toni and me toward the back of the field to the bleachers. They're old metal ones, a bit rusty and sunken slightly crooked into the soft earth. We climb to the top row and sit close together, with me in the middle. The sun is still shining, but it's lost most of its warmth. A nice breeze gusts past us.

"Grass-by-the-River, huh?" I comment. "Pretty literal name."

Our town's only river, small and shallow and unimpressive as it is, winds past the field. The wooden fence is open on that side, and there are a few benches right on the riverbank. It seems more like a spot for a picnic than a heavy rock concert.

"I think it's kind of poetic," Jordan says.

More and more people file in through the turnstiles and fill up the field below us. A few people join us on the lower levels of the bleachers, but most stick to the front of the crowd.

"I didn't know our town had this many people who were into heavy rock," I say. Our town feels so quiet and boring most of the time.

"You always see people you didn't expect at concerts like this," Jordan says. "It's pretty fun. Oh, look! That's my dentist."

We watch the crowd for a while, noticing a few familiar faces and expressing surprise or disbelief. We trade quips when we spot one of the science teachers from our school, who's so boring in the classroom. I even recognize a few police officers from yesterday; I make sure not to catch their eye.

A few minutes after eight, the band troops onstage to cheers and whistles. They look about like how I pictured them: lots of tattoos, long hair or no hair, angry-looking beards. They gather their instruments, their lead singer shouts a few rousing words into the microphone— something about making a lot of noise—and they kick off. The bleachers hum underneath us in time with the bass, and a flock of crows explodes from a tree by the river, cawing in annoyance.

I burst into laughter, but I can't hear my own voice over the music. Beside me, Toni smiles up at the flock as it wings its way overhead and disappears into the sunset. She seems less nervous than before, and her relaxed smile makes her face radiant. My heartbeat speeds up, almost as fast as the drumbeats.

On my other side, Jordan bounces in her seat in time with the music and murmurs a few of the lyrics. It's rare to see her this excited; she usually keeps her cool a lot more, even when she's happy. I grin. The music might be a little painful to my ears, but it's worth it to see both Jordan and Toni look so carefree.

"You should go to the front," I say loudly to Jordan, almost yelling—that's the only way she'll hear me, even all the way back here.

"Are you sure?" Jordan asks.

"Do it," I insist.

"Either of you want to come?"

Toni shakes her head, smiling, and I say, "We'll be here. Come find us later, okay?"

Jordan grabs my hand, squeezes it briefly, then hops down the bleachers and into the crowd. I follow her shiny black hair with my eyes as she weaves between the adults, making her way closer to the stage.

"What do you think of the music?" I ask Toni.

She purses her lips in thought. "I'm trying to decide."

"Me, too."

We watch the show for a few songs. At least, I think it's a few songs. It's hard to tell when one ends and another starts, since most of them have multiple instrumental interludes that seem to go on forever. There's a guy on the synths who makes all sorts of unexpected noises, so at some points, it sounds like an orchestra is backing up the band, while at others it sounds like aliens might have hacked the sound system. The bass and the drums are relentless, the beat echoing in my bones.

"Have you ever been to something like this?" Toni asks.

"No. You?"

She shakes her head. "No, but my ex . . . she really liked this kind of music. We used to watch concerts on YouTube. We would blast the volume and annoy the nurses."

"Oh." I look back down at the crowd. "Um, is it . . . does it make you sad?"

"Kind of. It's not as bad as I thought it would be, though." She smiles wanly. "I'm actually pretty relieved at how okay it feels to be here."

"Good," I reply. She's being so open with me, as if we've known each other a lot longer than we have. "I mean, I'm glad. That you're okay."

The band shifts to a more mellow song that isn't loud enough to rattle the bleachers. The sun is tucked behind the horizon, with nothing but the last rays peeking out. Lights come on, illuminating the stage, and dried ice puffs up around the band's feet to catch the rays of different colored spotlights.

"To think I could be at Vic's party right now," Toni says. The quieter music lets her speak at a more normal volume. She's so close; her breath smells like mint.

"Were you actually planning on going?" I ask, suddenly nervous. I think back to the sight of Vic flirting with Toni by the school lockers. What if I misread the situation and Toni was actually flattered by his attention?

Toni laughs and shakes her head. "No, of course not. That was supposed to be a joke. I'm glad I came to this instead."

"I'm glad you came, too." I hope I don't sound too relieved. I hesitate before blurting out, "I only wanted to come to impress you."

Toni's eyebrows go up, and I blush even more. My embarrassment makes it hard to meet her dark eyes, which blaze briefly with the last rays of the sun—but it's impossible to look away.

"Why would it impress me?" she asks.

"I don't know. I just wanted to say I had some kind of hobby so you wouldn't think I was boring."

Toni's mouth quirks up on one side. "Is that why you told me you could raise the dead, too? So I wouldn't think you were boring?"

I finally look down at my feet, too embarrassed to maintain eye contact any longer. I swing my legs, which dangle off the edge of the bleachers. "I guess so. I can't really remember why I said that. My mind sort of went blank."

Toni giggles. It's the first time I've heard her make that sound, all girlish abandon with none of her usual reservation. Something soft and cool rests on the back of my hand, which rests on the bench between us: her hand.

We're holding hands.

Well, sort of. Hoping my palm isn't sweaty, I turn my hand over and lace my fingers with hers. Nope, I'm definitely sweating; I can feel the stickiness. There's no way she doesn't notice, but hopefully she doesn't mind. My heart is just about shattering my ribs, and I'm so dizzy and shaky that I'm worried I might fall off the bleachers. Then she'll have to catch me and pull me back up. I guess that might be kind of romantic, but more than anything, it would be embarrassing as hell.

"You're interesting," Toni tells me. Her voice shakes a little. Is she as nervous and embarrassed as I am only better at hiding it? Or is she upset? I suddenly wonder if it's tactless of me to hold her hand right after she brought up her dead girlfriend.

"I'm really not," I say. Why am I doubling down? What's wrong with me? "All I ever do apart from raise the dead is watch TV and smoke weed. I used to read, but I don't even do that anymore. I knew a lot about animals when I was little. Did you know hummingbirds go into this sort of suspended animation thing at night, where their heartbeat and body heat go way down to conserve energy? I didn't even know I remembered that. I probably had a lot more facts before. But now I don't know anything interesting anymore."

Toni squeezes my hand. Maybe she's trying to get me to stop babbling. "You've put your life on hold. I know the feeling."

"You had an excuse. There's nothing wrong with my life."

Unexpectedly, tears trickle down my cheeks. I wipe them away with the back of my free hand. My mind wants to peel away from my body, escape my feelings, but I hold on as hard as I can. I don't want to let go of this moment. I don't want my hand to go numb when it's wrapped around Toni's.

Toni puts her thumb to my cheekbone, her touch feather-light, and catches one of my tears, whisking it away. I shiver. Is this really happening? She's so close, I can see the slightest bumps on her cheeks. The light below turns blue, bathing her chin and nose in its eerie glow. Her long lashes quiver as she blinks, her eyes shadowed as the sun fully sets. I can still feel her warm gaze on me, though.

"You don't need to qualify your pain, Amy. Everyone hurts."

I nod, my throat too tight to answer. Our faces drift closer together. The light turns orange, like firelight, and her lips glint as they part. I tighten my grip on her hand—part of me is convinced she's going to slip away from me, vanish into the night like she never existed. She squeezes my hand in return.

Our lips are so close to each other.

And then a familiar feeling rushes through my body like a fever chill. Before I know what I'm doing, I'm straightening, drawing back from Toni. Her eyebrows pull together as she searches my face, her expression wavering in confusion. My hand slips from hers and I jolt to my feet.

"Amy?" she asks.

"I . . ."

My heartbeat thrums in my ears. I've never experienced this feeling while I was fully awake, but I know what it is. It's telling me to climb down the bleachers and sink my hands into the muddy earth on the riverbank. It's telling me to reach out to wherever souls lurk before they move on and pull the right one into the malleable, silky substance between my fingers.

It's the Itch.

Holly's ready to come back.

CHAPTER FORTY-TWO

Itch

My hand has grown a lot colder without Toni's fingers laced between mine. I stand quivering on the top row of the bleachers, suspended between the world I see in front of me—Toni sitting there, staring at me, the band blaring and people cheering in the background—and the world I feel at the edge of my senses. It's like a shadow in the corner of my eye, a buzz almost beyond my hearing, a sweet taste almost obscured by salt, a mildewy smell I might be imagining, a feather dusting across my skin.

I've never been in this position before. Even though my family, including Maddie, insist I choose to raise the dead with my power and could stop if I wanted to, I've never consciously made the decision before. I usually wake in the middle of the night full of determination and purpose; I don't have to think as I slip out of bed and tiptoe out to the garden shed. In fact, I don't want to think—it feels like I'll chase away the Itch if I do, and in the middle of the night, that power, that magic, becomes sacred.

But now . . . now, it would be easier than breathing to break the spell. I could sit back down beside Toni, and we could pick up where we left off. I could have my first kiss. I've imagined kissing Toni so many times, I can almost feel her lips against mine. Except, since I've never kissed anyone, I wouldn't know if I'm actually imagining it right. It could feel totally different. If I walk away now, I might never know.

"Amy?" Toni asks. She's called my name a few times already. I hope she doesn't think I'm having a stroke or something.

"Holly wants to come back," I say.

It's hard to read Toni's expression now that I've moved away from her, the shadows lying thick across her face. Her voice sounds uncertain. "Why now?"

I shake my head. The answer to that question has never been clear to me with any of the creatures I've brought back, and Holly has been harder to understand than any other. Grandma thinks the dead are outside of time and able to see into my future to choose the ideal moment to come to me. Sarah thinks it has to do with my state of mind. Maddie has always just told me to trust that the time is right.

Toni looks down at the crowd and the band playing onstage, then at the river, then at the muddy parking lot outside the wooden fence that surrounds the outdoor music venue. "Where . . . where would you do it?" she asks. Despite her uncertainty, there's a definite note of curiosity in her voice.

That's a good question. I've never had the Itch when I wasn't at home, so I've never had to worry about finding materials or a workspace. Come to think of it, I've never had an audience, either. What if someone sees me pulling a small child out of the mud? What if they call the police again? Forget that; there are already off-duty police officers in the crowd. No one even has to call them.

I squint toward the river, straining to see despite the darkness and the glare of the multicolored spotlights. The wooden fence doesn't go all the way to the riverbank; I can walk out of the club if I go along the river. There should be plenty of mud down there. I try to remember what was beside the club, now invisible in the darkness. I must have seen it when Jordan's mom dropped us off.

"Is that just an empty field?" I ask, pointing past the fence.

"I think so," Toni replies. "You're not going out there by yourself, are you? In the dark?"

"I have to. Otherwise, Holly might never come back."

"Do you know that? It could be dangerous. There could be wild animals or . . . or people."

"Come with me."

I start down the bleachers. I don't know for sure if this is Holly's only opportunity to come back, but I don't want to take chances. What if she stays inside my head forever, haunting me with her memories? If she never finds peace, neither will I.

Toni catches my sleeve in her hand. "Wait. What about Jordan?"

"We'll meet up with her later."

Since Toni is obviously worried about the regular world, I'm making a huge effort to care about it, but it's not really working. My mind is hovering on the verge of an almost-there other world, one of shadows and whispers. I continue down the bleachers. Toni doesn't let go of my sleeve, but instead follows me, holding on.

We skirt the edge of the crowd and walk to the riverbank. A few concert-goers are sitting on the picnic tables to watch, drinking beer and cheering. None of them pays any attention to us. I lead Toni away from them, toward the gap between the wooden fence and the river. String lights drape along the top of the fence, casting a dim illumination onto the area just outside: scruffy bushes and tough, wild grass.

"This way," I say and continue along the riverbank. My shoes sink into the mud—there should be plenty of it here—but the Itch tells me to keep going.

Toni tugs on my sleeve. "No one can see. Why don't we stop here?"

"Just a little farther," I promise, and continue.

Toni keeps holding onto my sleeve. The part of me that isn't consumed by the Itch is surprised and grateful that she's still following me, still looking out for me. I'll have to thank her later. Now, I have only one goal.

The music is growing muted as we walk farther from the club, and we're well outside the area illuminated by the string lights. As my eyes adjust to the night, I'm able to navigate by starlight. An owl hoots somewhere nearby, and something rustles in the bushes. Toni presses close behind me.

"Amy," she hisses.

I stop. The Itch tells me this is the right place. I bend down and take off my sandals.

"What are you doing?" Toni demands.

I'm too focused to answer or even to remember how to answer. Mud squishing between my toes, I walk toward the water. Do I gather some of this mud? No, I keep going. That's what the Itch says, so that's what I do. I wade into the river, the water cool enough to send goosebumps up my legs in the warm night air.

"Amy," Toni repeats, almost begging.

The water climbs up my calves as I wade deeper, my bare feet finding purchase in the rocky riverbed. I squint; is that something floating in the water? Is that what I need to bring Holly back? I slosh toward it. Even though the river isn't wide or deep, the current's fast, and I throw my arms out to my sides to steady myself. The floating object is larger than I thought, maybe even the same size as me, and about to rush out of my reach. I lurch forward and grab onto it.

My hand closes around an arm.

Chapter Forty-Three

Alone

A chill runs through my body despite the warmth of the summer night. The current tugs at my legs as I lurch forward to grab the person floating in the river with both hands. The Itch is gone—I no longer have that certainty or that drive, and all that's left is me. Does Holly not want to come back anymore? I'm not sure, but I don't have time to ponder it, because the river's working against me as I try to tug the person out of the water.

"Toni!" I cry. "Help me!"

There are splashing sounds from behind me, and Toni appears at my side, the moonlight catching the whites of her eyes as she stares in shock at what I've found. She grabs the person's other arm, and we both pull with all our might. I slip on the loose rocks of the riverbed and lose my balance but catch myself by digging in my bare heels.

We drag the person through the water and onto the rocks. Hauling them against the current was tough, but now that they're on the ground, they seem to be ten times heavier. They're face-down, so we roll them onto their back. Their corkscrew curls settle around their head, an ethereal halo in the shallow water.

"Do you know CPR?" Toni asks. She's already dialing 911.

"Yeah."

Thanks to our family's mistrust of all authorities, including doctors, Mama and Grandma made me and my sisters all learn basic first aid. I crouch next to the person we rescued and check for breathing—nothing. I check for a pulse—nothing. I begin to do chest compressions while Toni relays the emergency to the 911 operator. Discarded Infernal still plays in the distance, the rumble of the bass and the drums the only sounds I can distinguish.

Overhead, a cloud drifts away from the moon, spilling moonlight onto the riverbank. The silvery light bathes the features of the person I'm resuscitating.

Jessica.

Without my CPR training, I would have panicked, but the familiar motions are easy to keep performing. I channel my shock into my work: pushing the heel of my hand into her chest in a quick, even rhythm. Periodically, I check for breathing—still nothing. I keep pushing, muttering the numbers under my breath to keep track. Toni crouches on Jessica's other side, watching us with her wide, fearful eyes.

Jessica coughs and hacks up a bit of water. I stop chest compressions—her chest is rising and falling erratically as she tries to breathe, chokes, and coughs. I roll her gently onto her side, and she coughs up more water. It takes her several minutes to clear her airway and settle down. She's shivering. I wish I'd brought a jacket.

"There's an ambulance on the way," Toni tells Jessica.

Jessica doesn't answer but stays on her side, her eyes out of focus. I can't tell if she's conscious.

"Jessica?" I prod. "What happened?"

"I fell in the river," she mumbles.

"Did you hit your head?" I ask. I don't see any blood, but it would be hard to tell when the moonlight makes everything nearly black-and-white.

"Maybe."

She has on the same clothes she wore to school today. Why would she be in the river in her clothes in the first place? I guess I was in the river in my clothes, but I'm hardly an example of normal behavior. Not only that, but she can't have been floating in the river too long, or she would have died. The club is far away from her house. What was she doing not far upriver from here, all alone, at night?

"Jessica, were you with someone?" I ask.

"No."

"Did someone hurt you?" What if whoever hit her and left that bruise on her face wanted to go even further and drown her in the river?

Jessica sweeps her wet hair out of her face—at least it's good that she can move her arm—and looks up at me, seeming to see me for the first time. I expect to see gratitude, confusion, maybe fear. But when her eyes lock onto my face, her expression grows furious.

"You! Why can't you leave me alone?" She covers her face with her hands, and angry sobs wrack her body. I glance at Toni whose startled expression mirrors my feelings.

"Why didn't I leave you alone to drown in the river?" I ask, incredulous.

"Yes!" she cries into her hands. "At least then it would be over."

An uncomfortable weight settles on me. I rest my hand gently on her shoulder "Jessica . . . did you try to kill yourself?"

"Leave me alone!" she repeats and jerks my hand off her shoulder. Her sobs turn into coughs.

I decide not to try to push her anymore. There's really not much I can do, especially since she's so mad at me. I sit back on the rocks, not caring that my shorts are soaked through and getting wetter in the half-inch or so of water under me.

Holly, did you want me to find Jessie? Is that why I got the Itch? Did Holly not want to come back at all, just to get me to the riverside in time to save her sister? I had no idea the dead could manipulate me that way. I've never felt the Itch and not brought something back from the dead. My body twitches with pent-up tension. Though maybe that's just the adrenaline.

We sit there for a few minutes while Jessica cries. Toni convinces her to move up onto the riverbank so she's not in the water, and Jessica follows Toni's directions mechanically, still sobbing. I guess it's better to let Toni handle this, since Jessica doesn't have anything against her. I try not to feel irritated at Jessica; I know this situation keeps throwing us together in ways that are painful to her, but it's not my fault. I don't appreciate being her punching bag.

After a while, we see the ambulance pull up by the club. Flashlights swing left and right through the overgrown thicket of the empty lot between us and the road. I get to my feet and call, "Over here!"

The EMTs make their way to us, carrying flashlights and a stretcher. They check Jessica, who stops crying and falls silent, refusing to answer their questions. Toni and I tell the EMTs what we know.

"Are you girls okay?" one of the men asks Toni and me as the others load Jessica onto the stretcher.

"We're fine," I reply.

"You should make sure to change into dry clothes," he tells us. "You can get hypothermia from being wet, even if it's not very cold."

"Thank you," Toni says.

We watch them carry a silent, motionless Jessica away. Toni and I stand there for another few minutes, dripping water onto the riverbank.

"Are you okay?" I ask Toni.

Toni nods, still staring toward the road where the ambulance disappeared. I start to reach for her shoulder and chicken out. What if she's upset at me for dragging her into this? For interrupting our romantic moment?

What if she doesn't want to kiss me anymore?

"We should go back," I say miserably, wrapping my arms around my torso. "Jordan might be wondering where we are."

Toni finally turns to me. "Yeah, and we don't want to die of hypothermia."

We stand there facing each other for a moment. I can't read Toni's expression in the dim moonlight. I look down and shift my weight from one bare foot to the other, my toes squishing in the mud.

"Thank you for coming in to help me," I murmur.

"You kind of remind me of my ex-girlfriend."

I look up, startled and blushing. "In a good way?"

"I'm not sure. Going into the river without telling me what you're doing, scaring me like that . . . it's the kind of thing she would have done."

"I've never run around naked through the night," I point out, remembering the story Toni told me about her ex. My attempt to lighten the mood doesn't seem to work.

Toni shakes her head. "You scared me."

I take a step toward her, my hands hanging awkwardly at my sides. "I didn't mean to. It's the Itch—it usually tells me what to do to bring the dead back, and I follow it, only this time it told me to wade into the river. I think maybe Holly wanted me to find Jessica."

"I don't know if that makes it any better."

"I'm sorry, Toni." My chest is so tight it's getting hard to draw enough breath to speak.

"We were only together about two months before she died." She wraps her arms around her torso and stares at the rocky riverbank between us. "I hadn't even made up my mind how much I liked her before she was gone. She was a lot of fun sometimes, but other times she was too much."

I don't know what to say. I've never dated anyone before, let alone someone who died. I'm completely out of my depth here.

"I'm sorry I couldn't give you closure yesterday," I murmur.

Toni shakes her head. "That's not what it was about. She . . . we were both about to die, or thought we were. Then she died, and I didn't. I'm still here."

I think I understand now. That look of desperation on her face when she came to my house yesterday wasn't grief, or not entirely. She wanted to know what would have happened to her if she'd been the one to die instead of her girlfriend. She dangled so close to the afterlife for so long. It must have been terrifying and confusing, not only to go through that but also to come back to the normal world where everyone goes about their lives without worrying about what comes after.

At least that's what I think she means.

If I could only explain that I feel something similar, that I walk around with death in my heart every day and feel like no one outside of my family understands, but my throat has completely closed up now. I'm too scared of messing things up worse than I already have. What if I'm wrong? I don't want to presume to understand what she's dealt with, what she's dealing with.

Toni turns away from me, toward the club with the colorful spotlights shining into the sky and the string lights strung across the fence surrounding it. "You're right. We should go back."

Feeling heavier with every step, I pick up my sandals and follow Toni along the muddy riverbank.

CHAPTER FORTY-FOUR

Warmth

"Where were you?" Jordan demands, emerging from the crowd of concert-goers and grabbing me by the shoulders. "I was so worried when I couldn't find you! And then I saw the ambulance pull up . . . "

"I'm sorry," I mumble, though I can barely hear my own voice over the music. It seems I'm worrying everyone around me tonight.

"Why are you all wet?" Jordan asks, looking between me and Toni. "Did you fall in the river?"

I'm shivering now even though the air is warm against my skin. I guess the water is sapping my heat, like the EMT warned us would happen.

"Holly . . . " I begin, but it seems to take so much energy to explain. My mouth won't form the words. It doesn't help that I have to talk so loud for Jordan to hear me over the music.

"Is Holly back?" Jordan asks.

I shake my head. "No, I thought she was . . . but it's not what . . . "

"We found Jessica in the river," Toni explains. "The ambulance was for her. We think she tried to kill herself."

Jordan's eyes get wide. "Jessica? How did you know . . . Why would she . . . " She shakes her head, her lips trembling.

It's rare to see her unable to find the right words. "I . . . Let me call my mom to take us home early."

"No, don't," I say quickly. The last thing I want to do is ruin Jordan's night by cutting the concert short.

"You need dry clothes," Jordan chides, more motherly than my own mother. "Besides, you look terrible. You should rest."

"I don't want to ruin the concert." My eyes sting. I try to will myself to be okay, but it's not working.

"There's other concerts," Jordan says, pulling out her phone. "You're both more important than seeing the whole thing."

"Thank you, Jordan," Toni says.

My throat is too tight to chime in, and besides, it feels like a simple thank you wouldn't be enough. I don't feel worthy of Jordan's concern when it comes at the cost of something she's been looking forward to for months, especially after Toni admonished me for being reckless. If I'd been more careful—if I were a normal person—I wouldn't be putting Jordan in this situation, and I wouldn't have ruined things with Toni.

Jordan grabs my arm and walks over to the riverbank to call her mom. I guess she doesn't trust me not to get lost if she doesn't keep an eye on me. Toni follows, wrapping her arms around herself. I wonder if she's cold or just upset.

"She'll be here in fifteen minutes," Jordan tells us as she hangs up. "Will you be okay until then?"

"Are you girls cold?" a male voice calls from nearby. We all turn. There's a group of young men at one of the picnic tables on the riverside, drinking beer.

"They fell in the river," Jordan says, right as I'm getting ready to snap that we're fine and don't need their help. I try to glare at her surreptitiously, but she's turned toward the men, still holding my arm. You'd think I was a toddler or something.

"Here," the guy says, and takes off his leather jacket. He's wearing a sleeveless white shirt underneath, and his arms are covered in full sleeves of tattoos. He offers me the jacket as one of his friends removes his and offers it to Toni. Jordan takes the one for me and drapes it over my shoulders before I can refuse, while Toni hesitates before accepting her guy's jacket.

"How'd you fall in the river, anyway?" the second guy asks. He has a mohawk dyed three different colors, though in the concert lighting, it's hard to tell exactly which colors they are.

"Yeah, we've been right here and didn't see you," the first guy adds. "Were you outside the club?"

"It was an accident," I say coolly. I have to admit the warmth of the jacket feels nice, though.

"Wait, was that ambulance for you?" a third guy asks, this one with glasses and a bit less of a biker look, though he does have several tattoos, too.

Jordan glances at me. I shake my head slightly, hoping she'll get the message. "No, it was for another girl," she says, ignoring my warning. "She got taken away."

"Wow. Seems like you girls were having a party," Mohawk Guy jokes.

"Yeah, it was a lot of fun how she almost drowned," Toni mutters.

Mohawk Guy laughs nervously, and the guy with the tattoo sleeves slaps him lightly in the back of the head.

"Sorry about him," Sleeves says. "Is your friend going to be okay?"

"We don't know," I say. I start to take off his jacket. "We're leaving soon, so I should give this back to—"

"You can sit here and wait if you want to," Glasses interrupts, jumping to his feet.

"No, thank—" I begin.

"That's really nice of you," Jordan says. "You know we're all sixteen, by the way?"

"Oh, Lord," Sleeves laughs. "We didn't mean to come off that way. We're just trying to be nice. We're all happily married." He shows us his ring.

"To each other?" Jordan asks.

The guys all laugh uproariously at that. Soon, we're cramming together at the picnic table, and they're showing us pictures of their wives, kids, and pets. We learn everyone's names, but I forget them immediately. Then Jordan and the guys are discussing the song Discarded

Infernal is playing, which is apparently off their new album, and comparing it to their previous work. I tune them out. I'm getting toasty in the leather jacket. Toni is pressed against my side, but she's not looking at me, so I hunch down and try not to seem too miserable.

My mind returns to Jessica. What could have made her try to kill herself? I don't know for certain that's what happened, but a few things she said all but confirmed it. *At least then it would be over.* Did she mean the pain of losing Holly? Or something else? If her stepdad is the one who hit her, her home life might be pretty miserable; could that be what she was trying to escape? Or is it my fault? Did it become too much for her when I brought Holly back into life, only for Holly to disappear again?

Holly, I could use your help right now. You know your sister way better than I do. If Holly purposefully led me to the river to rescue her sister—and it seems like too much of a coincidence to just be chance—she's obviously trying to help. Maybe that's why she hasn't come back yet? Because Jessica's not ready to see her? But without Holly's guidance, I have no idea what to do. If I'm just supposed to wait around until she decides to give me another Itch or send me another vision, I don't know how I'll stand it. I'll be stuck between my real life and my responsibilities as a necromancer, unable to entirely fulfill either.

"Mom's here," Jordan announces, checking her phone.

She and the guys exchange numbers—I'm not sure how her mother will feel about that—and Toni and I return their jackets. Then the three of us head through the crowd and out of the club into the muddy parking lot. We climb into Mrs. Nguyen's car.

"Are you all okay?" she asks, twisting around to frown at Toni and me in the back seat.

"Yeah, we're fine," I murmur. With the help of Sleeves' thick jacket and my body heat, I've mostly dried off. I would probably have been okay without having to go home, but now that the music is muffled by the car, I realize my head has been pounding. Maybe I really should go to bed.

"Jordan said you fell in the river. Is it unsafe? Maybe I should talk to the people who run this place."

"No, it was all my fault," I say quickly.

"Hmm." Mrs. Nguyen frowns at me for a moment longer before turning back to the wheel and pulling out from the parking lot. "How was the concert, then? Apart from the accident?"

Jordan excitedly relates her experience—leaving out her new friends, I notice—allowing me and Toni to sit with our own thoughts. We ride along in silence for a few minutes, Jordan's voice and the rumble of the engine melting together into a pleasant background hum.

Suddenly, something warm touches my hand. I look down and see Toni's fingers curled around mine. She gives me a quick squeeze before returning her hand to her lap.

"I'm glad you're okay," she whispers.

My heart stumbles. "I'm glad you're okay, too."

She looks out the window, her elegant profile outlined against the passing streetlights. She obviously doesn't want to talk, and she might still be upset at me, but she doesn't hate me. She's glad I'm okay. Why did she take my hand? To reassure herself that I'm still here? To comfort me? I'm not sure, but in this moment, I think I love her.

Calm down, I tell myself. *You've only hung out with her for three days. You can't fall in love with someone that fast.* Can you? Maybe there's a different standard for people who go through a lot together. Sarah might say it's my raging hormones or something. Whatever the case, I should definitely cool it. I don't want Toni to think I'm immature on top of being reckless and irresponsible.

But when Mrs. Nguyen stops in front of Toni's house and Toni gives me one last, enigmatic look as she's getting out of the car, all I can think about is how close we came to kissing. And how right her hand felt against mine.

CHAPTER FORTY-FIVE

Regret

That night, I can't sleep. I keep thinking about Jessica's furious sobs when she realized I saved her from the river. *At least then it would be over.* Did she really want to die? Sometimes, I've considered my own death and whether it should come sooner rather than later, but I've never carried those thoughts very far. What would it take for me to contemplate actually doing something to myself?

Why can't you just leave me alone? I know it wasn't a mistake to save Jessica's life, but other than that, am I making everything worse by trying to help? Is it my fault that she was floating face-down in the river tonight?

I sit up in bed, frustrated with just lying there with my thoughts, and climb down. Sarah's sleeping over at a friend's again, so I don't have to worry about disturbing her. There's a light on in the kitchen, and I slow down as I approach, trying to figure out who's there. Earlier, Mama and Daddy asked me how the concert was. I don't think they believed me when I said it was fine, but they didn't press me. I don't want to face further questions.

"Come in, Amy," Aunt Betty's tremulous voice calls from inside the kitchen.

I sigh. I used to think Aunt Betty had other powers in addition to her ability to speak to ghosts, but she could probably just tell who I was by my footsteps or something. I drag my feet into the kitchen and find her sitting at the island counter, drinking a mug of tea. She has a paperback book at one elbow, the spine so worn and creased that its yellowed pages lie open without any effort on her part. It's probably one of her old romance novels—she has a trunk full of them. Sarah and I used to steal them and read the steamy scenes.

"There's a whole pot of tea if you want some," Aunt Betty offers.

"Is it one of Maddie's herbal blends that taste like socks?" I ask.

"Chamomile."

"Great."

I pour myself a mug and sit across from my aunt. She returns to reading her book, and I sip my tea in silence for a few minutes.

"I saved Holly's sister tonight," I say finally. I don't know what Aunt Betty might offer in the way of comfort, but the words just come out of me.

"Yes, I thought you had a scent of death about you."

"No one's dead," I protest. "I just said I saved her. I mean, Holly's still dead, but she's not around lately."

"She brushed death," Aunt Betty says calmly. "Holly's sister. It rubbed off on you."

I shake my head and decide not to ask what she means or how she can tell. She never has satisfactory explanations.

"She tried to . . . " I begin, "I mean, I think she tried to . . . do it to herself."

Aunt Betty nods without any surprise. I guess that part of the experience rubbed off on me, too.

"She was mad at me for saving her." I stare down into my half-drunk mug of chamomile, watching a few loose particles floating around near the bottom. "I think she was mad at me for a lot of things. Earlier today, I . . . Holly made me . . . Well, however it happened, I channeled Holly in the cafeteria and asked her ex-boyfriend if he had hurt her."

"Had he?" Aunt Betty asks.

"I don't know. She has a bruise on her face. But anyway,

it didn't help anything when I shouted it in front of everyone."

"How do you know?" Aunt Betty asks.

"How do I know it didn't help anything?" I demand. "Because he didn't admit anything, no one got caught, and nothing changed except Jessica got more depressed. What if that was the final thing that made her jump in the river?"

"Have you had any new visions?" Aunt Betty asks.

I didn't expect her not to address my question at all, so I'm confused for a moment. Did she even hear me? Is this how she talks to the dead? I don't think I'd be any less frustrated if I was a ghost.

"No," I snap. "Well . . . I got the Itch. I thought Holly wanted to come back. That's what led me to the river."

Aunt Betty nods. "The dead sometimes sense when someone close to them might join them. Holly thought you were the person to save her sister, not that you were the reason her sister needed to be saved."

"Holly is three years old. Or was. Don't you think it's kind of ridiculous to expect her to know anything? Now that I think about it, having an outburst in public sounds just like a three-year-old. To her, having me yell at Peter in front of everyone might have been a good idea."

"Don't underestimate children," Aunt Betty says. "I often find children make much smarter ghosts than adults. Adults spend too much energy on denial."

"I don't want to talk about this anymore." I take a gulp of chamomile. After I'm done with this mug, I'll go back to bed and see if the tea helps me sleep. This conversation is going nowhere.

"Do you know where our family gets our powers?" Aunt Betty asks.

"What?" I ask, surprised out of my frustration. "What do you mean where? Aren't we just born with them?"

"Yes, precisely. We receive our gifts at birth. Every girl in our family line—and we do seem to have almost exclusively girls—is born with the umbilical cord tied around her neck like a noose. It's a dangerous way to be born. All your mother's daughters survived. None of mine did."

I stare at Aunt Betty, my mouth practically hanging open. Aunt Betty had stillborn children? I always thought she was a lifelong spinster. She never married, though I guess it was pretty old-fashioned of me to assume that meant she never got pregnant.

"I'm sorry," I say when I can form words again. "I didn't know."

"Our family teeters on the edge of death," Aunt Betty says, her voice and expression still serene, if a little sad. I've seen her cry while watching soap operas or reading a book she's read dozens of times before, but talking about her dead daughters either affects her in a different way . . . or affects her so strongly she can't even express it. "There's a wisdom that comes from peering over at the other side before you've even taken a breath in this world. The dead who linger, and I think particularly the youngest ones, share some of that wisdom."

"So you're saying I should trust Holly and myself. Just like Maddie told me to do."

"Maddie is a smart girl." Aunt Betty reaches across the table and takes my hand. Hers is cold, even though she was just gripping her tea mug. "You're like me, Amy. We both deal with the ones who linger. Everyone else, your mother and Maddie and Sarah, deals with cleaner deaths, cleaner boundaries. It's easier sometimes."

Something inside me unravels like a coil of barbed wire. I must have gotten used to the pricks, because I didn't notice them until I didn't feel them anymore. Is this why I've always seemed to have more trouble with my powers than the other members of my family? No, it can't be the only reason—I'm also just different from them in other ways. But it could in some measure explain why I've always felt so uncertain about death, about my role in it. Or maybe it's the other way around—my uncertainty might determine the nature of my powers. Whatever the case, I feel a little less incomprehensible to myself than I did a minute ago.

"Thank you for saying that," I tell my aunt. I look down at my hand and Aunt Betty's slender fingers curled around it. "But that still doesn't tell me if I'm the reason Jessica did . . . what she did. Or part of the reason. What if trusting my instincts was the wrong choice?"

"How would you know?" Aunt Betty asks. I frown at her and she adds, with uncharacteristic straightforwardness, "I've spoken to plenty of spirits left behind by people who took their lives, Amy. None of them had a singular reason for it. Every one of them regretted it. You did the right thing. It's not wrong to question yourself and learn from the past, but the best you can ever do in the moment is what feels right."

I stare at Aunt Betty's hollow, bony features, thinking I finally understand. "It's not going to get easier, is it?" I ask.

Aunt Betty releases my hand and picks up her paperback romance. "Quite the opposite."

CHAPTER FORTY-SIX

Garden

The next day after breakfast, I'm whiling away the time in the living room when Maddie marches over to my couch to ask for my help in the garden. Grandma's taking the day off since her back is bothering her.

"Do you really need an extra person?" I ask.

I've been watching a sitcom but not paying enough attention to understand what's going on. Mostly, I've been zoning out, thinking about everything and nothing, unwilling to get up to pour myself a drink or turn on the fan despite the heat. It's going to be sweltering outside, and I have zero motivation.

Maddie stands over me, her smile a small consolation for her intimidating height and closeness to my couch. "It'll go a lot faster with two."

"What will?" I ask.

"Sowing the new summer seeds," Maddie explains patiently. She's probably already told me. "I want to plant them all today. They need time to grow before the first frost."

"Can't you just . . . tell them not to die?"

"No, Amy. Magic can't make up for disregarding the basics of gardening." She pats my shoulder. "Come on. It'll be good for you."

I shoot her a disgusted look. She should know the worst way to get someone to do something is by telling them it will be good for them.

"Holly might need me," I say.

"She can find you in the garden just as easily as here."

Maddie picks up the remote and turns off the TV. My frown turns into a glower, but she gestures for me to follow her, unperturbed. I sit there staring at the blank TV screen for a few seconds before struggling to my feet and lumbering after her. I know she's not going to leave me alone until I help her.

Maddie and Grandma don't till the soil, which I guess makes sense considering Maddie can communicate with it. "Turning over the soil destroys most things living inside it," she explains as she leads me to the garden shed. "It strips away all the nutrients."

She chatters on while handing me homemade seed packets, telling me all sorts of facts in between explaining where and how to plant the seeds. I'm not retaining most of what she says, but I don't want to hear it all again, so I don't say anything and hope I won't mess things up too much.

I walk back into the sunlight with my packets of seeds—spinach, lettuce, cucumbers, beets, carrots. It's not as hot as I was afraid it would be, but it's heavy and humid, as though the air handed me a backpack on my way out the door and I'm having to lug it around. The ground is dry; the rain's just biding its time.

Maddie is planting seeds on the other side of the garden, so I eye her to make sure I do it right. I crouch down by one of the raised beds, part the soil with one finger, and place a seed inside the small hole. I do remember she said not to bury them too deep or pack the soil too tightly. What I don't remember is how far apart to put each crop, so I try to estimate the size of a cucumber plant.

It's kind of soothing once I get into the rhythm of it—the silky black dirt under my fingers, the crouching shuffle along the edge of the raised bed, the satisfaction of imagining each seed as a full plant. This must be what Maddie meant about it being good for me. Of course, I'll never admit that to her.

I reach the end of the first raised bed and stuff the empty seed packet into my jeans. On a whim, I plunge my hand into a soft patch of seed-free soil and close my eyes. I think back to the mud at the edge of the river last night, to how sure I was that Holly would come back. She hasn't spoken to me, or whatever it is she does, since I rescued her sister from the river.

How is Jessica doing? I imagine she's in the hospital. Her parents must have been told what happened last night and come to see her. Was she trying to escape her stepdad? If so, having him come to her hospital room after she took such desperate measures must be unimaginably painful.

I open my eyes and pull my hand out of the dirt, glancing self-consciously at Maddie to make sure she didn't see me. I'm being like Adela, letting my speculations about other people's lives run out of control. I don't even know if Jessica's stepdad is what made her do what she did. Like Aunt Betty told me last night, there probably isn't one singular reason for her decision.

I move onto the next raised bed and start planting carrots. I can't fix Jessica's problems for her, especially if she doesn't want my help.

My thoughts turn to Toni. Her expression after Jessica was taken away by the EMTs: her worry and something else—disappointment, maybe?—is burned into my brain. She compared me to her ex-girlfriend, saying I was just as reckless. At the time, I thought the main reason she was upset was that she was worried about me. But what if it also upset her to be reminded of her dead ex? Judging by how she came to question me about the afterlife the other day, she's still pretty hung up. That's totally understandable, of course—I have no idea how I would recover if Toni died, or if I ever would. I realize I don't know how long ago her girlfriend died. Is it too soon for her to be with someone new?

I pat down the earth on top of a carrot seed a bit too forcibly. Maddie notices, even though she's on the other side of the garden.

"Be gentle," she calls.

"Got it," I call back, trying not to sound irritated, and loosen up the dirt a bit.

I've never dated anyone, never even had someone I was interested in who was interested back. Maybe I'm not ready for a relationship, either. But the thought makes my chest ache. I don't want to give up on my chance with Toni. Most of the time, it seems so right, so perfect. I have to remind myself, again, that I've been hanging out with her for less than a week.

Am I being ridiculous and immature? It's so frustrating to have no idea what I'm doing. If only I'd dated other people before—if only I had something to compare this to. It's not like my friends have much experience, either, except for Harper, and I'm afraid they would make fun of me if I tried to voice my worries to them. They can be kind of tactless sometimes.

I finish up the carrots and put away the empty packet. I've been picking where to put each vegetable more or less randomly, so I hope Maddie isn't upset with me when they sprout in unexpected places later this summer. I stand up to plant the spinach, and my head spins. I sit back down before I fall.

"Are you okay?" Maddie asks, coming up to me.

"Yeah, I think it's just the heat," I mumble.

"Drink some water."

Maddie hands me a bottle that must have been frozen solid at one point, a core of ice still bobbing in the middle. Of course she'd be prepared. I accept the bottle gratefully and take several sips of blissfully cold water. My head has stopped spinning, so I start to get up again, more carefully this time.

"You can rest if you need to," Maddie tells me.

"I'm fine. Probably stood up too fast." I get my feet under me and swig some more water.

"You seem to be enjoying yourself," Maddie says. "Maybe you should help me in the garden more often."

"Don't get too excited. This is a one-time thing."

Maddie grins and shrugs. I cap the bottle and set it beside me as I crouch down to plant the spinach.

But when I try to make a small hole for the first seed, I feel like I'm plunging my hand into icy water. The Itch roars through me, completely unannounced and even more powerful than last night. I clear the dirt away and find a fingernail. A finger. A hand. I keep digging, uncovering an arm, the edge of a yellow sleeve. I trace up the shoulder and find the head. I have to rip up a tomato plant to uncover it. How is this happening? I brush away the dirt and reveal Holly's face, her eyes closed and her expression peaceful, like she's sleeping. She's fully formed, not muddy and uncertain like when I first brought her back. Her skin feels cool to the touch, the same temperature as the bottom layers of soil.

Holly's eyes open. Dirt falls away from her eyelashes as she blinks. Her free arm reaches up, and the dirt shifts where her other arm must be. I help her clear the dirt away and grab her under the armpits, hauling her out of the plant bed. She wraps her arms around my neck as her familiar weight settles on my hip. My brain is sluggish as I try to put a coherent thought together. The Itch is already fading, receding from my mind as quickly as it appeared.

"What . . . what were you doing in there?" I ask.

"She must have been dormant," Maddie murmurs. She sounds almost as shocked as I feel, which is rare for her. "Not really gone, just waiting. Like a perennial that waits for conditions to improve before blooming again."

"How have conditions improved? Jessie just . . . " I stare down at Holly's face. She looks up at me with her wide eyes, her expression just as still and peaceful as when she was sleeping underground.

"Maybe it's you," Maddie says. "Maybe you're more prepared to help her. Or maybe Jessie is more ready to talk to Holly now."

Jessica didn't look ready to do anything last night, but who knows how she feels now? I think about Aunt Betty's words to me last night, about the wisdom of small children, especially dead ones. Holly must know what she's doing.

I'm not going to trust her blindly like I did last time I took her to meet Jessica, though. "This time, stick with me," I tell her. "Don't disappear on me again."

"I see Jessie," she says.

"In the hospital?" I ask, a sinking resignation in my chest. "Your parents will probably be there, too."

Holly doesn't answer but keeps staring at me. I take that as acceptance.

"Do you need a ride?" Maddie asks.

CHAPTER FORTY-SEVEN

Backup

Mama intercepts me as I walk back into the house, Holly on my hip. She smiles at Holly as if she's a recurring guest who decided to stop by again rather than a dead girl who dissolved into mud and showed up days later in our garden.

"Jordan's on the phone for you," Mama says, handing me her cell phone.

I adjust Holly's weight to free one of my hands and grab Mama's phone. "Hey Jordan. Sorry, this isn't a good time. Holly's back."

"Oh, wow," Jordan says. "Is she okay?"

"She's still dead, but other than that, she's fine. We're on our way to see Jessica."

"Then this is actually a perfect time. Remember last night, Sam said he works at the courthouse?"

"Uh, Sam?" I ask.

"One of the guys we met last night? Short hair, glasses, a nice smile?"

I remember the three thirty-somethings who gave Toni and me their jackets and hung out with us while we were waiting for Jordan's mom to pick us up. I didn't retain their names, let alone their occupations. "Oh, yeah. Glasses."

"Well, this morning, I remembered that you said Jessica's stepdad is a judge and you were a bit suspicious of him. I asked Sam if he knew him, and he told me Judge Myers hasn't taken a single day off since Holly died. Apparently, he came into work the day after she died, though Sam didn't find out that was when she died until later because they kept it so quiet."

"That doesn't necessarily—"

"Wait. I told Sam I was worried about how Judge Myers treated Jessica—"

"Jordan, you shouldn't have," I interject, horrified that Jordan might have essentially done the same thing I did when I had my outburst in the cafeteria yesterday.

"It's okay, Amy. I told Sam I was just asking because I was worried about Jessica. I didn't accuse anyone or suggest anything. I just asked if Sam thought Judge Myers was a good dad."

I let out a frustrated breath. That doesn't sound like much of a distinction to me. Holly's getting heavy on my hip, so I set her on the island counter of the kitchen to rest my arm. Holly stares at me with the same peaceful but intense expression she's worn ever since I dug her out of the ground.

"Anyway," Jordan continues, "Sam said Judge Myers has been a real pain to everyone lately. He's been getting less and less patient, and he takes out his frustration on the people who work under him. Apparently, he had a hard year, even before Holly died. Sam doesn't know what was going on, but he said everyone's afraid of him at the courthouse."

I meet Holly's gaze. "Do you think your daddy might hurt Jessica, Holly?" I ask.

"Daddy get angry," Holly murmurs, a flicker of uncertainty in her otherwise calm eyes. "I don't tell Daddy."

My guts clench, and my knees get wobbly. Is this why Holly came back? To protect Jessica? Not just last night but in general? She's always insisted there's something she can't say because Jessica asked her not to, because her daddy would get angry if he found out. What if he did find out, and that's what got Holly killed in a fit of her father's rage? I have no idea what the secret might have been. Maybe Jessica didn't tell her parents she was dating Peter, or she rebelled in some other way.

Whatever the case, Holly led me to the right place to save Jessica last night. Maybe she's doing it again now.

I should hurry.

"Thanks for letting me know, Jordan," I say. "I have to go."

"The police won't be any help," she reminds me. As if I don't know that. "Please be careful. You're not going alone, are you?"

"Maddie said she would drive me."

Mama, who has been waiting patiently beside the island counter for her phone, points to herself.

"Mama's taking me," I amend.

"Can I come, too?" Jordan asks.

"It's probably not the best idea to mob Jessica's hospital room," I hedge.

"I won't go in with you. I just want to be there to back you up."

The tight feeling in my guts eases up a bit. It's good to have good friends. "Thank you, Jordan. I really appreciate that. We can stop by and pick you up on the way."

I hang up and return the phone to Mama. She's dressed in a button-down and nice jeans, her typical work clothes.

"I have a client at the hospital," Mama says before I can ask. She turns to Holly. "You have good timing, Chipmunk."

"I didn't realize you already had a pet name for her," I say, reaching out to pick up Holly again. She cooperates, making it easy to settle her back on my hip.

"She's always keeping things tucked away," Mama explains. "Secrets. Memories. It seems appropriate."

It's pretty cute. Chipmunk. I look down at Holly. After this is all over, she's probably going to disappear, this time for good. I'm not going to miss all the stress she put me through, but I think I might miss her. I've always been the youngest, so I never got to experience being an older sister.

I glance back at Maddie, who nods—she's coming, too. It will be a crowded truck. For a second, I wish Toni would come as well, but I squash the notion. Last night was a lot for her. I don't want to impose any more of this drama on her before we've even figured out how we feel about each other.

Besides, it doesn't really matter who all comes with me for the ride or the walk through the hospital halls. At the end of the day, this is all on me and Holly.

CHAPTER FORTY-EIGHT
Remember

Rain sheets down on Whaleback Hill as Mama drives us along the switchback road toward downtown—and the hospital where Jessica and her parents are waiting. I ride with Holly in my lap, hoping we don't get pulled over for not having a car seat.

Holly rests her head on my collarbone, watching the houses roll by. Her scent keeps changing. At some points, it's the muddy soil of the garden with a hint of decay; at other points, it's lemonade and fresh laundry. Like Aunt Betty said last night, she's lingering at the edge between life and death, teetering back and forth. One way or another, I know today will be the last day Holly walks the earth. After this last time seeing Jessica and their parents, she's going away for good.

We stop at Jordan's house, and Jordan hops in the back seat with me. She has her hair tied back in a ponytail, the end of it and the loose strands at her temples dripping rainwater onto the well-worn canvas seat of the truck. She's out of breath, even though she only ran from the front door of her house to the street, and there's a flush on her cheeks.

"This is it, isn't it?" she asks.

I don't know if she senses it from me or from Holly, but

it must be in the air somehow. I nod, my throat too tight to speak. When did that start? My pulse is beating against my seatbelt, too. It's not that weird for me not to be aware of my feelings, but now that I've noticed, I focus on my physical sensations, trying to ground myself rather than escaping. I need to be present and be fully conscious of what I'm doing. I can't afford to mess this up, and I have no idea what Holly will need from me.

"Are you sure Jessica's still at the hospital and not back home?" Jordan asks.

"I called the hospital and asked," Mama explains from the driver's seat. "They know me there."

"Wow," Jordan says. I'm not sure if she's surprised at Mama's connections, at Jessica's extended stay in the hospital, or just at the situation we're all in. After a moment, she turns to me. "I told Adela and Harper what was going on. You don't mind, do you? They wanted to be updated."

"Sure, that's fine." I'm sure my other friends are almost as invested in this thing as Jordan is.

"Adela said to be careful about Judge Myers. She thinks he might want to . . . finish the job or something. Or cover it up by getting rid of you, too."

I shake my head. Is that a real possibility? It seems so removed from my everyday life, the idea that someone would want to hurt me so I wouldn't get in their way. Holly won't be in any physical danger, but her soul might be at risk if her father prevents her from resolving what she needs to resolve before she can move on.

"We'll be right outside Jessica's room," Mama says, calmly but firmly. "No one will get rid of anyone."

"My mom would be so freaked out right now," Jordan murmurs to me. "She would never let me do this."

I don't doubt it; it took years to wear Mrs. Nguyen down enough for her to allow Jordan to go to concerts. Sometimes the concept of a mother protecting me by making demands and prohibitions rather than letting me take full responsibility for my life is kind of comforting, but would I actually enjoy it in practice? Probably not.

My eyes catch on Toni's house as we pass it. The living room curtains are open, and I can see inside. Toni is sitting on the couch, her feet curled under her, reading a book. It's such a perfect vision, framed in lace curtains, that for a second, I doubt whether it's real. Just before we drive out of sight of her window, Toni looks up. Our eyes meet through the two layers of glass. Or is it my imagination?

"Sad girl," Holly says. She's still looking out the window on my side.

"Do you remember Toni?" I ask. Holly was not being very responsive when Toni came to my house, so I'm not sure she even registered Toni's presence.

"Sad," Holly repeats.

"Yeah, she was pretty sad, wasn't she?"

Holly watches the double-wides and prefabs give way to gas stations and grocery stores as we leave Whaleback Hill and head into downtown. I wonder if she's gone back to being focused on Jessica and forgotten all about Toni.

"I don't remember," Holly says softly.

"What don't you remember?" I ask.

"The sad girl ask me what happen, Howee? What like? I don't remember."

It takes me a moment to figure out what Holly's talking about. Now I remember sitting on the roots of the old oak tree with Holly in my lap as Toni begged her for some hint of what the afterlife was like, Holly's disappearance, the trip to the police station, and everything that came afterwards drove the earlier parts of that day out of my mind.

"That's okay," I say, giving Holly a squeeze. "You don't have to remember."

Like Aunt Betty said, Holly's experience with death isn't a clean one. She might not even have experienced what comes after if she's been hanging on this whole time. According to Aunt Betty, ghosts never seem to know what death is like, either. Their souls or spirits might have moved on, but the imprint they leave behind is usually as clueless as the living about the specifics of death.

It's strange to see Holly expressing interest in anything other than Jessica—especially today, her last day. Maybe it's because I've stopped resisting her, so she's able to pay attention to other things. Or maybe she feels a kinship to Toni, who lost someone close to her the way Jessica lost Holly.

I wonder if I should tell Toni what Holly said. It might at least help to know that Holly listened to her and remembered her question, even if her reply isn't very reassuring.

The hospital looms over us like a storm cloud as Mama pulls into the front parking lot. Jordan touches my hand, and I try to smile at her. I'm not sure if it works. At least Holly is undisturbed in my arms, content to know that I'm doing what she wants me to.

I hoist her onto my hip as I step out of the truck. My eyes flick from one window to the next, wondering which of them belongs to Jessica's room. Where will I meet her? How will she react this time? Is she truly ready to face Holly?

And what about Jessica's parents? Her mother seemed nice enough when Jordan and I met her, though clearly still in the midst of grief. The only time I saw her stepfather was the other night outside the police station. He seemed so tall, so stern, his hands so big. I didn't want to go anywhere near him.

But this time, Holly has accepted that she will see her parents as well as Jessica. She came to me—she's been asking for my help this whole time. If she can face her parents, possibly even her killer, I can do it, too.

Chapter Forty-Nine

Progressive Care

Mama talks to a woman she knows at the hospital's front desk. At first, the woman is hesitant to give us Jessica's room number, since we're not her family, but Mama tells her Holly is Jessica's sister.

"But . . . " the woman begins. She stares at Holly for a moment, confusion melting into shock. Judging by her reaction, she either knows Jessica's sister is dead or heard the stories about the dead girl who visited the ER a few days ago. She might even be putting the two things together as we watch.

"It will just be a short visit," Mama says in the same calm, reassuring voice she uses when speaking to her clients and their families. It makes her words sound reasonable, even though they don't explain anything on their own.

"A short visit," the receptionist repeats, her eyes still fixed on Holly.

Then she looks at me. Did gossip spread about me as well, the weird teenager who brought in the dead girl? Until now, the rest of my family—especially Aunt Betty, whose graveyard exploits can sometimes be pretty public—were more likely to generate rumors than me. To my surprise, I'm somewhat gratified. Maybe because I'm so used to everyone overlooking me or dismissing me. Then my vision blurs, and I take a few steady breaths before I can start hyperventilating. I guess I'm not actually ready for notoriety.

"Jessica can't have visitors outside of her immediate family right now," the receptionist says. "Um . . . Holly . . . will have to go in by herself."

"That's all right," Mama says.

The receptionist shakes her head. "Progressive care unit, room 38."

She explains how to get there, even though I'm pretty sure Mama knows the hospital like the back of her hand. Mama listens patiently, nods, and leads me, Maddie, and Jordan across the lobby toward the elevators. I duck my head, trying to pretend the receptionist has stopped staring at me, even though I can feel her gaze on me. Holly holds onto me, her small body relaxed in my arms, staring straight ahead.

I'm not sure what a progressive care unit is, but it sounds intense. What state is Jessica in, physically? She wasn't breathing when I found her; who knows how long she was like that. What's more, the river wouldn't be strong or deep enough to drown someone all on its own, which is why I was looking for head injuries at first. If she really wanted to end things, she probably did something else to herself before getting in the river. Took pills or got drunk or something.

What if seeing Holly again—no, I have to stop thinking like that. Holly knows her own sister. She told me how to save Jessica last night, and she's the one who decided to come here today.

"Do you want to press the button, Chipmunk?" Mama asks Holly, indicating the correct floor as we file into the elevator.

I expect Holly to ignore Mama. Pressing the button is something living children like to do, and Holly showed hardly any interest in other childish things like toys or cartoons. But Holly stretches out one chubby arm and jabs the number 2 with her tiny index finger. The doors close, and Holly settles against my side once more. I guess it's a small gesture of independence, pressing the button to make the elevator take us toward her sister.

"Mama, do you think it's okay for me to go in, too?" I ask. "The receptionist said—"

"Oh, we'll just do a little rule-bending," Mama assures me. "It's a special circumstance. I know you want Holly to have someone there who's on her side."

I nod. After everything I've gone through, I want to be present when Holly finally confronts her family. But like Mama said, I also think Holly *needs* me there. Yes, I'm older and able to communicate a lot more things than Holly can, but on top of that, I'm alive. There will always be a disconnect between the fully living and the mostly dead unless someone who understands both worlds is there to translate. Like Aunt Betty told me, I deal with the ones who linger. Even among necromancers, among my family, that's a unique position to be in.

Jordan puts an arm around my shoulders and gives me a squeeze. I can tell words are failing her, but she's still trying to comfort me.

"Hey," I say, "thank you for everything."

"Sure."

"Really, though."

I'll have to think of something nice to do for her after all this is over. Something nice to do for all my friends. I know I haven't been a good friend recently; I've been too focused on my own messed-up life, barely able to deal with my own mind. Right now, there's only enough space in my brain to put together that thought before I have to go back to focusing on Holly and what's ahead of us.

The elevator doors slide open, revealing a hallway lined with relaxing watercolor paintings. We follow it to a quiet waiting room with several vending machines, coffee dispensers, and a play area for little kids. Obviously, a place where people spend a lot of time.

A nurse looks up from her desk. "Hello. Are you here to visit someone?"

"Jessica Myers, room 38," Mama says. She points toward a branching corridor, then indicates Holly. "This is her sister."

The nurse consults her computer. "Okay, it looks like she can't have any visitors right now. Her sister can go in, since she's part of her immediate family, but—"

"We'll wait here," Mama says, steering Maddie and Jordan toward a row of seats. "Good luck, dear," she calls over her shoulder, smiling at me.

"I'll just take Holly over there," I say, my dry throat almost snapping my voice in half. "Thank you."

I turn around before the nurse can tell me no and walk down the corridor Mama indicated. I pass a few other nurses and doctors, but they all seem too busy to try to stop me. Holly's arms tighten slightly as we reach room 38. I struggle to swallow. My feet put down roots in the tile floor in front of the door.

There's a window looking into the room, but the curtain's closed, obscuring the room's occupants. I listen for voices, trying to determine who's there—maybe I'll get lucky and Jessica's parents will be gone, so it will just be me and Jessica and Holly. Then I can help resolve things between the two sisters without pulling anyone else into this, without having to face the man who may have murdered Holly and driven Jessica to try to end her life. But I can't hear anything. Maybe that's a good sign.

I expect Holly to urge me on when I stand there for almost a minute, but she waits quietly in my arms. Her grip around my neck is a little tighter than usual, though nowhere near as tight as it's been a few other times. I also expect a doctor or nurse to ask me why I'm staring at this door, but no one questions me.

It seems I'll have to be the one to convince myself to take these last few steps.

It will all be over soon, I tell myself. *One way or another, this is it.*

The thought makes me nauseous. I'm not great at reassuring myself.

I take a deep breath—one of the deepest breaths of my life, like my lungs keep finding new corners of my ribcage to expand into. Then I let it out as slowly as I can.

I step forward and push open the door to Jessica's hospital room.

CHAPTER FIFTY

Brianna

The door to Jessica's hospital room swings open, and I'm standing there in the doorway with Holly on my hip, staring at Jessica and her parents. Of course, I should have known I wouldn't be lucky enough to face Jessica on her own.

Jessica lies in the hospital bed, hooked up to a heart monitor and saline drip. She's curled on her side, facing away from the door. Her mother stands at the window, one hand tight around her opposite wrist. Her stepfather sits on a folding chair at the foot of the bed, holding a phone but staring at the floor. Jessica doesn't move—she might even be asleep—but both adults look up at me. Then they both look down at Holly. For a moment, no one says anything.

Jessica's mother opens her mouth as if to speak, but no sound comes out. The cell phone drops from her stepfather's hands and clatters to the floor, the screen shattering on impact; he doesn't seem to notice.

Should I say something, or should I wait for them to get over the initial shock? Is Holly going to speak? I wait a few seconds. Holly is not going to speak. I probably should have prepared some kind of introduction. *Hello, my name is Amy, and I'm a necromancer. I brought your daughter back to life but not really back to life. Her body is made of mud. She doesn't have a heartbeat and doesn't need to eat, sleep, or breathe. She's been giving me visions, and I think you might have killed her, Mr. Myers. Judge Myers. Whatever.*

"Um," I begin eloquently, "I'm sorry to int—I mean, Holly wants . . . I mean, this is . . . well, you obviously know who . . . She wants to talk to—"

Jessica's mom asks in a trembling voice, "Holly? Baby, is that you?"

My stomach clenches again, and I think I might throw up. I've been dreading this moment ever since Holly first emerged from the mud. Jessica, if nothing else, seemed to know from the start that Holly was dead. She didn't take it well to say the least, but I didn't have to break the news to her. But how do you tell someone that their dead child isn't really back?

"No," Judge Myers snaps. "Of course it's not." He jerks to his feet and takes a step toward me, his large frame suddenly seeming to swallow up half the space in the room. "I don't know what game you're playing, girl—"

"It's not a game," I retort. I resist the urge to retreat. Judge Myers won't hurt me while I'm standing in an open doorway with doctors and nurses in the hallway. And if I have to choose between dashing a mother's hope and squaring off against an angry man, I think Judge Myers is easier to deal with right now. "Holly's still dead. But she came back because she wanted to talk to Jessica."

Judge Myers stares at me, a vein pounding in his temple, his jaw muscles tensed so hard I can make out their outline despite his scruffy beard. I can tell he's working hard not to look at Holly, as if ignoring her will make her disappear. His waxy skin and the bags under his eyes speak of lots of sleepless nights. I'm torn between pitying him and wondering if he's unstable enough to do something reckless. Like attacking me in front of witnesses.

"Holly?" Jessica's mom asks again, her voice now almost inaudible.

Holly doesn't answer.

"Jessica, are you awake?" I call. Jessica still lies with her back to us; she hasn't moved this whole time. "Please, Holly needs to talk to you."

"Jessie, I come see you," Holly says, finally chiming in.

At the sound of her voice, her mother's knees buckle, and she catches herself on the windowsill, shivering violently. Judge Myers staggers back, retracting the step he took toward us as if I shoved him. I avert my eyes from his face. I don't know if I can stomach his reaction, whatever it is.

"Go away," Jessica murmurs without turning. "You're not real."

Is this Jessica's new strategy for dealing with Holly? I would be surprised if she believed it herself.

"I real," Holly says. "I come see you." She looks up at me. I guess she trusts me now, enough to expect me to do what she needs rather than having to demand it of me. She knows I'm on her side.

I nod and eye her dad to see if he seems like he'll approach me if I come into the room. He's running a hand through his hair, almost missing it in his distraction. He looks at Holly, then closes his eyes as if she emits a blinding light and shakes his head slightly. I think we're safe from him for the moment, but just in case, I leave the door open.

Jessica doesn't turn when we reach her bedside. Holly reaches out and touches Jessica's arm. Her sister jerks away, curling into a tighter ball, and buries her face in her pillow, her tangled curls falling across her cheeks.

Her mother rushes around to our side of the bed and tears Holly from my arms. I'm too startled to resist. She squeezes Holly against her, rocking from side to side, tears streaming down her cheeks. I don't know if it was seeing Holly reach out for Jessica that finally convinced their mother Holly's really here, or if it's just that we came closer, within easy reach, and she couldn't hold herself back any longer.

"Brianna," Judge Myers says. I realize that must be Jessica's mom's name; I don't think I ever knew that. I don't know his first name, either, now that I think about it.

Brianna ignores him and holds Holly, crying quietly.

Holly allows it, but she's looking over her shoulder at Jessica, almost not seeming to notice her mother is the one holding her. She's never once asked for her mother, and when I mentioned she'd be at the hospital, she didn't seem interested. I don't think that means she doesn't care about her mother, though it would look that way to most people. Aunt Betty says ghosts are single-minded creatures and almost impossible to distract from their goal; I guess that applies to Holly, too. She came back for Jessie and only Jessie.

"Let go of her." Judge Myers stalks forward to stand beside his wife and reaches for Holly, but Brianna backs away, flattening Holly against her chest. "That's not . . . this isn't real."

Brianna shakes her head and doesn't speak.

Judge Myers rounds on me. I back into the bedside table, knocking over a plastic cup that spills its contents down my leg, and shoot a glance at the door. Still open. Though there's no one in sight at the moment, I'm sure there's someone a few steps from visibility. A nurse carrying a tray of medications or a doctor with a clipboard or a janitor pushing a cleaning cart. Someone. He won't hurt me when it will be so easy for someone to see. He went to all the trouble of covering up—no, I don't know that. I don't know that he's a murderer. With him looming over me, backlit by the sallow hospital light and shaking with some suppressed emotion, it's hard to remind myself of that.

"What are you doing here? What do you want?" he demands.

"I came to help Holly." My voice comes out squeaky and breathless, like a rubber toy that's been stepped on. "She wants to see Jessie."

"Holly is dead."

"Look at her," Brianna says. "She's not dead, she's—"

"Yes, she is," I say. Whatever else happens, I need to make it clear Holly isn't back for good. I can't look at her mother as I say it, though. "I'm sorry, but she is."

"Then how is she here?" Judge Myers asks. He smells sour, like sweat and bad breath.

I can't look at him, either. "I'm a necromancer. I bring back people who die without being able to accept their death. They come back for a short time before they move on."

"You expect us to believe that?"

I'm strongly reminded of being interrogated by George at the police station, except he didn't loom over me like this, and he smelled better. "Look at her," I reply, echoing his wife. I know that if you look closely at her, it's unmistakable that Holly is Holly—and that she's dead. There's nothing I can say that's as convincing as them figuring it out for themselves.

Judge Myers glances at Brianna, who holds Holly by the window, her face blotchy from crying. I lift my eyes to his face, which is a lot easier to do when his attention isn't on me. He's pale with a sickly yellow undertone, his jaw muscles still tense. Sweat beads his receding hairline. He shakes his head slowly.

I lay a hand on Jessica's shoulder. "Jessica, you have to—"

Jessica lurches upright. Her heart monitor spikes, and the saline drip jiggles on its pole. Her feverish eyes bore into me, her face contorted with fury.

"Leave me alone, Amy! I told you to stay out of my life!"

"I can't!" I take a deep breath to try to steady my nerves. I want to yell at her that I'd be happy to stay out of her life if I could. "Look, this is the last time you'll ever have to see me outside of school, and I won't bother you there anymore. Holly just needs to talk to you."

"Then talk!" She turns her furious gaze toward Holly. "Tell me what you want to tell me and then go away!"

Holly wiggles out of Brianna's grip enough to twist around and look at Jessica. "Jessie." She frees an arm and reaches for her sister.

Jessica screams and buries her face in her hands, pulling her knees up to her chest. "Why can't you all just leave me alone? Why are you doing this to me?"

"Jessica, baby," her mother says.

"That's enough," Judge Myers says. He scowls at me. "Young lady, get out. This is a family matter."

I open my mouth to protest, but before I can, Holly pipes up. "Amy has to stay."

No one says anything for a moment. The two adults and I wait for Holly to continue, while Jessica keeps her face covered, her back quivering. The heart monitor beeps irregularly, but there are no alarms and no one comes running, so I guess she's not in any danger. I have no idea what Holly will do next. This is the chance she's wanted ever since she remembered her name.

"Jessie," she insists, reaching for her sister. Brianna carries her over to the bed, still holding her close.

"Jessie, she wants to talk to you," Brianna says. Tears still stream down her face, but her voice sounds a little stronger. Maybe feeling like there's something she can do to help her daughters makes her able to keep going.

Jessica lets out a small whimper and laces her fingers together behind her head, pushing her face down between her knees. Holly leans over enough to put her small hands on Jessica's back. Jessica shudders, but there's nowhere for her to retreat. It's hard to decipher Holly's expression. Longing? Regret? Frustration? I don't know if it looks wrong on her because she's dead or just because it seems like too big an emotion for a three-year-old to have to feel.

"No," Judge Myers says.

I freeze—everything, from my muscles to my brain—as he turns back to me, his eyes dark and his mouth pressed into a thin line. In two steps, he's right in front of me.

He grabs my arm so hard I can feel my pulse pounding against his fingers.

"That's it," he says.

CHAPTER FIFTY-ONE
William

Jessica's stepfather, Holly's father, holds my arm so hard that my fingers start to go numb. His are a tourniquet.

"That's it," he says, and yanks me forward. I stumble.

"William!" Jessica's mother exclaims.

So now I know his name.

William Myers stares down his long, angular nose at me. His dark eyes seem to see through me, like I'm a shadow. His face twitches. Less violently than before, but about as gently as a shovel slicing into the dirt, he pulls me toward the open door of the hospital room.

"This is a family matter," he says. I don't know who he's talking to; it doesn't seem to be me.

"Amy has to stay!" Holly repeats. Her voice has all the authority of a toddler play-acting a queen.

William Myers stops and glances over his shoulder at Holly. "You can't be real," he mutters.

"She's real," I say, the words tripping out of my mouth. "Look at her."

I've had to argue my case so many times these past few days, but it's never mattered as much as it does right now. Who knows what will happen to Holly if I let her father kick me out? If they keep ignoring her words, dismissing her, she'll collapse into mud again—and this time, she won't come back.

I also really, really want William Myers to get his hand off me. I don't think a grown man, a stranger, has ever grabbed me like this. My parents almost never get mad at me, but if they do, they show it in words, not with their hands. I *hate* how small and breakable I feel in William Myer's grip, like a twig that could snap.

I'm not used to feeling powerful, or strong, or confident. I'm average height for a girl my age and not the least bit athletic—I've never thought I could beat anyone in a fight. But I guess I must have had some confidence, some sense of power, of strength and security.

Because I've lost them all now.

And what I say next isn't the least bit helpful. "Did you kill her?"

William Myers stops dead halfway to the door and stares at me with wide eyes. He tries to speak but can't. He lets go of me and walks unsteadily over to the door, closing it. Cutting us off from the view of nurses and doctors. Witnesses.

I back up until my butt hits Jessica's hospital bed. At least now I'm not out in the open in the middle of the room. If he tries to attack me, maybe Jessica or her mom will help. My pulse pounds in my stomach, compounding my nausea. Why did I have to ask that?

William turns his back on the door and stares at me, then Holly, then me again. "Is that what you told the police the other night?"

For a moment, I have no idea what he's talking about. My entire life up until now seems to have vanished from my mind. Then I remember the first time I saw him, outside of the police station after being questioned for hours. Did he think, back then, that I was a threat to him? That I might know something? I have no idea what Jessica told him—if she said I brought Holly to see her or if she kept quiet about that whole evening.

"No, I didn't tell them anything. I don't have any proof." Should I have pretended I did? Should I have pretended I already told the police everything, so there's no point in hurting me? Too late now.

William closes his eyes. I can't tell if he's relieved or trying to control his emotions. Behind me, Brianna's crying softly. Jessica and Holly don't make a sound, and I can't take my eyes off William to see their faces.

"She came to me and asked for my help," I babble. "Holly did, I mean. She wanted me to take her to see Jessie. But at first, I thought it would be a bad idea. I know something traumatic happened to her. I know she's afraid of men, and she thinks there's something you shouldn't know, that she shouldn't tell you, because she promised Jessica that she wouldn't tell."

Why am I saying this? God, am I digging my own grave?

William opens his eyes. "So you think I killed her?"

"I don't know anything. I just came here to help her talk to Jessie, to make sure you all listened to her and understood what she was trying to say. I'm a link between the living and the dead."

"That's what you believe, is it?" William asks.

"I *know*," I reply. I realize I just said I don't know anything, but I might as well accept that I'm contradicting myself with every other sentence. I can't keep my words under control. I'm just trying to stay alive. "I know I am. My whole family is. The women are all born with our umbilical cords around our neck, and sometimes they're stillborn—"

That doesn't matter. *Change the subject.*

"We understand death. Holly and I are connected. She's sent me visions, and sometimes I feel what she feels."

"Visions?" William asks. He's very calm for someone who was just accused of killing his daughter, though his dark eyes are haunted. I don't think either of those are good signs.

"I don't always understand them. Holly's somewhere dark, and she can hear voices outside. It might be a closet. I heard Jessica and Peter, her ex-boyfriend, talking outside. That's all."

"That's enough, Amy." The voice is Brianna's, tremulous but adamant. "William, she should go."

I finally look away from William and back at Holly's mother. She stands on the other side of the hospital bed with Holly on her hip. She's not crying anymore, though tears still shine on her face in the morning sunlight.

Jessica still sits on the hospital bed with her head between her knees, her fingers laced together on the back of her neck like she's bracing for an earthquake or airplane turbulence. Holly's expression is serious but a lot less upset than I expected. Has she been paying attention to my conversation with her father? You'd think talking about her possible murder would bring up some intense emotions for her.

"Don't you understand?" I plead to Brianna. "I'm trying to help—"

"You're not," she tells me. "Please, just leave us alone."

"No telling, Amy," Holly says unexpectedly.

I blink at her. "You don't want me to . . . Who am I not supposed to tell? What am I not . . . what are you talking about?"

Holly shakes her head. "No talking."

I'm at a loss. Isn't that why I'm here? To do the talking? To explain to her family the things she can't explain? Maybe I'm not doing a good job, but shouldn't I keep trying until I get it right? Why else would she be so insistent on making sure that I stay?

Then it finally clicks. I've been misunderstanding her this whole time. She's three years old; she didn't come here to talk to Jessie or her family. Talking has never been what it's about.

"Jessica," I say. "I'm sorry, I was wrong. Holly doesn't want to talk to you. You don't have to say anything."

I search Holly's feelings, which are tucked somewhere inside mine. I've tried to rationalize them, to figure them out, but I was too wrapped up in my own interpretations to really understand. I remember that time in the emergency room when my instincts told me to ignore what the adults were talking about and put Holly in Jessica's lap.

"She just wants you to hold her," I finish.

CHAPTER FIFTY-TWO

Sorry

"I can't," Jessica says into her hands.

"Jessie—" Holly begins, reaching out for her sister again.

"I can't do it! Leave me alone!"

Brianna takes a step back, pressing Holly close to her again. "I'm sorry, baby, but your sister can't hold you right now. It's too much for her." To me, she repeats, "It's too much."

"Holly won't be able to move on," I say. "This is all she wants. She just wants Jessica to hold her one last time, and then she'll be okay. She'll be able to leave for good."

Maybe that wasn't the right thing to say. Brianna squeezes Holly tighter and takes another step back, her eyes growing a little wider. If William Myers looks like he hasn't slept in days, Brianna Myers looks like she hasn't slept since Holly died. Of course she doesn't want Holly to move on—she wants to keep her baby girl here by any means necessary.

"I'm sorry," I tell her, though I know how little it means. "I'm so sorry this happened. I know you don't want Holly to go, but she has to. She doesn't belong here anymore. The body she has now is temporary, and—"

"It's her," Brianna snaps. "She feels like my daughter.

She smells like my daughter. Her voice . . . " She swallows and presses her cheek against the top of Holly's head, flattening her curls. "This is my daughter."

She's lying to herself. A mother should be able to tell better than anyone that Holly isn't like she was. Yes, the basics are there, and I'm sure she feels and smells and sounds similar to how she did when she was alive, but there's also the stench of death and decay, faint but unmistakable. Her skin might be as soft as it was before, but it's also colder. Serenity, the nurse from the other night, took Holly's temperature several times and consistently got something in the low eighties, only a bit warmer than room temperature and way below normal body heat. And with Holly pressed so close against Brianna's chest, there's no way she can miss the lack of a heartbeat, the absence of breath.

I guess it's not enough to convince her.

I've gone about this all wrong. I didn't understand what Holly needed until a few minutes ago. I let everyone freak out before I could explain; I confused them, confused myself. But I have to stop regretting everything I didn't do right, everything I'm not good at. Sure, Mama or Maddie or Grandma would have done a better job, but it *isn't* their job. Holly came to me.

I don't think she latched onto me just because I'm the one who brought her back or because I'm the same age as Jessica. I think she came to me because she felt, in some way, that I could understand. She asked me to be her sister for a short while, to take over the role when her real sister couldn't fill it.

"Holly," I say softly.

I can't help but glance over my shoulder at her father before continuing. He's still by the door; he hasn't moved any closer to me. I have to set him aside for now. I don't think Holly would lead me to my death or to serious harm. Though she is just a toddler, so who knows how sharp her sense of danger is.

That doesn't matter right now. This isn't going to be resolved with me cowering in fear of William Myers.

"Holly," I say again, "I'm sorry. I'm sorry I didn't understand. I'm sorry I kept you from your sister for so long. I'm sorry I wasn't able to help you last time you saw her."

She peeks out at me between her mother's arms. "You okay," she says softly. It's the same thing she told me when I got upset over the obituaries.

"Thank you." Tears sting my eyes. I really am going to miss her. "You've got a sweet kid," I tell Brianna.

She just stares at me as if I'm speaking a foreign language.

"I'm sorry I didn't do this right," I say. "Look. Holly came back because . . . " I sigh. "Because she needs something she didn't get while she was alive."

"How can you say that?" Brianna's voice is choked, angry.

"I'm not saying *you* didn't give her what she needed," I clarify. "But she died suddenly at three years old. Of course she was missing something. I don't know why it's Jessica that she needs, but it is." I fix Brianna with a steady stare. "Keeping her here without giving her that won't stop her from disappearing. You'll just let her leave restless and unsatisfied."

Brianna shakes her head slowly back and forth, back and forth. She seems unable to process my words.

Jessica lifts her head enough to blink bloodshot eyes at me. "Where will she go?" she asks. Her voice cracks like an eggshell.

"I'm not sure," I say truthfully. "Do you believe in Heaven?"

"I don't know," Jessica says.

"Well, maybe there," I suggest. It probably would have sounded a lot more comforting if Jessica had said she believed in it.

"Some necromancer," Jessica mutters. "You don't know anything about death."

I fight down the urge to snap at her. She's probably trying to pick a fight with me as usual. I'll be just as glad as she is never to have to talk to her again. Does Mama have to deal with people taking out their grief on her?

"I deal with the in-between," I say, and then change

the subject, because technicalities aren't going to reassure anyone. "Jessica, please. Can't you do this one last thing for her? Then it'll be over."

Jessica tugs at her hair. "Do you like butting into other people's lives?"

"No," I say, hoping that will close out this topic. "I really don't."

She stares at me for a moment. I wonder if she's doing that to avoid looking at Holly. "You really have no idea, do you?"

I assume she means about grief, about loss. She probably wants me to get mad or defensive. "I don't know what you're going through," I say, trying to make my voice soothing. An echo of Mama's. "I'm here for Holly. That's it." *I'm not here to help you deal with your pain, especially not by letting you go for my throat every five minutes.* I hope she gets the subtext.

Jessica tugs at her hair again. A few strands come out, tangled in her fingers.

I glance over my shoulder at William again. He's still standing by the door, watching us. I can't interpret his expression. Will he let me go after this is over? After Holly's gone? I did accuse him of murder. My heart stutters.

Witnesses, I remind myself. *Right outside the door. And in here—his wife and stepdaughter.* If he did kill Holly, I don't think it was in cold blood. That doesn't necessarily mean he's not prepared to kill me to cover it up, but it does mean it's less likely. I hope.

I have a job to do. I have to stay confident and calm. I'm probably blowing things out of proportion, thinking I'm in some sort of crime drama. After this is over, I'll leave the family to deal with their grief without distracting them and be on my way.

Right?

I focus on Jessica again. She's pulling out more of her hair. Without thinking, I reach over and grab her wrist to stop her. She yanks it out of my grasp with a glare, but she stops tearing at her hair.

"Okay, fine," she says. She straightens a little and turns toward her mother, though her eyes are on the window behind her. "I'll . . . I'll hold her."

Brianna rubs Holly's back. "Baby," she tells her younger daughter. "You don't have to go. Stay here with us, okay? You'll see when your sister holds you . . . you'll see you have to stay. It's . . . it's too hard without you." She takes in a shuddering breath and squeezes her eyes shut for a moment. "Stay with us."

I open my mouth to say that's not how it works, but I bite back the words. I doubt anything I say will convince her.

Brianna walks back to Jessica's bedside and holds Holly out to her sister. Jessica takes her mechanically, as if she's miles away from her body. I know the feeling. Holly settles into Jessica's lap, wrapping her little arms around her neck and pressing her face into Jessica's shoulder. Jessica pats Holly's back, still staring out the window with unfocused eyes.

"You okay, Jessie," Holly whispers. She holds her sister tighter.

Brianna puts a hand to her mouth and turns away, a choked sob escaping through her fingers.

A tear tracks down Jessica's cheek and sinks into Holly's curls.

CHAPTER FIFTY-THREE
Trade

With each tear that rolls down Jessica's face, she seems to deflate a little more. Her stiff posture melts away, her spine curves, and her arms tighten around Holly until they seem to become one being. Something unclenches within me, and I know it's almost done. Holly's time in this world is almost over.

"Okay, Jessie," Holly pipes up in her small voice. "You okay."

A sob wracks Jessica's body. She hunches low over Holly, pulls her even closer. This is why she hasn't wanted to hold Holly, has barely wanted to look at her: it's all she needed to unravel.

Brianna puts her arm around both her daughters. Her eyes are hollow, exhausted.

I step back toward the chair William occupied when I came into the room so I won't be in his way if he decides to come join his family. He doesn't. He still stands by the door, squinting at his wife and his daughters like Daddy when he tries to read without his glasses.

I can't help but compare him to Daddy. He'd never watch so coldly, so distantly, as any member of his family cried. Jordan said everyone who works for William is terrified of him; the only time Daddy's scared me was when he pretended to be a velociraptor and chased me around the house. He stopped and hugged me as soon as I started crying. I remember how he held me the night before last, when I came home from the police station—how safe I felt in his arms. It's awful to think of someone in his position, a father, making his children feel afraid rather than comforted.

"Holly saved you last night, Jessica," I say.

Jessica and her mother and Holly all ignore me, but William looks at me. I thought he might.

"She told me where you were going to be," I continue, still speaking to Jessica. "It's not a coincidence that I ended up in the right place at the right time."

"You were there last night?" William asks.

I realize they must not know all the details of how Jessica got out of the river. If her parents had known beforehand, they might have been more willing to listen to me when I was trying to explain about Holly. But then again, it seems cheap to leverage saving their daughter's life against them.

"Yeah, I was there," I say.

I can't quite meet William's eyes, but it's hard to keep speaking to Jessica when she's ignoring me and he asked me a direct question. I stare at his feet instead. He's wearing a pair of old sneakers beneath his faded jeans. I would guess that's not how he dresses for the courthouse.

"I . . . I went to the river and . . . I went in, and . . . there was Jessica. My friend and I, we pulled her out. My friend called 911."

"I see," William replies. "Well, thank you for that."

"Thank Holly," I say. It somehow ends up more like a question than an instruction. I'm not projecting as much confidence as I want to. I still haven't forgotten how scary it felt to have William's hand gripping my arm. "I think part of the reason she came back is to help Jessica. To save her." I force myself to look up at William's eyes—sunken, shadowed. "Is Jessica . . . safe?"

William stares back at me. Brief confusion plays in his expression before being replaced by a stony mask. He understands what I'm asking.

"Holly says you get angry," I press.

I know I'm pushing my luck. The whole family has fallen silent now. Even though Jessica is still wrapped around Holly and Brianna around Jessica and none of them are looking at me, I assume they're listening. This is for their benefit more than William's. I don't expect him to confess to me or anything, but I think seeing me—an unimpressive girl Jessica's age who a few minutes ago seemed to be at William's mercy—stand up to him and ask him these questions . . . well, I guess it's kind of a long shot, but I hope it might encourage them, Jessica especially, to stand up, too.

"I know Jessica had a bruise on her face from before the river," I continue. "No one can hurt Holly anymore, but Jessica might still be in danger."

William doesn't dismiss me outright as I half-expect him to. I don't know if it's the shock of the past few minutes, of my accusations, of Holly's reappearance, or if he's just cold-blooded enough not to show guilt or remorse or even a hint of uncertainty about the way he's treated his daughters. I like to think he wasn't expecting me to stand up to him.

Of course, he could just be extremely unimpressed.

"You know, it works both ways," I find myself saying. My voice has the calm tone I hear in it when I'm not entirely aware of my feelings or how they impact my decisions. I feel a lot more in control than I usually do when I dissociate, but I guess my overzealous survival instinct is trying to protect me.

Or maybe I'm just pissed off that he made me feel so afraid. That he made Holly and Jessica feel so afraid.

"I pulled Holly out of the earth," I continue. "All it took was water and mud. I can do the opposite, too. I could put *you* in the earth."

I've never said such an outrageous thing; I would never have imagined those words coming out of my mouth. My powers don't allow me to kill people. No one in my family—in our whole lineage, as far as we know—has ever had power to destroy. We're all about balance and peace, the opposite of fear and destruction.

But Judge William Myers doesn't know that.

He stares at me, his jaw set. I imagine it keeps his mouth from betraying any emotion he doesn't want it to. His gaze wavers, flicking to Holly and back to me.

"Would it bring her back for real?" he asks in a quiet rasp.

It takes me a moment to figure out what he's asking me. I told him it goes both ways, that I can put someone in the ground the same way I can take someone out of it. I guess that implies the two processes are connected.

He's asking me to trade his life for Holly's.

My heart staggers against my ribs, and a deep ache creeps through my stomach. This wasn't at all what I meant. I shouldn't have said something that suggested I could . . .

"No," I say. It's weird to have to pivot so quickly from trying to intimidate him to trying to . . . what? Take away his hope before it takes hold of him? "No, that's not how it works. I'm sor—" I swallow back more apologies; no number of apologies is going to make this okay. "Holly's dead. Nothing can change that."

William nods slowly. His shoulders don't exactly slump, but his posture softens, grows a little less imposing. His hand, which I didn't realize was balled up into a fist at his side, unclenches. Was he just doing that to suppress or channel his emotions, or was he thinking about hitting me? I can still feel his grip on my arm, see the bruise on Jessica's face. But at the same time . . . he's not nearly as scary with that defeated look in his eyes. I feel like I've broken his heart.

"You want to trade me, don't you?"

William and I both turn to stare at Jessica. She's still clutching Holly to her like they share one body between them, but she's looking up now, at her stepfather. The whites of her eyes are streaked with red.

"You wish I had died instead of her," Jessica chokes out.

"Baby," Brianna begins, resting her palm on Jessica's cheek as if to turn her daughter to face her.

Jessica pushes her mother's hand away, laser-focused on William. "You hate me, don't you? Tell me you hate me."

"Jessica—" William says, taking a few steps toward the hospital bed.

"Tell me!" Jessica screams.

"Shh," Holly says, patting Jessica's back.

William sits heavily in the chair beside me, his hands shaking.

Answer her, I think at him. *She's telling you what she needs to hear. Why aren't you saying anything?*

"Why don't you hit me again?" Jessica demands. Her old bruise stands out on her face, which is growing paler as she gets angrier. I wonder if she's forgetting to breathe like I often do when I get worked up.

"That's enough," Brianna says. "Not in front of—"

I don't know if she's going to say Amy or Holly, but Jessica cuts her off.

"Tell Amy, then. Tell her everything, since she won't stop sticking her nose in. Tell her why you hate me."

The ache in my stomach is growing, making me almost double over. I back up against the wall, wrapping my arms around my midriff. Maybe I should leave. I don't like where this is going.

"Shh, Jessie," Holly says. "You okay."

"I'm not okay!" Jessica pries Holly off her and shoves her little sister at their mother. "I'm not okay, so stop telling me—"

"Don't—" I begin.

"You came back to torment, me, didn't you?" Jessica asks Holly, tears falling fast now. "You came back to punish me, right?"

Brianna shakes her head as if she thinks that will stop Jessica from speaking. It doesn't, though. Jessica isn't paying attention to anyone except Holly, who now sits in her mother's arms, her face blank.

"Because I killed you."

Chapter Fifty-Four
Safe Travels

Jessica has to be lying. Or maybe it's an exaggeration, like she feels like she did something or behaved a certain way that ended up with . . . No. There's no way she killed Holly, is there? Not *really*, right?

"Stop," William orders. "Don't say—"

"I killed her," Jessica spits. "Are you happy, Amy? Now you know the truth. The answer to your little mystery. I—killed—Holly."

"No, you didn't," I say.

Jessica gives a little gasp of humorless laughter. "You know everything, don't you?"

"It wasn't—" Brianna begins.

"What?" Jessica demands. "Not my *fault*? That's not what you said before."

William Myers closes his eyes. He looks exhausted and resigned.

"You *did* cover it up," I say.

He doesn't answer, but he doesn't have to. William covered up the circumstances of Holly's death, just like I suspected in my most cynical moments. But he did it to protect his stepdaughter, not himself.

"Jessie!" Holly whines, reaching for her sister again.

"Why are you *doing* this?" Jessica cries. "You want me to confess? I did. You want me to feel sorry?" She cuts off a sob. Her next words are a whimper. "You want to hurt me?"

I take a deep breath in and out. I keep thinking I've grasped the whole deal, but I've only been seeing pieces of it until now. I didn't understand why Holly was obsessed with Jessica more than the rest of her family. I thought it might be because Jessica was taking her death worse than their parents, and Holly wanted to comfort her before moving on. When I found Jessica in the river, I thought I had my answer—Holly wanted to protect her sister from the pain her death had caused, so that Jessica wouldn't take her own life out of grief.

But now I get it, and I think maybe I've finally gotten the whole thing.

"She didn't come back to hurt you," I say quietly. "She came back to forgive you. She doesn't know how to say it—or maybe it's not important to say it out loud—but that's what she's trying to say."

Jessica stares at me, either not understanding or not wanting to accept my words. Tears are still streaming down her face. She doesn't try to wipe them away. I know the feeling when you realize there's no point in getting rid of the tears, because you're just going to keep crying until there's nothing left inside you. It's going to keep hurting no matter what.

"I was stupid," Jessica murmurs. There's an emptiness in her voice now that matches the emptiness in her mother's eyes. The force is gone from her words; they're flat. "I was . . . so stupid. They left me with Holly over the weekend. I said I could do it, could take care of her. I had Peter over. We . . . "

Her jaw clenches, and I can almost hear the creak of her teeth mashing against each other. I don't know who she's telling this to. Everyone knows the story but me, and I don't think she cares what I think.

"We got high. Just like we did every time we were together. We drank and got high and we binge-ate potato chips. And Holly wanted to play hide-and-seek . . . and we forgot about her."

Without warning, I'm in Holly's vision again. I'm in the dark with clothes hanging all around me and slats of light in front. A closet. Holly could hear Jessica and Peter talking somewhere in the distance, but they didn't come any closer, no matter how long she waited.

"No telling, Jessie," Holly murmurs, pulling me back into the present.

"Sh-she was playing with . . . She took some new shirts out of a bag and started playing with the bag. She was probably bored." Jessica almost sounds like she's laughing when she says that, and her face is contorted into something approximating a smile. "When I found her," Jessica continues, her voice higher than before, close to breaking, "there were those white letters on the bag over her face. It said to keep out of reach of children. Danger of suffocation. This is not a toy."

She digs the heels of her palms into her eyes. "William was right about . . . this whole time, he kept saying I was going to ruin my life. He kept saying I was a screw-up." She drops her hands and looks at him. "I proved you right. You didn't want a stepdaughter like me, and you were right."

I think about what Jordan learned from Sam, who works with Judge Myers, about how angry he's been this last year. He's been dealing with a rebellious teenager and dealing badly, taking out his frustration on the people who work under him. I imagine his frustration and Jessica's defiance fed off each other. Maybe she even resented Holly for being his daughter, for interrupting her life. I don't know. I don't think I'll ever involve myself enough in their lives to find out for sure, and I don't think I want to. I didn't even need to know this much; I didn't need to solve this mystery. I feel sick. I should have left it alone.

When I was little, Sarah—only a year older than me—alternated between being my best friend and being my tormentor. She would pinch me, break things and blame me, teach me bad words and get me in trouble when someone heard them. She got over it eventually. Funny enough: once she did, we grew apart. I wonder if she ever wanted me dead, even as a passing thought, knowing nothing would ever come of it.

I wonder if Jessica ever felt that way about Holly.

Maybe Holly identified with me not because I was Jessica's age, but because I was also the baby of the family. The one who annoyed her older siblings. The one who hogged her parents' attention, who needed the most looking after.

William gets to his feet and starts toward the door.

"Don't just leave when you don't want to answer me," Jessica says.

"What do you want me to say, Jessica?" William asks.

"Did you really hit her?" I ask.

He glances at me, then back at the door.

"Yes, he did," Jessica says. "When he found out what I did. I deserved it, didn't I?"

"Jessica, please," Brianna murmurs.

"Please what? It's not like I can disappoint you anymore than I already have. Might as well keep—"

"Jessie," Holly interrupts.

"Leave me alone!" Jessica screams, burying her face in her hands again.

"Jessica," I say slowly. "Whenever I asked Holly what happened to her, she would say you told her not to tell because your dad would get angry. She tried to stop you just now when you were talking about it. I think she must have been trying to keep—to keep William from finding out what happened. She didn't want him to take it out on you." I shoot a look at William, hoping he's not about to turn his anger on me. He stands rooted to the spot, halfway to the door, apparently unable to keep going or to turn back. "She, um, might have even worried he would . . . you know."

No one answers. Holly doesn't contradict me or agree with me; she just stares at me with somber eyes from her mother's arms. Brianna stares at me, too. They both look equally dead.

"If that doesn't convince you that she forgives you, I . . ."

I shake my head. "Jessica, I don't think she blames you at all. I think she wants you to be happy. It's why she came back."

Jessica's shoulders shake with silent sobs. Brianna stares at me for a moment more before setting Holly down on the bed next to her sister. Holly puts her arms around Jessica, as far as their stubby length will allow, and rests her head on Jessica's shoulder. She lets out a sigh like a contented puppy after a long day of running and playing. Jessica continues to cry softly. We all wait, and slowly, Holly's body begins to soften around the edges. It's entirely unlike the time she collapsed into mud in the emergency room. There's no violence, no anger, nothing sudden about it.

"Baby." Brianna puts a hand to her throat as if she can feel the knot that stifles her voice. "Baby, are you ready to go?"

Holly doesn't answer but continues to fade little by little. Her yellow dress grows duller, her curls sink against her head, and the creases in Jessica's hospital gown from where Holly's hands grip it smooth out, as though she's let go of it—even though she still hasn't.

William finally turns to look at his daughters again. He's crying now, too.

"Holly," Brianna says. "Remember that we love you. We all love you. Forever. Okay? We'll miss you so much . . . " She squeezes her eyes shut for a moment. She's clearly struggling to keep her voice steady. "But we'll be okay. You can rest in peace, baby. We'll be okay. Jessie will be okay— I'll take care of her, better care of her. You rest now, baby."

I don't know if what Brianna's saying is all true. I don't think this is the sort of thing you ever recover from, or if you just learn how to deal with the pain as the years go by. But Holly must be convinced that she's done her best to help Jessica heal, because she's finally ready to go. Warmth radiates from her, filling my chest. She doesn't have to thank me, just like she doesn't have to say out loud that she forgives Jessica.

"I'll see you again," Brianna continues. "I'll see you again one day, Holly. We'll all be together again. And then we'll live together . . . and be happy. We'll all be happy together."

I take a deep breath and slip past William toward the door. Just before I close it behind me, I peek at Holly one last time. She's almost completely gone—just the suggestion of a girl now—but her mom is still talking to her.

"I love you so much," Brianna says. "We all love you so much."

"Safe travels," I whisper, and close the door as softly as I can.

CHAPTER FIFTY-FIVE

Heartbeat

I walk into the waiting room, exhausted. Mama, Maddie, and Jordan all stand up, brows furrowed, probably trying to glean what happened from my expression. I try to smile, but I'm not sure it works—my face muscles are as worn out as the rest of me.

Mama steps forward and wraps me in a hug. "It's done?" she asks.

"Yeah."

"Is everything okay?" Jordan asks. "Is everyone safe?"

"I think so," I murmur into Mama's shoulder.

I haven't thought about what to do next. Should I tell someone what happened? I'm fairly sure there's no point in involving the police since they'd probably do more harm than good based on how useless they've been so far. Besides, I don't think jail will help anyone. William hit Jessica because of an extraordinary circumstance, but what if it opened the door for him to do it again? If they're still trying to cover it up, it seems to me like the family won't seek out the help they need.

"Let's go home," Mama says.

"Don't you have a client?" I ask.

"I did a short visit while we were waiting. They have some time left; I'll come back tomorrow. Right now, I'm taking care of you."

I hug her tighter and let her steer me back to the elevator. I lean my head on her shoulder and close my eyes as we ride down. Someone squeezes my free shoulder. I'm not sure if it's Maddie or Jordan, but I'm grateful

Soon, we're all in the truck again. Mama pulls out of the hospital parking lot. My lap feels empty without Holly's weight. I still haven't fully accepted that I'll never hold her again, that she's really gone now.

There's no point in trying to figure this out all by myself. I take a deep breath.

"Holly's death was an accident," I say. "Jessica was taking care of her when it happened, so I guess that's why they tried to cover it up. I think they were afraid she would get charged with something."

Jordan pales. Maddie turns from the front seat to face me, her expression sad. Mama glances at me in the rearview mirror but keeps her focus on the road ahead.

"That's why she tried to . . . " Jordan begins. "Last night in the river . . . "

I nod. "Yeah. And William—her stepdad—is the one who hit her. I guess he blamed her for Holly's death. But then he helped cover it up to protect her."

"Or to protect his reputation," Jordan mutters.

"Maybe," I say, though William seemed a lot more focused on his family than on the outside world. None of them tried to tell me not to tell anyone, either. "I don't want to tell the police, though."

Maddie nods, understanding. Jordan bites her lip.

"Do you think I should?" I ask my friend.

"No, that's not it," Jordan assures me. "They're pretty terrible at handling domestic violence. Remember how they blew off Adela's mom when all that stuff happened with her mom's boyfriend?"

"Yeah." I have vivid memories of how much that whole situation hurt Adela.

"I think you should tell social services," Jordan tells me.

"You don't think *they'll* tell the police?" I ask.

"That's what I was worried about. Covering up how Holly died is a crime. If social services get involved, they might have to tell the police what happened. But I feel like they're still the people to talk to."

I squeeze my eyes shut and lean back against the headrest. "Why did he do that? Would Jessica have even been charged with anything? It was an accident."

"He must have thought she might be," Maddie says. "He's a judge. He would understand the legal situation better than we do."

"The police do tend to be harsher on Black kids," Jordan adds.

I can't argue with that. William must have had his reasons. Who knows how clearly he was even thinking in the hours after his daughter's death?

I rest my eyes the whole way back home. I must drift off because I start in surprise when Jordan touches my arm. The four of us head inside. I'm looking forward to some more peace and quiet, but the living room is full of people: Adela, Harper, Sarah, Grandma, Daddy. Only Aunt Betty is missing. I'm resigned but not disappointed by the company.

Fortunately, Mama, Maddie, and Jordan explain what happened, saving me the trouble of repeating my story to everyone. Adela and Harper make room for me on the couch and I settle in, hugging a throw pillow to my stomach. Predictably, Maddie brings me some herbal tea. I drink it down, even if it does taste like socks, and feel a little less achy.

"You did well, Amy," Grandma proclaims.

"You're so brave," Adela adds.

Jordan and Harper clamor in agreement.

"Calm down," Sarah tells them, "she doesn't need an even bigger head."

I glare at her, though her jab was weirdly comforting. She shrugs in reply.

"What will you do?" Harper asks me.

"Maybe you should leave it alone for now," Daddy suggests. "See how things work out."

"Maybe," I say. "I don't think I'll decide anything today."

There's a reason "sleep on it" is such a common expression. It really does feel like things might make more sense, might be clearer, after I've had a night's rest. Though it might just be that I want to put it off as long as possible.

Everyone fusses over me for a few minutes. Sarah has friends to meet. Daddy has to stop by his construction site to check on things. Grandma's back is still bothering her, and she wants to lie down again. But first, they all want to make sure I'm okay. I feel warm, grateful, and a bit overwhelmed.

As the living room empties out, things quiet down. Mama and Maddie head off, each giving me a hug before leaving. My friends pivot to talking about how things turned out, speculating about what will happen next, connecting the pieces we'd gathered before.

"I guess Peter knows," Adela muses.

My temples pound; I'd forgotten all about Peter. But of course, he was there when Holly died. He carries half the blame.

Harper nods. "That must be why they broke up. Can you imagine staying with someone after you helped get your girlfriend's sister killed?"

I shudder, and I'm not the only one who does.

"Why do you think Holly made you shout at Peter in the cafeteria?" Jordan asks.

"Oh, right." That's another thing I'd forgotten about. It would be nice to erase it from my memory. "Jessica got that bruise after Holly died. Holly probably didn't know who did it. It could have been her dad or Peter, either one. They must have both been really upset."

Adela, who's sitting on the rug in front of the couch, wraps her arms around her knees. "So Holly really forgave Jessica? Forgave her completely?"

"I would be so angry if my sister got me killed," Harper mutters. "I'd haunt her as long as I could."

I'm not sure I'd be as quick to forgive as Holly was, either. I can't know, though. There's the fact that she's three years old and might not fully understand things, but I don't think that's the reason.

"She knew it was an accident," I say, suddenly even more exhausted than a minute ago. "She loved Jessica so much, she didn't want her to suffer because of what happened."

Adela sniffles. Everyone's quiet for a moment.

"You look beat," Jordan tells me.

"A bit."

Adela gets up from the rug. Harper, who's perched on the armrest of my couch, and Jordan, who's sitting beside me, both stand. They take turns giving me hugs—except Harper, who gives me a fist bump—and start toward the door.

"Thank you, everyone," I say. My friends all turn back to me. "I couldn't have gotten through the past few days without you. Can I do something nice for all of you soon?"

"We're just glad you finally told us the truth," Adela says.

"Sorry it took me so long." I hesitate for a moment, but I'm too tired to think it through. I'll just go ahead and say it. "Things have been hard for me this past year or so. Or maybe a bit longer, I'm not sure."

The other three exchange a look. "We know, Amy," Adela assures me. "We can all tell you're messed up or whatever."

Jordan elbows Adela.

"I guess so," I admit.

"Did anything happen?" Harper asks, uncharacteristically gentle.

"No, not really. Nothing specific." I try to smile, but I don't have much strength in my face. "I'm supposed to be a necromancer, but I can't really handle death. It gets to me. Everything gets to me. All the little things just keep piling up until I just . . . I just feel like I'm buried in it, sometimes. I've been going to a therapist, though I obviously can't tell her everything. Maybe I'm not cut out for this."

"Maybe not, but you did pretty good," Jordan told me. "You saved Jessica's life, maybe more than once. You helped Holly move on."

"I guess so," I say again. Something feels strangely light about my body, though it's different from when it fades away through dissociation.

"Let's talk more later, after you've rested," Adela says. "We can have that back-to-school sleepover we've been talking about."

I feel exhausted just thinking about it, but hopefully I'll have more energy when the time comes. And maybe it'll be easier now that they know all my secrets. "Yeah, sure. Thanks, all of you. I promise I won't keep making everything about me."

"We can make it all about me," Adela proclaims. Jordan and Harper snort.

They wave goodbye and head out. I sigh and relax into the couch cushions again, realizing I've built up some tension since I first sat down. I'm finally alone. My bed seems so far away, and I don't have the energy to climb the ladder to the top bunk anyway, so I might as well rest on the couch. It seems unreal that I've finally told my friends not just about my powers, but a bit about the battleground inside my head, too. My therapist, Mary, will be proud of me.

"It's done, then," Aunt Betty says. "Holly's gone."

I jerk in surprise. I didn't see her come up beside my couch. "Yeah, Holly's gone. She's not lingering anymore."

She stares at me impassively, her white nightgown hanging around her bony frame.

"You were right," I say. "It didn't get easier. It's not any easier now. I have no idea what to do."

Aunt Betty sweeps forward and sits on the coffee table in front of me. She smells like the garden; she must have gone outside, which is rare for her to do during the day. She doesn't say anything. I realize she knows intimately what it means to lose a child; I'd suggest that she talk to the Myers, except she'd probably terrify them.

"I guess you don't have any advice for dealing with the living," I mumble.

"I've tended to avoid that sort of thing."

"Yeah, I know." I give her a half-grin. "I don't blame you. It's even more confusing than dealing with the dead, and I don't have any special powers to help me."

Aunt Betty touches my cheek, her hand cold as always. "You're a good girl. You have a good heart."

My eyes prick with tears. "Thank you."

Without warning, Aunt Betty gets up and leaves. I guess I shouldn't have expected any different. I'm alone again, but now I don't want to be anymore. Everyone's off to do their own thing, whatever that is, and I have nothing to do but stew in my thoughts and doubts. What *am* I going to do now that I know the circumstances of Holly's death? And what about next time the Itch comes? Holly was the first human being I brought back from the dead, but I'm sure she won't be the last. Can I deny the Itch like Maddie suggested, leave the next lost soul in the ground? Maybe if I can focus on getting better first, on putting my life back together and figuring out who I want to be, I'll be able to handle raising someone else from the dead and helping them deal with the things they left undone.

I turn those thoughts over in my head for a few minutes before a knock comes at the door. I heave myself out of the couch and open it.

Toni stands on the front step, her eyes wide with worry. She relaxes a bit when she sees me, and then we just stand there, each waiting for the other to speak.

"Um, you want to come in?" I ask.

She nods and steps across the threshold. Now we're standing just as awkwardly, except we're both inside instead of at the door. She's wearing a solid-blue, crisp, short-sleeve T-shirt and jean shorts along with those cute sandals that make me feel self-conscious about my ragged footwear. Blue really is her color. I don't bother looking down at myself; I can't remember what I'm wearing, but I know it's not cute. I run my fingers through my hair, hoping it's not too messy.

"I saw you drive by with Holly," Toni begins.

"Yeah, we were heading to the hospital to see Jessica and her family."

"Did you?"

"Yeah."

"Is it over? Is Holly gone?"

I nod.

Toni folds her arms over her chest as if she's cold, even though she can't possibly be that. We don't have air conditioning, and it's a blazing early afternoon outside. She looks at the rug, then back up at me. My cheeks burn, but I hold her gaze. I'll only make myself more embarrassed by trying to hide my blush, and I'm too tired anyway.

"What are you going to do now?" she asks.

I shrug. "I'm trying to figure that out. It's not going to be easy, no matter what." I explain the bare-bones of what happened, what Jessica told me about the day Holly died.

Toni listens. When I'm done, she shakes her head. "That's awful. Are you okay?"

"I'll be okay after I rest. How are you after last night?"

"It sucked," she admits. "But we did a good thing. You did a good thing. You saved a girl's life."

"We did it together."

"You're the one who knew she was going to be there and dove into the river to get her out."

I snort. "You make it sound a lot more heroic than it was. I feel bad that I dragged you into—"

She holds up a hand. "No, Amy. Don't go there. You didn't drag me. I'm the one who chose to get involved with you."

My cheeks get even hotter. "Involved with me?"

She looks down at the rug again, scuffing the edge of her sandal against it.

"I didn't mean to make it weird," I say quickly.

"You *are* weird."

"Yeah, I guess so."

Without warning, I start laughing. It's the kind of laugh you let out when you've just fallen on your butt—a mixture of self-deprecation and relief that it wasn't worse. Toni looks up at me, grinning and rolling her eyes a bit.

"Anyway, I just came by to make sure you were okay," she says.

"Thank you."

She nods and turns toward the door. My stomach clenches. She's leaving already? Does this mean she's still upset at me? Is she trying to get *un*involved with me? Am I about to lose my chance to make up for last night?

"Don't go," I burst out.

Toni raises her eyebrows. "You look tired. I was going to let you—"

"I don't want to be alone."

We stand there staring at each other for another moment. Why do we keep doing that? It was so easy to talk to her last night. Before I knew it, our faces were so close I could feel her breath on my lips. If Holly hadn't interrupted . . . Now that I want to pick up where we left off, I don't know how.

I take a step toward her. Maybe I'm making a mistake. Maybe she'll think I'm even weirder than she did a minute ago. Maybe neither of us is in a good state of mind to do this. Maybe we're too young or too distraught or have too many unresolved issues of our own. Maybe it's too soon after her girlfriend died or too soon after our multiple brushes with death over the past few days.

Toni licks her lips, losing her usual cool, self-contained demeanor as she shifts her weight from one foot to the other. Her eyes flick between my eyes and my mouth. She's thinking about last night, too.

I'm tired of dealing with death and its consequences to the living, which are even worse. If I'm going to have to deal with life and all its complications, I might as well also enjoy it.

I don't know which one of us closes the distance or if it's both of us at the same time. Next thing I know, my lips are pressed against hers. They're even softer than I imagined, warm and alive. At first, my arms hang awkwardly at my sides, until she puts hers around my waist and pulls me to her. I fumble, putting my hands on her shoulders, and when that feels odd, I slide them to the back of her neck. She laughs softly against my mouth. I return the laugh.

Then we stop laughing and deepen the kiss. I close my eyes, wrapped up in her scent, citrus and sunshine. Her heart beats against my chest, setting the beat for my own.

Epilogue

The tombstone reads simply *Holly Myers* and has her date of death and birth underneath. No epitaph. I guess even picking out something to inscribe on the granite slab would be too painful for her family. Flowers spring from vases and bouquets all around it; after the news of her death became public knowledge, a lot of people came to pay their respects at the graveside.

"That does sound very unpleasant," Aunt Betty agrees with the air.

She sits a few feet away from me, perched on top of a blocky tombstone in her gossamer white dress. The full moon hangs high in the sky above her, illuminating the strands of silver in her dark hair. She's staring straight ahead at someone I can't see. She's been talking to the ghost for the past half hour, though the ghost seems to be doing most of the talking because she only occasionally interjects.

I shiver in the early autumn air and zip up my jacket. I don't know how Aunt Betty can stand the chill in that dress. Mama gave her a sweater on her way out the door, but the sweater pools in the grass beside the tombstone, unused.

I'm sitting on a small, faded picnic blanket on the

grass in front of Holly's grave. It's surprisingly peaceful here, even though my skin keeps getting goosebumps from the proximity of all the ghosts. I've never come with Aunt Betty on her full-moon cemetery visits before, but I'm oddly glad I did this time.

"You're absolutely right," Aunt Betty says. "It sounds like your mother was quite unreasonable, and I don't blame you in the least."

The conversation seems to be wrapping up. I'm starting to feel sleepy; we've been here for hours, and I have school tomorrow. Maybe I'll tell Aunt Betty I'm going home after she finishes talking to this ghost. I'd obviously never interrupt her.

My mind wanders, as it usually does these days, to Toni. We've been taking it slow, mostly just hanging out and talking. Well, and kissing. But we have a lot to talk about, and it feels like we're just getting started. It's a good place to be. Comfortable. Safe. I think we both need that.

Goosebumps flush across my skin and I turn back to Aunt Betty. Her pose has relaxed somewhat, a slight slump in her shoulders. The ghost she was talking to has left—maybe it's moved on to the afterlife, or maybe it's just faded for now. It usually takes more than a single conversation to release souls from the mortal realm.

"Are you okay?" I ask. It seems to take a lot of energy out of her every time a ghost leaves, as if they take a piece of her with them.

"Oh, yes," Aunt Betty says, her voice steady. "We had a good conversation. Have you made your decision?"

Right—I forgot the reason I'd given Aunt Betty for coming with her. I've been sitting here so long, enjoying the chirp of crickets, the flutter of bats at the edge of darkness, the scent of dewy earth. I was supposed to be thinking about my dilemma. To be honest, though, I had already decided; I've mostly been working on strengthening my resolve.

"I'm going to stop," I say. The words leave me like one of Aunt Betty's ghosts. My stomach unclenches and my spine curves. "For now. I'm going to try to put the Itch to sleep until I'm ready to use it again."

Aunt Betty nods from her seat on the tombstone. "That seems wise. It might not be easy, you know."

"Yeah. It woke me up a few nights ago. I had to fight it really hard, and I had a stomach ache the next day."

"Could you tell what it was?" Aunt Betty asks conversationally.

"I couldn't at first, but I've been having intense dreams ever since." I stuff my hands into the pockets of my jacket and stare at the flowers around Holly's grave. "I think it was a bird. A swallow. I keep waking up feeling like a hawk's diving out of the sky toward me. I flap my wings, but I'm too slow to escape its shadow."

Aunt Betty doesn't reply, but gazes off into the darkly intertwined treetops that surround the cemetery.

"The dreams are manageable," I add.

"And the guilt?" she asks.

I blow out a breath. "I don't feel guilty. I really believe I can do good with my power—and I want to. I want to be like you and Mama. It's just that I'm . . . I'm not ready. I have to take care of myself before I can help anyone else, otherwise I won't be able to keep going."

"That's very astute of you."

Now if I can only convince myself that it's true.

Toni and I have spoken about it a lot. She agrees with my decision. Everyone seems to agree. The dreams are still fresh in my mind, though.

"It'll probably be harder next time it's a person who tries to come back," I murmur, mostly to myself.

"It may get easier to resist, with time."

I nod. I'm counting on that.

One thing I'll miss is the certainty that comes with the Itch. When I'm half-awake, digging my hands into the silky mud and feeling it solidify into a living form, I feel a sense of rightness. That certainty vanishes the next morning, though.

Every day, I question the choices I made with Holly and her family. Jessica still hasn't been back at school; there are all sorts of complex legal procedures going on with her and her family, but they've done a good job of keeping it private. Not even Adela has been able to find out any details. I tried to keep the details sparse when I called Social Services the day after I found out the truth. They had a lot of questions, though, and I ended up telling them more than I meant to. I assume the rest of the story came out when Social Services visited the family.

Holly got what she needed. I go back and forth over whether I think Jessica got what she needed, too. Her sister's forgiveness was obviously a huge deal, but would she ever forgive herself? I'm not sure it's possible.

"You know, Amy," Aunt Betty tells me, "even if you wait until you're eighty years old, you won't always be sure what to do. Not with the dead, and not with the living."

I frown at Holly's tombstone. "I know. It's not about that. I just need to get better before I can think about everyone who needs me. Sometimes I feel like I'm barely here. How can I help anyone deal with their death if I'm like that?" I glance back up at Aunt Betty. "Did you ever stop talking to ghosts? After . . . after your daughters . . . "

She sighs. "For a while, my girls were the only ones I spoke to."

"They came back as ghosts?" I ask.

"I'm afraid I kept them here for longer than they should have stayed."

I think of Brianna, Holly's mom, begging Holly to stay. It was bad enough that day in the hospital; I can't imagine dragging it out over weeks, months. I wonder if I could have used my power to keep Holly with us against her will. I wonder if I would have been tempted to try if Holly was my sister instead of Jessica's.

"Death is too much a part of me, I think," she says. Aunt Betty sounds matter-of-fact, though I think I hear an edge of regret in her voice. "It will be good for you to only be around the living for a while."

"Yeah, I think so, too."

Aunt Betty and I both look up as a cloud brushes over the moon, deepening the shadows of the tombstones and the trees. The leaves rustle with a gust of wind that bites through my jacket. An owl hoots nearby. I curl my fingers into the grass beside my blanket, feeling the cool earth beneath.

Tomorrow, I'll tell my friends what I've decided. A smile twitches my lips at the thought of seeing Toni again, even though I saw her earlier today, and every day before that for two weeks. My cheeks warm with the memory of her kisses.

In this moment, I'm completely here. I feel every inch of my skin like it belongs to me. I'm grounded in the world of my body—in the world of the living.

Acknowledgements

I originally released *Amy of the Necromancers* as a free serialized novel on my newsletter throughout 2020. It was incredibly gratifying and encouraging to hear from readers as I wrote—it was a small point of human contact in a year marked by intense isolation. Thank you so, so much to everyone who was with me on that journey.

Thank you, too, to the person I spent all of quarantine with: my partner, Stephen Energia. I think if you're not tired of each other after months trapped together in a tiny studio apartment, that's a pretty good sign that you're good for each other.

Thank you to all the usual suspects: Charlie Knight, my editor; Molly Howard, my proofreader and trusted writing accomplice; and Lena Yang, my amazingly talented cover designer. Thank you as well to Shannon Waldman, Ellen Willmann, Dylan Morison, and Celeste Flahaven for your thoughtful feedback.

Other books by Jimena I. Novaro:

The Phyrian War Chronicles

The Relic Spell (Book 1)
The Warlock Snare (Book 2)

Standalones

Codex of Mechanical Dreams
Blue Rabbit

About the Author

Jimena Novaro always knew she would be a writer. She wrote her first stories before she could spell and hasn't stopped since. She was born and raised by wildlife biologists in the arid steppe of Neuquén Province, Argentina, identifying stool samples, dreaming up other worlds, and climbing mountains without her pants (that one time). She recently graduated with a B.A. in Creative Writing from Warren Wilson College in Asheville, North Carolina. She currently lives in her home town in Argentina with her family, her partner, and one very needy cat.

Sign up to get the latest news about Jimena's writing, as well as free serialized stories, at **www.jimenainovaro.com**.

If you enjoyed this book, please consider leaving a review on your website of choice. It's an incredibly helpful and deeply appreciated show of support for any indie author.